Boned
Every Which Way

A Collection of Skeletal Literature
2018

BONED EVERY WHICH WAY

A Collection of Skeletal Literature
2018

Edited by
Nate Ragolia

SPACEBOY BOOKS

Denver, Colorado

Published in the United States by:

Spaceboy Books LLC
1627 Vine Street
Denver, CO 80206

www.readspaceboy.com

Content from BONED: bonedstories.wordpress.com

First printed June 2019

ISBN-13: 978-0-9997862-9-1

Profits from sales of this book will benefit the National Network of Abortion
Funds. Find them online at abortionfunds.org.

For all the creators building that which cannot be torn down.

TABLE OF CONTENTS

THE SUNSET BRUISED THE BOTTOM OF THE SKY
- CAMERON LOVEJOY

The sunset bruised the bottom of the sky.
Our long day hangs on memory's edge;
Were we but a blemish in a bird's eye?

Our young winter walk with fingertips tied
Renewed the veins and marred cartilage.
The sunset bruised the bottom of the sky.

From afar, we watched the slip of avalanche pry
Away the mountain's fleshy ledge.
Were we but a blemish in a bird's eye?

It thundered to cover where bones still lie,
Skulls of stone to the hammer sledge.
The sunset bruised the bottom of the sky.

Trees were snapped, the sap of love dried,
Timber split by the axe's wedge.
Were we but a blemish in a bird's eye?

And we, now farther from memory's cry,
Grow deaf to the yells in the burial sludge.
The sunset bruised the bottom of the sky.
We were but a blemish in a bird's eye.

CR   SO

Cameron Lovejoy is a poet, gardener, and Lindy Hopper. After ten years on the road, he's been adopted by New Orleans where he now resides, sweaty and content. You can find him on the street writing poetry on demand.
https://www.cameronlovejoy.com
https://www.patreon.com/cameronlovejoy

BONE / LOVELY BONES - TOMOKO IRIE

Bone

My eye sockets pain me, prickling,
Sinking needles into my skull, ever
so slowly, smoothing the edges, the
corners lost to the numbness;

Over coffee, it changes like fickle
Weather, whispering of thoughts not
spoke out loud, of words withheld,
dropping into empty eyes, empty sockets;

Crushing the tendrils of color, weight,
Twirling into the abyss, the click of
annoyance, the tongue flickering,
a snake ready to spring, coiling, coiling;

(The tethered bone creaks with ancient curses.)

Lovely Bones

I rested my head upon
your lovely bones, as time
wasted away the last embers
of the fire that encircled
the world for one day; After the smoke
had cleared, all that remained
were your lovely bones

ଔ   ଓ

Tomoko Irie is a Los Angeles based writer / poet who has yet to decide what her future holds. She loves cats, the rain, cloudy days, and coffee shops. Her recent personal goal is to try as many chai tea lattes as possible (hot or cold). She takes inspiration from people-watching, dreams, and traveling. She went to the UK for the first time this past summer and cannot forget the beautiful Scottish countryside. She writes online under a pen name at http://www.wattpad.com/user/nashipo

WHAT OF FOREVER / DAYBREAK / THERE COMES A POINT - P. C. SCHEPONIK

What of Forever

I will not leave my life unwritten,
though I will go into that night untyped.
My words lying on pages the color of moon
reflecting the light of sun my eyes no longer see.
My words, drying on these lines, growing brown
and brittle around the edges, like the crisp bodies
of fallen leaves—
those left along the edges of walks and roads
and the root-gnarled bases of trees.
Who will love the piles poised on the promise
of being read, of reaching out and speaking
after I am long dead?
Such a Lazarus tease that plays in my head...
that plays in my head.
I have sanctified the pen.
I have made a paper bed for my heart to
lie down upon, for my mind to pretend
that my soul might live forever.

Daybreak

The morning wind combs willow's hair,
strand by weeping strand.
Trembling silver edges, teeth made of air
slide softly through the green-leaf mane
with a mother's love or a lover's care.
All is peace and gentleness.
Sun's golden hands softly caress
the edges of glowing clouds.
Heaven's blue cheek is brightly rouged
with dawn's blush, and drowsing moon,
a bit confused, seems in a rush to clothe
her pale nakedness with an indigo robe of sky.
While robin sings a matin song and starlings fly
in black star throngs to celebrate the break of day.
My heart rises with each note, and my soul longs

---

to find its way deep into the beauty this world shows,
into the perfect truth the body knows when it's
seduced by morning.

There Comes a Point

There comes a point when the best thing
we can do for our children is die.
Before the mindlessness and madness
pry self from body, turn consciousness to dust,
proving there is a purgatory and therefore must
be a hell, where the body becomes a fragile shell
crushing hopes and breaking hearts—
a horror show of creeping parts that break and
bleed and ooze.
But most of all to show us how little we are and
how much we have to lose.
Such great capacity to wound and leave nothing
behind but the scar to serve as a reminder we are
never far from suffering.
How an hour becomes an eternity in time,
and the only hope for escape we can find
is through death's merciful door.

CR BO

P.C. Scheponik is a lifelong poet who lives by the sea with his wife, Shirley, the love of his life, and his shizon, Bella. He has four collections of poetry and has been published in numerous journals.

CONSTELLATIONS – AMANDA MARTIN

I'm perched in the shadows, darkness is my home
Harshness is the tone that world takes
When they juxtapose my role
With those who decompose
The humans who complain
About my presence near the expired
Are the ones who only desire to
Remember the dead
When they're huddled around
A hole in the ground where
The souls of loved ones
Will never be found

My thing is Harvesting
There's no consuming souls
No leeching of life
I bring beauty into the night
The lights in the sky you strain to see
Thanks to a city that never sleeps
Are because of me
It's not my fault you waited to care
Until your person was no longer there

Starlight is a drug to me
A resource just out of reach
A privilege restricted by a scorned lover
Who has long since forgotten the sound of my voice
So I'm forced into the creation
Of delicate constellations
Forged from the power of souls
That serves two goals
The dead's and mine—
I hope they let this one go this time

Her soul is ripe and despite the pleas
And gripes of the family
There is no God in sight
No, there is only me tonight

The room is sterile
White walls, white tile, white sheets
The hollow air incessantly repeats
The steady mechanical beeps
Of a machine that is stronger
Than the patient's heartbeats

There she lay, five days from seventy-five
One side of her head shaved from
When the brave woman gave the okay
To stave off the cancer
That rattled her relatives to the core

Then she rises, translucent, unaware of her demise
Her movement's unsteady but she seems ready
For what lies ahead
There's a thread suspended from wall to wall
Intended to guide, as per protocol
Laced with magic, only the deceased can see
One step. Another. Then three.
Now she appears just shy of sixty
The years melted off, pooled on the floor
A peachy drip following her to the door

Salt and pepper hair, more grey than not
Three more steps and she's in a different spot.
Now she's back to forty
The way she was when she watched
Her son walk across the stage
A high school grad
With siblings and a mom, no dad
Then he's off to wage a war
Against minimum wage

A few more steps, she's half across the room.
Her hair's long and strong
A moderate brown
The breaths she takes don't make a sound.
Down to only twenty-two
When her first born
Was barely delivered from the womb.

A final reason to make her escape
To write the constant abuse out of her fate

Her final steps lead her to the edge
Of my shadowed corner
Shedding down to a soul's last defense
It's skeletal armor
I reach out, put my hand on her shoulder
Her bones crack into splinters
Held together like shimmers
In a diamond's facade
She radiates light
Her core growing bolder
Till I can't hold her any longer
And I let her go into the night sky
To build her own castle of Versailles
To watch down upon her lineage
From her side of the bridge

And I retreat into my corner
To come down from my high
Until the next soul
Can be cast into the sky

CR   SO

Amanda Martin is a poet and writer living in North Carolina. She spends much of her free time reading, watching TV, and writing (or at least attempting to). In December, she will graduate with a BA in English with a Concentration in Creative Writing.

THE FLOW OF THE RIVER HAD STOPPED - MARIAH NOEL

We had heard no water rushing for near a week | Our downstream
cabin was sore dry and throats dusty
Young travellers in their wagon stopped to board a meal and bandy
words
Over potatoes they brought, the mush meat we shared — they tell us
news from the east — and upriver
-You hear the skirmish last week?
–Ay, geste.
-Twixt the brutes of the hill and the swine of the plains?
–Ay, geste. Stayed hid and hoped they would nay come.
-Follow us
Follow we did
The river on our side reduced to dry bedrock and crunched crayfish
There, a great blockade stood / one of mud and sticks
Shook our heads – but the young travellers beckoned us to step round
| They had washed downriver |
remnants of a victorless battle
| Swept away among cannon debris and fellow bodies |
Beavers swimming around a dam built from bodies and bones.

CR   BO

Mariah Noel studies Acting and Literature. Her flash fiction piece, "The
Patch of Darkness", was featured in Sick Lit Magazine.

THE SKELETON OF A FEMALE FOX / YARD SALE / COPSE / AS IF IN A DREAM - YUAN CHANGMING

The Skeleton of a Female Fox

There is a fairytale told, and retold again
In Ming Dynasty, about the skeleton of a coquettish fox
That takes on the shape of a beautiful young woman
Ready to offer herself to a poor obscure guy

Like a magician she brings rich food and wine
To him during the day, and uses her two mouths
To suck up all his yuanqi (energy or masculinity)
At night until he dies in ecstasy of sexual love
Then, the immortal woman would marry another
While many hungry boys would rather become
That lucky guy. I enjoy thinking of that fox
Like a deformed soul wearing a human mask
With hair behind, which makes it feel itchy
While all men are waiting, in anxiety

Yard Sale

A whole box of human hearts, each
Still beating fresh like skinned toads
Two rows of shiny skeletons of unknown gods
All fingers longer than legs, toes bigger than skulls
Three sets of knives, blades extremely blunt
With evil spirits and devilish impulses
Four giant alarm clocks, making thunderous noises
Waking up all dead from as many directions
Five bottles of wine filled with soaked souls
As colourful as the rainbow above the styx
Can I just have the reddest heart please?
Sure, it's free

Copse

Posted on by
Standing straight against the frozen sky
Your skeletons are the exquisite calligraphy
Of the season
Your name is writ
Not in water
But with wind

As If in a Dream

Flying between sea and sky
Between day and night
Amid heavenly or oceanic blue
I lost all my references
To any timed space
Or a localized time
Except the non-stop snorting
Of a stranger neighbor
Then, beyond the snorts rising here
And more looming there
I see skeletons of tigers, lions, leopards
And other kinds of hunger-throated predators
Darting out of every passenger's heart
Running amuck around us
As if released from a huge cage

CR ঞ

Yuan Changming published monographs on translation before leaving China. With a Canadian PhD in English, Yuan currently edits Poetry Pacific with Allen Yuan and hosts Happy Yangsheng in Vancouver; credits include nine Pushcart nominations, Best of the Best Canadian Poetry (2008-17), BestNewPoems Online, Threepenny Review and 1,369 others worldwide. Links: poetrypacific.blogspot.ca & happyyangsheng.blogspot.ca

SHADOW CITY – KG NEWMAN

On an Uber's final fumes we made it
to the spirits tour, where pricey beers
and an up-close look at walled-off
smuggling tunnels brought back
bone-ridden märchen of the Red Light District—

upscale LoDo juxtaposed against
powerful Mesdames sneaking politicians
around under nefarious warehouses
strengthened by the Brick Ordinance—

and still no elite officially wanted
association with saloon-laden Market Street,
originally named for mountain man
William McGaa, who also got to dub Wazee
and Wewatta after his Indian lovers before
drunkenness did him in, freezing to death
in the town jail in December 1867.

                ର   ଡ଼

KG Newman is a sports writer for The Denver Post. His first two poetry collections, While Dreaming of Diamonds in Wintertime *and* Selfish Never Get Their Own, *are available on Amazon. The Arizona State University graduate can be found on Twitter @KyleNewmanDP.*

SOMETIMES IT FEELS LIKE THE BACK OF MY HEAD OPENS UP AND I CAN BREATHE AGAIN – RIN BAATZ

The background radiation came,
softly, smoothly
tearing at the edges of my mind
and dissolving tenuous social relations

I felt it coil behind my eyes
and weave between the ridges of my brain,
smoothing gray matter as it went

My body slowed and fell,
limbs heavy and eyelids weak.
My back curved over the edge of the sofa,
opening my ribcage with a soft crack

Radiation pools in the cup of my skull,
thoughts collecting and vanishing
in the smoldering green glow

Fingers decay in perfect unison
as they reach out to touch,
desperate for understanding
and finding only empty confusion

Edison bulbs shatter and hum
growing louder, brighter with each second

Electricity shorts out and the
backup generators
belch themselves awake,
scrunching their moving parts in confusion

My vertebrae slip to the floor and I ooze,
lazily,
to the nearest outlet

Melted bone meets soft plastic and
cold, metal wiring
A cool click, and then nothing more

ଔ   ෨

Rin Baatz is a college student currently studying creative writing. Her focus is in poetry, but she also works with creative nonfiction. She has been published in Khroma, Germ, and Beautiful Losers.

THE LORD OF THE BLUE ABOVE - RAJNISH MISHRA

The moving specks of brown have gone. The parched grey ground is
dried of them, my talons clutch cracked bark. I cry shrill and low.
The small grey spots of feathers too, are gone, all gone. The cruel
yellow and the ugly blue above, they smile today.
They smile for I search for food I can't find, and I'm the one: the lord
of the blue above, the god of the grey below.

Enraged eyes range the grey beneath, the blue above, ahead. Now
this, my home, is dead for me. Friends I had none, have none, won't
have, yet can't forget my kind is gone, all gone, but me.
No, I won't die, for I'm the one: the lord of the blue above, the god of
the grey below.

It shines, my beak, it lusts for pink. My talons glisten, they thirst for
red. I can't stay still. Yes, I must kill.
If not to feed, then just to kill, or else, I die while the yellow smirks
and the blue cackles.
How can I die so young, I, who they called the lord of the blue above,
the god of the grey below?

My lazy wings stay folded long. Once spread they hide the smiling
yellow. My talons clutch no bark; cut through the belly of the blue.
I fly and search. No, close to grey won't help. Rise I must, and cut
through the blue, up where eyes can't see, then dive.
Or, do nothing I said, I don't need to, for I'm the god of the grey
below, the lord of the blue above.

At last, I see small white things four: three small, one big. I choose the
one that nibbles alone. My glistening beak and shining talons laugh at
the blue, deride the grey.
I go close, so close I see the big one's eyes widen. One bleating sound
and two run back but not the one I singled out.
It's slow. My eyes are fixed on it – the offering for the lord of the blue
above, the god of the grey below.

My talons, glistening red, clutch white. My shining beak tears red to
the white. The little one is slow no more. It runs, but not away from

me. I ride it.

Its neck not near, I tear away the pink from the side, then snap the bone. Mistake in haste: its red covers my eyes. Can't see a thing yet work as well.

I know how it ends for it, for me. You know that too for I am the lord of the blue above, the god of the grey below.

⋘　⋙

Rajnish Mishra is a poet, writer, translator and blogger born and brought up in Varanasi, India and now in exile. His work originates at the point of intersection between his psyche and his city. His work has now started appearing in journals and websites. He runs an ezine: PPP Ezine.

QUEEN JO - JOHN GREY

Take it off,
take it all off-
she sates her words
with sarcasm,
repeating the chants
of her fat and sloppy,
drunken clientele.
Before the dressing room mirror,
off comes the makeup,
mascara scrubbed
from purple lids,
blood-red washed
away from lips,
powder flushed from
the pores in her cheeks.
Take it off,
take it all off-
she snarls.
She removes the
the blonde tresses
from her bald dome,
pops blue eyes
from their sockets,
drops them in a glass,
unclips the ears,
twists the nose free,
then sets about her flesh
with more hideous cries of
take it off,
take it all off.
They only want her for her body
but her skeleton will have to do.

CR SO

John Grey is an Australian poet, US resident. Recently published in *Examined Life Journal, Studio One* and *Columbia Review* with work upcoming in *Leading Edge, Poetry East* and *Midwest Quarterly.*

CHARON BE MY SONG! - CARL TEEGERSTROM

Charon be my song! Great Goddess of Life and Death, Persephone, Mistress
of Hades who was taken under the earth to rule as queen, sing through me!
Sing of the Ferryman and aid me in remembering his tragedy.
Sing of his loss, his grief, of his journey to your husband's gloomy kingdom.
We've sung of dead heroes' greatness for too long, so sing of their Ferryman!
Glorious Persephone I pray that you will aid me to remember
what other, blind poets have forgotten! So be my muse and inspire me!

Charon was not a god or some other spirit. He was a mortal who lived
with his wife Stygia on the slopes of Mount Pelion where one day
seeds of the Trojan War would be sewn. Charon was mortal, but more
than a mere man because he was the grandson of the river god
Peneus. Charon's mother Diotima was Peneus' daughter and his
father was Emporos who met Diotima while hunting by the Pineios
River. He fell in love and eloped with her. They lived in the city of
Sesklo and one day Diotima gave birth to a son. Emporos went to a
priestess of Apollo to learn his family's fate. The priestess prophesied
that their son would ferry them to the Underworld and live a life of
eternal suffering. Emporos and Diotima feared her cryptic words and
decided to expose the child in the wilderness to prevent their own
deaths and spare him from a life of eternal suffering. But nothing can
defy fate. One day Artemis and her nymphs happened upon the child
while hunting in the woods. She took him to the humble home of
Iomori and Amphansia; a pious couple that lived by the Pineios River.
Artemis appeared to them in disguise and asked if they would care for
the babe. Iomori and Amphansia wanted children for a long time, but
Amphansia was barren, so they gladly accepted the babe and named
him Charon. They lived happily together until they tragically died in
a plague when Charon was ten. With no other family to support him
he put grief out of his mind and forced himself into adulthood. He
became a successful merchant on the Pineios River. Though he could
have lived the rest of his life as a humble merchant he saw
opportunities for wealth and fame in Sesklo's army, so he earned
enough money to afford arms and armor and joined when he was
twenty.

Sesklo declared war on the northern kingdom of Scythia three
years later. The war was not long, but it was a terrible war. Sesklo lost
more than three quarters of its army and the brutality was so great
and costs so high that poets refused to sing of its horrors to this day.

Charon distinguished himself in the war, but lost all of his comrades, including his dear companion Elegeus. Elegeus and Charon deeply loved each other ever since they joined the army. The two were Sesklo's most skilled warriors, and when the two fought together they were nearly invincible. They had saved each other and their comrades on many occasions, but, as the campaign wore on, more and more of their friends were killed or maimed. Once a sling had knocked Charon unconscious, and Elegeus tried to protect him while Scythians, who thought Charon had died, tried to loot his arms and armor. Charon recovered from his head wound to find Elegeus had driven off the Scythians but was dying of injuries he sustained in the fighting. Charon held his beloved as he died. Charon then cut a bloody, vengeful path through the Scythian army and even killed its general. Thus, Charon earned the respect of Sesklo, but lost all of his friends and the one man he loved so dearly.

Years after the war Charon married Stygia; a daughter of one of Sesklo's generals and built a home on the slopes of Mount Pelion. The marriage started as a happy one, but as the years wore on their relationship strained. Charon loved Stygia very deeply, but he spent less and less time with her. He had many nightmares from the war. Sometimes he dreamed of burning his parents on the pyre and others he relived the war and Elegeus dying in his arms. He did not want to talk about his nightmares or his anxiety to anybody out of shame, guilt and many other reasons he could not begin to explain. He often went back to the River where he was raised, where he would fish and ferry pilgrims to try to take his mind off of his parents, the war and death whose specter haunted his thoughts. They tried to have children, but, unfortunately, Stygia had several miscarriages. She began to resent Charon for his coldness and distance, and many in the town whispered of a possible divorce.

Events seemed to change for the better when Stygia became pregnant and carried the child without complication for eight moons. Charon was elated at the prospect of being a father. He spent less time wandering the wilderness and the two loved each other as they once had so many years ago. Charon had fewer and fewer nightmares until they became like a distant memory. The two never felt better and were excited to finally start a family.

One day Charon received a lucrative commission to help build ships for Sesklo's navy. Although his wife looked ready to give birth any day he took the commission. The shore was only a day's walk from the house and he promised to drop everything to come to her when the pangs of labor set in. He expressed his regret and tried to assure his wife that he would not be gone long, though, in truth, he wanted some time by himself. The nightmares returned as Stygia entered her ninth moon of pregnancy. But these nightmares were not about the past, they seemed to be prophetic. Even worse was the fact that each new nightmare was worse than the last. Stygia noticed her husband's anxiety and, though she desperately wanted him to stay, she had spent enough time around him to know when he needed to be alone. She was angry with him for leaving, but hoped that when he returned and their child was born he would finally change. He departed on the last day of fall. They kissed coldly when they bid each other farewell for Stygia was still frustrated and Charon was plagued by worry and grief, but as Charon started to leave he turned around and passionately embraced Stygia. She returned her husband's embrace as she was also deeply worried. The night before she dreamed Charon was drowning in a dark river, but as he drowned he also melted; his flesh boiling away as he dissolved into the gloom. They hugged tightly and for a long time, but both remained quiet. If only she had spoke. Charon also had the same dream, but saw her drowning and melting into a dark river. If only he had learned to speak with his wife, to admit to his nightmares, then they both would have seen it as the omen it was.

Charon helped design and build an enormous trireme for three days, putting a superhuman amount of energy into his work. The harder he worked, the fewer nightmares he had. The darkness in his mind receded and he began to look forward to each day. As he stared at the ship he dreamed of taking his family on a voyage one day. He imagined forgetting about the war, about Scythia, about the nightmares, and living far away by a wide, gentle river, perhaps in Ionia or even further east. Charon dreamed of leaving everything behind and starting anew as his family grew.

He woke early on the fourth morning. Winter had arrived, and the icy wind blew across the water. He shivered and grabbed a cloak his wife had made him. Stygia was a weaver without equal, and she wove him a cloak depicting the forested wilderness, the dancing of nymphs, and the Pineios River winding its way through the wood. He wrapped the great garment around his shoulders, feeling the warmth of the fabric as it blocked the bitter winds. He then took a skiff to go get breakfast. He was an excellent diver and after some trips down into the rocky sea floor he had gathered a large collection of oysters. He put ashore, wrapped his cloak tighter around his shivering body and ate the oysters. He found an enormous pearl in the last oyster. It was nearly as large as his palm, and did not just shine but glowed like the full moon. It reminded Charon of his wife's beautiful, pale-blue eyes. He put it in his bag, thinking it would be an excellent gift for her. He walked up shore, wondering what color his child's eyes would be but stopped when he saw somebody running toward him. His heart sank when he saw his half-brother Toxon. He was a famed runner in Sesklo and delivered messages between villages. He volunteered to stay with Stygia while Charon was away and would run to tell him if Stygia was in labor. Charon considered how fast he ran, and knew the message would not be good.

"Stygia...blood...go to her..." Toxon gasped when Charon was in earshot and then collapsed on the shore. Other workers ran to help him, but Charon stood there in shock. Everything fell silent for him. He could hear his heart thumping, pushing and bursting against his chest. He ran. He ran to his home as fast as he could, cutting his feet on the jagged stones. His legs burned. His muscles felt as though they would burst and slide off his bones. His chest felt empty from the constant gasping, and his ribs felt stretched and torn. He made the day's journey in just a couple of hours. Finally, he could see his home, but stopped when he saw Stygia's sisters wailing and beating their breasts outside the door. He collapsed unconscious.

When he regained consciousness he learned that he would have had a son, but he was strangled by the umbilical cord. Stygia died from blood loss just before Charon reached the house. He spent the night wailing and tearing his hair by the bloody, pale body of his wife. He had again lost someone he loved.

***

Charon stood outside of the mound where his wife was buried. His cloak flapped in the cold, winter wind. Many days had passed since his wife's death but he often returned to her tomb to sit in silence. He wanted to be left alone and vehemently rejected the consolation and company of others. He did not have any nightmares since the night she passed. In fact, he had no dreams at all. He did not return to his house and often laid down and slept anywhere and woke up not knowing how much time had past or where he was. Today he brought the pearl he had found. The pearl he would have given his wife. He hoped to burry it at the foot of the mound to dedicate it to his wife and son's souls.

He was startled by the sound of somebody approaching. He turned and saw an old man walking to him. He stood next to Charon and rested on his staff in silence for a while.

"Who?" the man asked Charon after some time.

"My wife," Charon responded, "and my son."

"I'm sorry, it is difficult to lose your family" the man said in a soft, soothing voice. Charon nodded. The man waited again and said, "Are you Charon?"

"Yes, but," Charon paused, confused as to why he would know his name, "but how did you know?"

"Apollo gives me foresight, and in return I carry out his will as a faithful servant. He told me to come to Sesklo and find you Charon, adopted son of Iomori, husband to Stygia and would be father to Acheros," the old man said. He paused to let his words sink in. Charon was astonished this stranger knew his mother, his adoptive father, the fact he was adopted, his wife, and what the name of his son would have been. Only a prophet could know so much. The stranger then said, "Have I convinced you?"

"Sure," Charon said after a moment of hesitation.

"Good. Now listen. Apollo sent me here to guide you to a place where you can see you wife and son to say goodbye or, maybe, bring them out of the Underworld," the stranger spoke.

Charon stood there in disbelief. He did not know how to respond. But, if a God sent him, then it was in his best interest to listen.

"Why?"

"I never question the will of far-shooting Apollo. That never ends well for any mortal."

"Indeed."

"Listen, this is a blessing from an Olympian, a chance to save your wife! Come with me, there is nothing for you here." Charon pondered the stranger's words. There was so much he wanted to ask, and even then he felt like he could never fully understand everything. He reached into his bag and felt the pearl. He remembered his wife's beautiful eyes and how happy she was to start a family. His heart painfully swelled in his chest. He sighed and tightly grasped the enormous pearl. He told the stranger, "old man, I do not know you, but there is no denying your knowledge, and you are right that I have nothing left here. Wandering with a madman in the wilderness is as good a fate as returning to my home, which would never be the same without her. Lead on, wherever you want to take me. I would do anything to properly say goodbye, and even more if there is even a chance to save her and my son."

"Then come, fortune favors the swift," the stranger responded and smiled. He turned and started walking down a nearby path. He was much faster than Charon had expected, and he almost had to run to keep up with him.

"What is your name?" Charon asked.

"Eupedilos," the stranger responded with a smirk. Charon followed him, but paused by one of his footprints. There was a white feather with a golden shaft in the footprint. Tthe feather did not appear to belong to any bird he knew of in Greece. "What is it?" Eupedilos asked, then he saw the feather Charon was now holding.

The smirk briefly vanished from Eupedilos' face. For a brief moment his face looked like a liar whose tricks were unraveling. But he smiled and said, "That's a pretty feather, maybe you should keep it around. It would make a beautiful gift for your wife." Charon knew he was hiding something but decided not to question him. He stuffed the feather into his bag. He did not know what to think about it, but he knew there was more to Eupedilos than he was letting on.

The two walked through Greece and the weird feathers continuing to appear in Eupedilos' footsteps. Eupedilos explained they were heading to the Necromanteion; a temple dedicated to Hades and Persephone, the rulers of the Underworld and the Hosts of All. A mystery cult worshiped there, and they had been known to bring pilgrims and travelers down to the realm of the dead. Though few have returned from the Temple. Some said madness drove them to stay in the Underworld. Still others spread more sinister rumors. Charon shuddered when he heard the rumors Eupedilos told him, but he was willing to risk madness or worse.

On the way to the Necromanteion, Eupedilos told Charon they needed to pluck a pear or some other fruit. He explained the one ritual he knew from the temple. If the dead eat fruit of the living, then they can return to the world above. If the living eat the fruit of the dead, then the living could never leave. Eupedilos planned to save Stygia through this ritual. Charon asked how they could save his son if he was but a babe and could only suckle. Eupedilos chuckled and explained that Apollo thought of everything, and explained that if Charon's son suckled from his mother after she ate the pear, then both of the could leave. Thus, Charon and Eupedilos spoke with each other on their long, hard, cold and lonely journey to the deathly temple, the Necromanteion.

Charon traveled with Eupedilos for three days. Eupedilos was a friendly guide with a razor sharp wit who told many stories of his life. The most incredible anecdote he told Charon was of a scheme he devised to steel his brother's cattle by getting them to walk backward. They otherwise spent the time passing truisms and other ideas between each other. Charon had not felt this contented in such a long time. Though he never forgot Stygia and suffered from an even greater insomnia than when she was alive and would usually spend the night wandering around the fire and observing the stars.

They reached the Necromanteion at the beginning of the fourth day. On the way Eupedilos gave Charon a pear he had stolen from a nearby farm. Charon still had his doubts, but took the fruit regardless. When the two could see the Temple in the distance Eupedilos told Charon to stop.

"My journey with you ends here," he told Charon, "Apollo calls me elsewhere, but I am glad to have meet you Charon, you must be of the noble line of heroes or a descendent of some god. Now listen. The Necromanteion is a place of mysteries and does not admit many non-initiates. However, the priestesses of that temple must heed Apollo's will, so present them this coin when you ask to enter." Eupedilos reached into his billowing cloak and pulled out a golden coin. Charon was awestruck by that coin, which seemed to glow in Eupedilos' palm. The surface did not have a single dent or speck of rust and was polished brighter than any metal he had every seen in his lifetime. A regal eagle was cast on one face of the coin and the other face bore the image of a lyre. Eupedilos explained to him that the coin was from Olympus itself and bore the insignias of Zeus and Apollo, so any of the priestesses should recognize it and grant his request to rescue his wife and son.

"Eupedilos," Charon said, "I can not even begin to express my thanks. I could never repay you." The doubt Charon had once held in his heart shrunk when Eupedilos gave him the divine coined. Charon told him, "I will pray for your health. Fortune go with you!"

"Fortune go with you, Charon," Eupedilos responded, putting his hand on Charon's shoulder, "you will need it my friend. Few mortals return from the Underworld. As they said: 'Easy is the descent to Hades, difficult is the return to the world above.' Good luck." Eupedilos turned and began to walk down the road, away from the temple and east toward the sun. Charon waved him farewell, then started down toward the temple. But turned when he heard the rustling of feathers. He saw a trail of gold and white feathers leading down the road. The breeze started to scatter them, so he snatched one up quickly. He held it between his thumb and forefinger and saw it had a golden shaft. He reached into his bag and pulled out the curious feather he saw in Eupedilos' footsteps four days ago. The old feather was mangled but was identical to the one on he just found on the road. He did not know what to make of his discovery. He did not know whether it was an omen sent by a god or the sign of a god. All he knew was that in some way he could not wholly understand the gods of Olympus were with him. He took the two feathers he held and put them back in his bag for safekeeping.

Charon turned around and continued to the Necromanteion. The road lead up a mountain on which the Temple was perched like a carrion bird. The walls and columns were dark and smooth like onyx or obsidian. As Charon approached he could hear music coming from deep within the building. The temple, though small compared to others Charon had seen, echoed as if it had an enormous cavern as wide as the world hidden within. The ghostly hymns were carried by the wind and soon he heard their somber lyrics:

Sing through me great muses of the Lady of the Dead and Hostess of All.
Daughter of Thunder Wielding lord Zeus and the Great Demeter. Abducted
by Hades, Demeter rebelled against Zeus' and starved the world to save her
dear daughter, but what she did not know was that she'd already chosen to
stay and rule by him as Queen of the Underworld and ate the three red seeds.

So each year Demeter curses the world with winter while they live below.
Hades and Persephone wed here when she first returned to her mother
and they then instructed us to build our Temple here and honor them
and celebrate their marriage every year as winter sweeps through the land.

Life is but death's short dream, for ages souls have strewn your ashen banks like the
autumnal leaves that fall on the still surface of a cold lake, the ripples fading as the
water becomes silent and still like nature's true mirror.

Let us drink Lethe's forgetful waters. Send us through the Horn gate not the
Ivory gate of false dreams and shades. Remember us as we honor you.
Hail to you Persephone! Hostess of all! Lady of the Underworld!
And hail to you Hades! Host of All! The King of the Underworld!
Now we all will remember you and another song as well.

He was mesmerized those ominous hymns sung in soothing tones. Entranced, he nearly forgot everything as the song flowed through his mind. But, he stopped and shuddered as he remembered where he was, what he was doing and, most importantly, the dreaded place he was going to.

Charon wanted to turn back. He shuddered as he thought about descending to the land of the dead. The cursed realm that had stolen everything from him, but at that moment he remembered Stygia. He remembered her beautiful blue eyes and her sweet voice that was warmer and more beautiful by far than the ghostly sighs of the Temple. He remembered hearing her heartbeat while they lay together in bed. He remembered when she was pregnant and he could hear his son's heartbeat in her belly. The flood of memories rushed over him. His mind raced as if in a revelation or a Dionysian trance. He mercilessly insulted his own cowardice while every fiber of his body seemed to demand he turn back. His body seemed to battle his memory. His spirit wrestled with his vessel as his mind rushed and his legs shuddered. Then, the wind suddenly stopped. The landscape was quiet and the hymns had even stopped. It was as if the world itself; from Chronos deep in Tartarus to Zeus on Olympus to Poseidon deep in the sea all waited with bated breath to see what Charon would do.

Charon reached into his bag and pulled out the pearl that glowed like Sirius, the cursed star that brings fever and plagues to suffering humanity. It was as if the pearl brought plagues, fever and death to Stygia. He gripped it tightly in frustration, but then remembered why he kept it. He held it up to his eyes. It shone like Stygia's eyes on their wedding day, a long time ago, when they were happy. He knew at that moment he could set things right. He put the pearl back into his bag and walked toward the temple. The earth seemed to sigh after as wind picked up again, but the breeze carried an odd, faint sound; something like a cord being cut.

Charon stood on the steps of the Necromanteion. The glossy, black stone of the columns reflected the grey, overcast clouds creating the ghostly illusion as if the temple was made of mist. Between the columns were black, silk banners embroidered with silver. He still heard those ominous hymns behind the billowing silks. He walked through the columns and entered the temple's portico. Columns and silken banners bordered three of the four sides. The back wall was plain, solid and made of the same black stone. There was one gate to the temple. Marble busts of Persephone and Hades were mounted on the gate. A circle of six women stood around one women standing upon a raised dais in the center of the portico. All of them wore black tunics with crossed, silver embroidery. Each of them held something: two held bright, golden bushels of wheat, two held bushels of grey wheat that seemed almost made of ash and dust, two held golden censers with embers that smelled of sulfur and charred flesh, and the woman on the dais held a narcissus flower. Charon noticed that woman on the dais had her right arm bandaged with black silk like her tunic. That arm also had an uncanny aura, something otherworldly.

The woman upon the dais saw Charon step into the portico. She was in the middle of a hymn, but locked eyes with Charon and nodded. He understood the nod and waited by one of the columns. The women in the circle formed a procession some minutes later and disappeared into the temple while the woman on the dais stepped down and approached him. She held a commanding presence like that of a general or warrior. She exuded authority greater than any priest of any god that Charon ever met, but there was still something uncanny about her that he did not know how to explain. He kneeled before the woman, assuming her to be of high rank.

"Who are you and why are you here?" she spoke tersely, without the eloquence of her hymns.

"I am Charon," he swallowed, paused, but then continued, "I have come to go to Hades. To bring back my wife and son."

"Leave." the priestess spoke and turned to leave.

"Wait! Apollo sent me!" he said. The priestess paused, and turned back around.

"Do you have proof?" she asked. Charon nodded and reached into his bag. He pulled out the coin Eupedilos gave him, but as he pulled the coin out of his bag one of the feathers Charon found fell out of the bag and was carried off by the breeze. The priestess saw the feather and her eyes widened. Charon did not notice the feather being blown away, but he did notice the priestess' eyes widening.

"What is it?" Charon asked.

"Nothing, show me your proof," she said. Charon showed her the coin and her eyes flashed again. She knew at that moment the feather was no coincidence. She knew he was not there by foolishness or madness. She knew where she must take him. She told him: "You were sent here by more than just Apollo. So come in. Come in. Fortunate favorite of Olympus – or else – not so fortunate." She gave him a look of sorrow as she spoke; the sorrowful look somebody gives to a poor, naïve soul unknowingly approaching a terrible fate.

The priestess led Charon into the main chamber of the temple. A great, golden tripod was in the center, encrusted with every jewel known to man. The fire of the tripod flickered in the dark, but gave no warmth. Instead, Charon felt colder than he had outside. He felt a wind come from the back of the temple. The wind felt strong and bit through his cloak, but, looking around him, the flame did not flicker with any type of wind and the Priestess's tunic was not moved by even the slightest breeze. She led him to the back of the large chamber where there was gate carved from ivory. She grabbed a torch mounted on the side of the ivory gate. Charon looked through the gate and saw a tunnel with torches lining both sides of the tunnel for some distance, eventually leading to darkness. The cold, windless wind he felt earlier emanated from deep within that tunnel and he shivered from uncanny cold.

"Do you have some fruit?" the Priestess asked. Charon took out the pear from his bag and showed it to the priestess. She nodded and Charon put the fruit back in his bag.

"If I might ask, priestess," Charon asked, "What is your name?"

"Aitheremia."

"Aitheremia," Charon said, "it's a beautiful name."

"Thank you," Aitheremia said, smiling slightly before continuing, "Charon, fortify your heart as we descend to a grief-stricken land of lost shades." The two then crossed the doorway and began their descent into the Underworld.

The tunnel smelled of sulfur, was as cold as ice, and the air was thick and humid. Multiple arches held up the tunnel, and the red torchlight that flickered on the walls made the passage look like the throat or belly of a giant serpent. The shadows cast by the arch looked like ribs, the shifting red and pink lights made the stone look like flesh and the sulfurous smell was like putrid bile. Charon did his absolute best to keep his calm while descending to the realm of the dead, but he was nonetheless filled with dread. He had not felt that way since he stood in the ranks of Sesklo's armies in the brief moments before the trumpets to charge sounded. His heart felt like it was made of lead. It sank down into his gut, ripping and pulling the rest of his chest with it. His breathing became heavy as the air felt colder and colder.

He could still feel the cold windless wind he felt earlier. The cold windless wind passed through his cloak and into his skin. But just like earlier his cloak did not flutter and the torch flames were not disturbed. He felt emptier and emptier as he descended. The sulfurous smell even felt empty. It did not smell as if it came from anywhere. It did not smell like decay, but instead smelt toxic smoke. The air itself seemed to be pushing him away. All of these paradoxes of a windless wind and an empty yet noxious smell strained his mind. It was as if he were in some sort of dream. Perhaps, he thought, he was in a nightmare. Maybe he was already dead and was serving his punishment in Tartarus. The torches were coming to an end ahead of him, and after walking for what seemed like hours he could not stand it anymore.

"Aitheremia, wait," she stopped and turned to hear him, "I feel a cold, windless wind burrowing through my cloak, my skin, my muscles and my bones. It feels like walking through a storm, but our clothes are still like there is no breeze. The air feels empty, but it smells like poison. I feel like I need to hack out my lungs, but you are not affected? Am I going insane? Am I dreaming? Am I dead? In Tartarus? What is this?."

"Calm yourself." Aitheremia said.

"I may not even be here," said Charon falling to his knees as realization after realization came over him, "my wife might just be an trick! This might be a dream, and I might not even have a wife!"

"Be still!" Aitheremia shouted at the bent over Charon. "Listen, you are here. I feel windless wind and the toxic air. The Underworld is an otherworldly place and has otherworldly wind. So many shades come to this place that it reeks of death, but not decay. So please, Charon, calm yourself. You are here with me."

"How can I feel the wind and smell the stench of shades if I am alive?" Charon asked.

"We are shades carrying corpses" Aitheremia answered.

"I might be more shade than corpse" Charon said and hung his head, staring at the dirt floor. The two were silent for a while. Aitheremia was at a loss as to what to do. Then she had an idea and asked: "Tell me, what was your wife's name?"

"My wife's name was Stygia," Charon told her. She sat beside him and then asked: "What was she like?"

"The most perfect woman I ever knew. She had beautiful eyes like stars and long, flowing hair dark as a night. She was so kind to me, and everybody she met..."

"Anybody would say that about anybody they loved," Aitheremia interrupted, "so instead tell me something unique. Something special." Charon took a deep breath, thought for a moment and the started telling his story.

"I remember one time, after we were married, when we were walking along the Pineios River. I could not sleep that night, so I decided to walk before dawn. As I got up to leave Stygia woke up. She looked up at me, playfully sneered and asked, 'Going anywhere?' I turned looked away in embarrassment. I told her I was going for a walk. She smiled and said, 'without me?'

"'You want to come?'"

"'Of course, I have always loved watching the dawn. And besides, I got to make sure you do not wander off anywhere,' she winked. She then got up and got dressed in one of my old hunting tunics. We left our home and wandered along the River. As the sun started to rise above the horizon my wife asked me, 'I bet I'm a faster swimmer.'

"I agreed to her challenge and made our wagers. If she won, then she would win my belt. If I won, then she would give me her girdle. She threw off all her clothes except her girdle and dove into the River. I threw off all my clothes except my belt and quickly followed her. But, we didn't agree on a finishing point, so we swam for hours. She was quick and powerful, and we were neck and neck for what seemed like miles. My muscles burned and yet she was still right next to me. I pushed harder and harder, but I could not get a lead. By the time the sun rose high into the sky we were both weary and near to treading water so we both swam to the shore. We clawed onto the sandy beach at the same time, and collapsed with exhaustion. We spent the rest of the day resting on that sandy beach. We even saw the stars rise into the sky.

"Eventually, we broached the subject of who won, and we decided it was only fair we exchanged gifts, so we did, and I won her girdle and she won my belt."

Aitheremia smiled at the story, then she said: "She sounds like a strong and delightful woman. You must have been very happy."

"Not always. I kept having nightmares from a war. About those I lost. My heart always felt so heavy in my chest. You could say I really did feel like a shade carrying a corpse. We grew more distant as my nightmares became worse. She wanted to help, but I just wanted to be left alone. I didn't deserve her but we stuck together. When she was with child I started having fewer nightmares. I thought things were turning for the better until she was in her ninth moon. The nightmares returned, more terrible than ever. So, in my cowardice, I took a job away from home," Charon paused, his eyes watering, "and she died trying to give birth to my son. I wasn't there. I failed her, in all the ways she knew I would. In fact, you could say that I killed her. She died trying to give birth to my son."

"I know what you're feeling" Aitheremia said, "I have seen it before. I once had a sister who died in childbirth. Her husband felt the same way you did but I will tell you what I told him," Aitheremia paused to make sure Charon was looking at her and, without breaking eye contact, she said, "she wanted to have your son as much as you did. She knew the risks. Many women die in childbirth, which is why a successful birth is a blessing. You should not blame yourself for what happened. Death in childbirth is a tragedy," Aitheremia paused briefly, and Charon saw her stroking her bandaged arm, the she continued, "a terrible tragedy, but never the fault of the husband or the wife."

"I'm sorry for your loss, but thank you for everything Aitheremia," Charon said after a moment of silence.

"Do not thank me yet, we still have a long way to go," Aitheremia said, standing up. She then helped Charon to his feet and the two continued. Along the way, she asked him, "What was you son's name?"

"His name would have been Acheros," Charon said.

"We'll get them, I promise." Aitheremia said. She then looked at her bandaged arm. Charon saw she opened and closed her bandaged hand, watching its fingers move. He knew she was hiding something under those wrappings, but he did not want to ask what.

The two walked downward. The rows of torches ended and the tunnel became dark. The blackness was so thick that the pair felt like they were wading through it the same way one wades through mud. The torch seemed to get weaker as they continued, barely illuminating even the ground at their feet. Charon noticed that the walls of the tunnels appeared to be growing farther and father apart. The tunnel itself was widening into a large cave. Ahead, he began to notice a faint light that grew larger as they approached, but not brighter. The pair eventually reached the exit to their tunnel and the entrance to the Underworld. The entrance was a tall as a giant and wide as a ship. A blue mist shrouded the whole of the entrance like a curtain. He had no idea what would be on the other side, though he knew, or hoped, that Stygia and Acheros would be there so took in a deep breath and walked through the mists.

The entrance opened into an impossibly wide cavern. Enormous walls made of cragged and dark stone that looked like flint rose up all around. The walls seemed to have no ceiling, but instead rose to a void. The whole space seemed dimly lit by some unseen source. It was bright enough for Charon and Aitheremia to see, so she put out her torch. Charon stepped out from the cave and noticed that the floor was like a desert made out of black sand. The sand clung to his feet and stained his cloak as it dragged across the floor. Charon inspected the strange sand. It felt fine, finer than any sand on earth and felt like ground ash. He surveyed the space. An enormous river flowed to his right. The river seemed like a narrow sea, and he could only barely sea the dim outline of the opposite shore. The river itself flowed strongly and even though it appeared to have rapids at some places it gave off no sound. The water itself was dark like tar, but it seemed lighter and quicker than water. The shore gently rose to Charon's left, but he could not see a crest. Instead the shore rose like a hill on and on to a foggy horizon.

"This is Hades?" Charon asked.

"Yes and no. This is the Underworld. The dead are here. But Hades is across that river." Aitheremia then pointed to the River. Charon looked at the wide gloomy River and saw something strange. The surface broke and white foam formed around the break in the surface. Charon stared and finally recognized a person was in the river, drowning and screaming. He started to the shore to dive in and save the person, but saw that he or she was dragged under. There were no bubbles or any other signs of a struggle. But, Charon saw something more unsettling; he saw more people drowning and being sucked into the river. He looked up stream and saw hundreds of people drowning and screaming.

"What is that river? Who are they?" Charon asked.

"That river is the nameless River that divides the lands of the living and dead. That River is a cursed one, an ancient one, and a powerful one. The gods themselves fear it. Some rumor that the River is a primordial goddess or the daughter of Tethys and Oceanus. Nobody can be sure. And as for them," looking at the drowning people, "I'm sorry to say you cannot save them. They are shades that tried to swim across the River to Hades. Though, as soon as a shade enters it he or she is sucked down into a bottomless abyss."

"You mean to tell me," Charon said in bewilderment, "there are no dead in Hades?"

"Yes. There is no way to cross that River, so the dead wander about this shore listless and grief-stricken. Many become so desperate that they try to cross, and they drown for eternity. The others wait here at the borders to Hades; the only place where they can truly find rest." Aitheremia then gestured to Charon and told him: "Come. Your wife will be this way." The two continued along the shore for some time until Charon spotted a large, dense crowd of people in the distance. "So many have died that the Underworld has become overcrowded," Aitheremia explained as they walked to the crowd, "stay close to me and do not loose yourself amongst the shades."

Aitheremia and Charon walked amongst the crowd of shades. There were thousands upon thousands of shades. After some hours of walking through the crowd a shade approached them. The shade was his beloved Elegeus who he lost during the terrible war, whose death tormented his dreams. Charon ran to embrace him, but instead passed through his ghostly form. He collapsed into the ashy sand and wept at seeing them but not being able to touch them.

"Why are you here?" asked Elegeus. "Are you dead?"

"No, I," Charon paused, "I am here to rescue my wife and my son." Charon looked at Elegeus, then said, "I'm sorry. I'm sorry I didn't come for you."

"Charon, I did not expect you to come for me. I was able to say goodbye to you before I died. And my life felt complete despite it being short. I bear no grudge."

"But," Charon interrupted, "you died in my arms. I failed to protect you."

"I was fated to die," Elegeus said, "I reached the end of my cord, cut to end on that day. There was nothing you could have done. But, perhaps there is something we can do now." Charon stood up when he heard Elegeus. "Charon, listen, if you loved your wife as much as I had once loved you, then I would gladly help you find her." Elegeus said.

"I could save you if you want to?" Charon asked.

"Charon," Aitheremia interrupted, "Listen, it's your wife and son or him. I'm sorry, but you cannot save all three."

"Then save your wife," Elegeus said to Charon, "Trust me when I say that if I can help you escape with your wife, then I can rest happily here."

"Thank you," Charon said.

"I think I remember a woman cradling a babe wandering amongst us recently. She wandered through the crowd asking for her husband for a whole day, but then she left the crowd and wandered further upstream. It might be her. Let me lead you to her," Elegeus spoke. He then started drifting across the sands, and Charon and Aitheremia followed him.

Elegeus led them upstream. They walked for hours maybe even days as the crowd dwindled and the sounds of drowning shades faded away. Out in the distance, in the mists by the River's shore, Charon saw something. A single shade stood on the shore. He walked faster and faster toward the figure, recognizing it was Stygia. He ran. He sprinted. His muscles ached and his lungs stung in the ashen air. Elegeus kept pace, but Aitheremia was left far behind. She kept shouting for Charon to wait, but her sounds faded as he ran toward his wife.

Charon saw Stygia more clearly as he approached, but noticed that tears stained her translucent face. She was undressing too, shedding the robes she wore as a shade. When she shed the last of her clothing she started walking to the River. Charon immediately realized what she intended to do.

"Stygia! Stygia! Stop!" Charon shouted. Stygia turned and saw him, stopping just before her feet touched the water. He stood before her and nearly collapsed from exhaustion but he kept his composure. He smiled as he looked into her eyes and saw her face. He moved his hand to touch her, but she backed away.

"Stygia? What's the matter?" Charon asked her.

"What are you? Are you dead too?"

"No, I came here for you!"

"No. My husband would never come so far. You must be some deceitful spirit." Stygia rebuked with contempt.

"But I have!"

"Why would you, if you are Charon? You never even came when I was in labor with your son."

"What? Did you not think I tried to reach you when I heard what happened? I ran, faster than maybe Hermes himself! I nearly died trying to get to you! I was just too late."

"That's not the point. You should never have left in the first place."

"I didn't want to."

"Then why did you go?"

"It's difficult to explain. I just wanted to be alone, away from everybody because I thought I didn't deserve anyone. I have nothing but contempt for myself. Too many have died because of me."

"There, was that hard?" Stygia asked with an accusatory sarcasm.

"What?"

"Talking. To me. Your wife? Did you think I wouldn't listen?"

"I didn't want you to think it was your fault. I didn't want you to leave me."

"So you left me alone. Multiple times. Even after I lost children? When I could have had your son?" Stygia saw that her words cut deep, so she continued, "So what now? You come here and just expect me to forgive you? To come back to you? Just so you can leave me again? Never talk to me? Maybe never even see your son? No Charon. You abandoned me so I would never abandon you. You rejected me so I would never reject you. Now I reject you. I let you go. If you left me in my time of need, then we might as well never have been married." Stygia then turned around and started walking into the River. Charon eyes lit up and he rushed to the very edge of the water.

"Stop! Stygia! You don't know what you are doing!" Charon shouted at her.

"Yes I do. My son and I cannot listlessly wait here forever. Rest lies there," she pointed to the opposite shore, "in Hades. I can feel it. There is where my son and I belong. I will swim over there and beg Hades and Persephone to ferry my son across." Stygia waded through the River. Charon paused and looked at the black water. He shivered in fear, but was determined to save her. He threw off his cloak and bag, and he then started to wade in after her.

"AAKH!" Charon howled. He looked at his feet, but he could not see them. The water seemed to boil around him and a thick, foggy vapor that smelled like rotting and burning flesh rose around his legs. Stygia shuddered at the sound but kept moving forward. Charon could feel skin sliding off of his feet. Elegeus went up to the River edge and shouted at his friend to come back. Charon, after a long moment of feeling the agonizing pain rip its way up his body, gritted his teeth and shouted at Stygia, "Don't do it! You'll drown!"

"I can swim as well as you, Charon, if that is who you are. Other, weaker shades may drown, but I swear by my son I will not. And if you are a trick, then I swear you will not lead me astray." The water was now up to her chest and she was ready to dive into the River and swim across.

"You don't understand" Charon said, waist deep in the River and feeling his muscles fall off his legs.

"No, I understand perfectly." Stygia took a deep breath but, suddenly, she was dragged under as if an undertow swept her away or an unseen serpent swallowed her.

"Stygia!" Charon shouted. He did not see her come up so he dove into the River.

The water felt cold, colder than anything he had felt before. But, he could feel his flesh melting away. Bubbles of steam erupted all over his body like the steam bursting from a red-hot blade quenched in water. The pain split through every sinew and nerve in his body but he swam onward. He opened his eyes, which stung as if somebody poured molten bronze into his skull. He saw Stygia dragged deeper into the depths. He pushed toward her as hard as he could. His muscles frayed and slid off his bones with each stroke. Stygia swam with all her might and it seemed like she was able to overcome the currents pulling her under. They came closer and closer together and soon Charon was in arm's reach of Stygia. He desperately reached out to her. His arm seemed to dislocate from its socket as its ligaments melted away. Then, for a brief moment, he was able to hold her. She was able to grab his hand despite being a shade. He did not know how it was possible but he was elated. He started to pull, but neither of them would budge. Then he could feel something pulling Stygia as if she were being swallowed. He tried to pull with all his might, but he too was being dragged deeper. He stopped when he felt her other hand releasing his grasp. He tried to shout at her to stop but she shook her head. She freed herself of him and started to sink down into the depths. She looked up at him one last time, and mouthed two word: I'm sorry. Suddenly, she was dragged with tremendous force down into the black depths and vanished. Charon stayed there in silence for some time, feeling his insides melt away. The whole River was so dark that he felt like he was in an endless shapeless void. He did not remember where the surface was, and he didn't care. He now knew for certain that he failed.

Suddenly, he remembered his son; perhaps he could still save him. This thought animated whatever was left of his limbs and he swam to the surface, using the bubbles from his still melting flesh to guide him upward. He still felt the River trying to pull him under, trying to swallow him, but he struggled to the surface with all his might. He pushed himself harder and harder until he felt a subtle release as he broke the surface of the water. Steam erupted all around him as he gasped for air, but he could not breath. He panicked and rushed to the shore. The current had carried him far down River, but he could still see Elegeus in the distance, calling his name. He swam to shore with the last ounce of his strength, battling the raging waters all around him until he finally felt the ashen sand beneath him and crawled onto shore. The last remaining bits of meat clinging to his bones splattered onto the sand, vaporizing as they touched the ground. He collapsed and lost consciousness.

He woke to see Elegeus and Aitheremia kneeling over him. He sat up feeling his cloak around his shoulders. For a moment he thought he was waking from a long, deep sleep but then remembered where he was. He pulled his cloak tightly around him and saw his hands. They were nothing but smoldering, flaking bone. His inspected the rest of his body but there was nothing but bone as well. He clawed at his head and only felt a skull. He tried to scream for help, but only inhuman howls echoed from his mouth.

"Charon! Stop! Listen to me!" Aitheremia shouted, "Focus on what you want to say and the words will come. Calm down and focus." Charon heard her, and eventually calmed.

He focused on what he wanted to say until his howls and moans congealed into an otherworldly voice that was not his own. He asked: "What happened to me?"

"The River devours everything that enters it. Shades that go into that River drown forever, but it does something even worse to mortals. It starts with the flesh, slowly eating it away. If the living person does not escape it, then the rest of him or her melts away into the currents. If the person does escape, then River takes away that person's death. You cannot die or be killed, Charon. You are not mortal, but not immortal."

Charon sat there, stupefied and overwhelmed. Elegeus sat beside him and placed an arm around his shoulder. Charon could feel Elegeus' arm. He realized he could touch him. He backed off in confusion.

"How can Elegeus touch me?" Charon asked, "Am I a shade?"

"No. You can touch shades, but I cannot explain why."

"How do you know this?" Charon asked Aitheremia. She did not answer, but waited for some moments. She hung her head as if in shame. She took a deep breath, brought her right arm forward and started to unwrap the silken bandages. Underneath the wrappings Charon saw her hand, or whatever was left of it. Her hand and forearm was nothing but bone that moved as if it had ghostly muscles. Her skeletal arm ended in a hideous stump at her elbow. The muscle and skin looked rotten and cauterized.

"Charon, remember when I told you about my sister? My older sister, Dystokea, died in childbirth. I loved her so much, so I decided to save her. I thought I could. At the time I was an initiate in the Necromanteion, and I knew of that tunnel we traveled through. So, I came here very much like you but found my sister already drowning in the River. I climbed on a stone overhanging the shore to reach her. When she was dragged past I reached out to grab her hand. But, my hand passed through hers. Then I lost my balance and braced myself on the stone with my other hand, but this one," she raised up her right, skeletal hand, "went into the water. The flesh melted away, and this is all I was left with. I tried to cut and burn it off, but nothing worked. Over the years I learned much about my curse, and that is how I know so much."

"I'm sorry," Charon said.

"I'm sorry too," Aitheremia responded. The empty words fell on deaf ears.

The three sat silently. The rippling of the cursed River echoed through the boundless cave. Then, they heard a soft crying. Charon stood and went to see what it was and found a small alcove in the shore about where Stygia went into the River. He looked inside and saw the shade of a babe, weeping softly, as if it had already been wailing for hours. He scooped up the child and held it in his arms.

"Acheros," Charon said softly. He knew this was the shade of his son. Stygia must have put him there, intending to return when she found a way across the River. The babe wailed in terror of Charon's skeletal form. Perhaps, he could feel that the thing, whatever it was, that held him was cursed and uncanny. Elegeus offered to take Acheros from Charon. Acheros quieted down once in Elegeus' arms.

"Acheros, I like the name," Elegeus said. Charon nodded, he would have smiled if he could. He turned to Aitheremia and he saw that she had his bag slung over her shoulder.

He walked toward her.

"Give me the pear," Charon told her.

"Pear?" Elegeus asked.

"Yes, if he eats is we can save him. We can bring him back to the world above," Charon explained and reached for his bag. Aitheremia tried to hold it from him but he wrenched it from her.

"Charon it won't," Aitheremia tried to explain to Charon.

"Shut up!" Charon shouted at her.

"Charon!" Elegeus shouted at him, the babe started crying again. Charon was quiet, then Elegeus explained to him,

"Charon, even if he could touch that," nodding to the pear Charon held, "he cannot eat it. You would choke him. He doesn't even have teeth yet!"

"He's right," Aitheremia said, "The only way it could have worked is if Stygia ate the fruit and then nursed your son. Your son cannot eat the pear. If you tried to force him to, then you'd only make things worse."

Charon was still as he listened to her words. He walked toward the shore, and threw the pear into the River, furiously shouting. Then, the cave became quiet as Charon collapsed to his knees and Elegeus quieted Acheros down.

Suddenly, Charon, Aitheremia and Elegeus heard a tremendous thundering. They heard the clattering of wood and the snorting of horses growing louder and louder. Charon stood up and backed away with Elegeus when a chariot came into view. Aitheremia bowed when she saw it.

"Bow!" Aitheremia whispered to her companions, "Hades and Persephone are coming!"

Elegeus bowed. Charon saw a golden chariot drawn by four sable-black horses. A cloud of black dust obscured the chariot until it came to a rest. He bowed as he saw two regal figures dismounting.

One figure was a slim man with pale-olive skin, curly dark hair and sharp blue-grey eyes. He was Hades, Host of All. The other figure was a woman that seemed to glow in the dark. She had bright blonde hair, green eyes and wore a sable robe with golden embroidery. She was Persephone, Hostess of All. Charon, Elegeus, and Aitheremia offered their respects but Hades waved them off. He then walked up to Charon begging him to rise. The God stood nearly twice as high as him.

"Charon?" Hades asked him, he nodded, "it pains me to see what has happened to you. I never meant for this to happen. Hermes arrived..."

"Hermes?" Charon interrupted.

"Oh," Hades paused, stroked his beard, and then continued: "Let me start at the beginning. You have seen the shades and that there are too many. They need to be in my realm, but there too few who could cross this River. The gods can cross the River but they all fear it, including myself. I am also King of the Underworld and cannot spend my days as a ferryman. My Queen cannot do it either. We both have other duties to our realm. Hermes could do it, and though does guide souls to the shore on occasion Zeus would never make his messenger my ferryman. And none of the other gods would ever do such a service to mortals. So for eons listless souls gathered on the banks, unable to rest. I begged my brother again and again for a ferryman but each time he ignored me.

"This all changed after the terrible war between Sesklo and Scythia. So many died that Zeus could ignore the problem no longer. He convened the gods to find a solution. Apollo proposed you to be the ferryman. You were the son of River god Peneus, so you could navigate Rivers better than most gods and mortals. In fact, that is what allowed you to escape it. You also fought in the war, so we hoped you would want to help your comrades find rest."

"So you killed my wife!" Charon interrupted.

"Your wife would have died either way. I am the lord of the Underworld, not death itself. I was ready to send for you and offer your family godhood and a home on the Isles of the Blessed in exchange for your service. But Thanatos told me he had already taken your wife and son. So I asked Hermes to lead you to my Temple. I planned to make the same offer when you arrived. But I could not have predicted what your wife did. I could have saved her and you, but I could not find you amongst the shades until it was too late. I am sorry Charon." Hades placed his hand on Charon's shoulder, and then he said, "Charon, I can still save her if you wish. I will make a new deal. If I make a large enough sacrifice to the River, then I could win a shade in exchange. Collect coins, Obols, just like the ones in Sesklo, from each person you ferry. Collect enough of them and I could save her." Charon stood in silence, thinking over the offer. Persephone then walked toward Charon. Hades backed away.

"Charon, I see the shade of your son survived? I can make sure he and your dear friend," she nodded to Elegeus, "have a home Isles of the Blessed. I know the task sounds daunting but you could save her. Think. There is nothing left for you in the world above. Here you at least have hope." Charon stood in silence. He remembered what Stygia said to him. He remembered how he failed, but now he had another chance to make things right and he was determined not to fail. He did not care if she ever loved him again. All he wanted was for her to be free. Charon finally looked up to the goddess and told her, "I will do anything to save her."

Hades gestured to the river as if beckoning somebody to come. Then, a skiff emerged from the darkness and beached itself on the shore.

"This will be your craft," Hades explained, then he knelt before Charon and continued, "I thank and honor you, Charon, for accepting this task. And, I swear upon this River, the most sacred of oaths to us gods, if you hold up your end of the bargain, then I will free her."

"How many Obols must I collect?" Charon asked.

"First, ferry all of these souls. Once word of the cost to be ferried to my realm has spread across Greece you can start collecting Obols. Then collect Obols until there are no more dead." Charon stared at Hades in shock as he said this, but the Host of All continued, "I know it sounds impossible, but this is the only way to appease this voracious, malicious River." Charon nodded slowly in understanding.

"I will serve you faithfully my lord and lady," he said to the Rulers of the Underworld. He then went to his skiff. He felt even colder and wrapped his cloak around him. The whole garment was stained black from the ashen sand and the landscapes and rivers his wife had so skillfully woven into the fabric were blotted out. Charon stopped at the shore, and as he looked out over the waters he remembered his wife. He took out the pearl that shone with the light of her eyes, the gift he was never able to give to his wife.

"It's beautiful," Charon heard. He was startled and turned around quickly to see Persephone standing behind him. She walked toward him and asked: "May I see it?"

Charon handed it to her. "Was it a gift?" she asked.

"For her. I thought she would love it because it shines just like her beautiful eyes," Charon told the goddess. She smiled as he spoke.

"Charon, I am so sorry for what happened to you, and there is little I can do," Persephone spoke, "but I can this for you." She clasped the pearl between her hands. Then pulled her hands apart, revealing a golden lantern growing around the pearl, which began to glow brighter than the moon with a beautiful, blue light. Persephone then gave the lantern to Charon and told him: "Let the light of her eyes forever guide you across those waters, and let this gift remind you of what you are struggling for." Charon held the gift and began to cry without tears. He bowed before the goddess and offered many thanks, but she stopped him and told him to rise. He did. She caressed his skull and, looking into his vacant eyes, said, "I too swear by this River that she will be free someday."

Persephone went to the chariot and took out a golden libation bowl. And there, on the shore, Hades, Persephone and Charon swore on their agreement; binding them all in the most sacred of oaths.

The Hosts of All then mounted their chariot. Hades said one final thanks to Charon. Persephone bid him a final farewell and promised him all will know his story and thank him for his sacrifice. The gods then departed, back into the darkness.

The three stood there in silence, each slowly realizing what had just occurred. Eventually, Charon knew he had to begin his task soon so he had to bid his friends farewell. He walked to Aitheremia.

"Thank you for everything," he said to her, "I will remember you forever, and when the time comes I will take you to the Isles of the Blessed myself." Aitheremia's eyes began to water, and she embraced him. The two hugged each other some time and Charon would have cried if he could. She had done so much for him and he was truly sad to see her depart, at least, until she returned to Hades' realm.

"You are welcome Charon and I will make sure everybody in the world knows your story," Aitheremia said with a wavering voice, "Farewell and may Fortune be with you." She then departed.

"Elegeus," Charon spoke, "come." He fastened the lantern Persephone had made him to the bow of his skiff, boarded the boat and waited for Elegeus.

"Master," Elegeus spoke, "you can trust me to take care of Acheros. I cared for my older sister's children before the war," Elegeus said, "I promise, he will be safe and happy with me."

"Elegeus," Charon said, "dear Elegeus, I know he will be happy with you. I know you will take care of him. I trust you."

"Thank you," Elegeus said.

"I loved you so many years ago, and you are just as brave, kind, and faithful as you were when I last held you in my arms. I trust you with my son but promise me this: if he grows up in the Isles (if the shades of children grow), then tell him about the Charon you knew. Tell him about his mother, the most perfect woman in the world, and how I am working to save her." Elegeus nodded.

"Come, beloved Elegeus," Charon said, reaching out his bony hand, "I laid you to rest many years ago, and I will lay you to rest again but this time forever." The three then crossed the Styx, the first souls to successfully make the crossing. Charon and Elegeus recounted stories of their time together at length. Charon also told Elegeus all about Stygia; the story of how they met, how excited he was to be a father and even the story he told Aitheremia. Eventually, the skiff landed on the opposite shore. Not far from the shore an enormous flint and obsidian cliff face rose upward into the void ceiling. There was one white, ivory gate starkly set into the cliff face. Elegeus and Charon saw the gate and departed from the skiff. They stood on the threshold to Hades' realm.

"Will we ever see each other again?" Elegeus asked, his ghostly eyes welling with tears.

"Probably not," Charon responded. Elegeus embraced him, and the two held each other for a long time. Charon then caressed his son's head as Elegeus held him, bidding him a final farewell and whispering a prayer. Charon then bid Elegeus farewell as he crossed the threshold to the Underworld. Thus, Hades accepted his first guests.

He eventually ferried the crowd of shades across the River including his adoptive parents, who bemoaned their son's state. Charon silently and tearlessly wept when he met them and when they entered Hades. One day he ferried Aitheremia and they spent their short time together recounting what had happened since they last spoke. She eventually left him with tears in her eyes.

Many, many years later a strange man and woman approached Charon, and handed him his first Obols. They were Charon's true parents Emporos and Diotima. They lived a long life and passed away peacefully, believing they had escaped the Oracle's fate. And thus the couple paid their son to ferry them to the land of the dead. A prophecy was fulfilled and an endless struggle began that day. From then on Charon would only take on souls who offered Obols. He wanted to ferry the pitiful, listless souls without Obols but even after centuries and millennia he remembered Stygia suffering because of him and he dogmatically stuck to his task, turning away anybody who could not pay his fee.

Thus, Charon ferries souls to this day, working and struggling to free his wife from torment. Unfortunately his story faded away, overshadowed by the works of a blind poet and a shepherd poet. However, Charon's story does live on in a certain sense. As his tale faded away the River he crosses took on the name of his wife and became the Styx, so we still honor the deathly ferryman and remember what he tirelessly struggles for.

I thus conclude my song. Thanks be to Persephone, muse who inspired
me to tell you of the man who others spoke of as little more than a
prop or automaton. So remember these words when others sing of Charon,
or if you think my myth false then wonder for just a moment who he is.
Who is the ferryman? Why have none sung of him? And so sing you own tales to
answer these questions. But for now I must leave. So farewell listeners!
And now, noble Charon, I shall remember you and another song too.

ೞ   ৪০

Carl Teegerstrom *is a Junior English and Classics major at Trinity University with a passion for myth, literature, sketching, poetry and the humanities in general. He was born in Houston, Texas where he grew up with his loving family of avid readers. He was inspired to write this story of Charon after his teacher challenged his class to create a myth for this mythless figure.*

After the Stroke of Midnight

After the stroke of midnight
when most are fast asleep
into the ancient graveyard
stealthy he does creep
Seeking out the marker
of a long forgotten soul
he digs into the hard earth
to obtain his unholy goal
He collects the fleshless bones
and gathers them to his sack
then quietly leaves the scene
with his booty on his back
Once inside his dark room
a single candle he does light
sorting all his treasures
working late into the night
Femora, tibiae, and ulnae
plus other skeletal remains
sorted by type and stacked
with such thought out pains
Grinding them into powders
for poultices and potions
carefully carved magic charms
and other ghoulish notions
After the stroke of midnight
another night of work begins
he sold his soul and must toil
to atone for all his sins

Freedom Journey

Among the ruins of broken lives,
they came across great expanses,

43

searching for a place to rest their weariness.
Empty from hunger.
Full from hope.
Carrying with them stories of their pasts,
and the bones of their ancestors.
Multitudes marching,
while looking out over myriad expressions,
in quest of a familiar face.
Grasping the future in clasped hands
tucked into worn pockets.
Afraid to let go,
lest dreams scatter like lost seeds
among devouring crows of indifference.
Tiredness overtaking,
broken bodies pitch tents
of sparse comfort.
Taking refuge along the never ending
journey of freedom.

Broken Calm

Pitch black
foreboding night
distant rumbles
a sharp crash of thunder
the sky is split in two
by a white hot bolt of lighting
mighty trees bow to the wind
awakening sleeping beasts
the hearts of men race
pounding in their ears
bones rattle
teeth gnash
horripilation
as all await the next imminent strike

Fallen

the sign said open
so she walked right in
checking her wings at the door

red papered walls
in a room filled with smoke
and the smell of cheap perfume
whispered conversations
in an unknown language
heard only by discerning ears
bleary red eyes staring out
from under thick mascaraed lashes
followed her every move
working her way to the back of the room
she finds a quiet corner
to wait her turn
all the while a neon sign flashes overhead
with the words
"Welcome to Gehenna"

The Waiting is the Hardest Part

The cold white hand of Death
reached out and touched his black soul.
He had no place left to run to,
it had been following him too long.
The waiting is the hardest part.
He knew it was coming for him,
we all do, deny it as we will.
Death has his way in the end.
Although he courted Death
for far too many years.
The bottle and the needle
being his only friends.
Now he sits alone on a street corner,
cold and shivering.
He knows it is his time,
as he takes a deep breath of relief,
for the waiting is the hardest part.

Who Will Be Left to Perform

Refined phrases,
sculpted like a statue.

Abstract images,
tickling the mind.
Becoming lost on
the road to nowhere,
sidetracked by the
mourning dove's song.
Questioning the outcome.
Was it worth the effort?
The man in the front row
just stood up and left;
wandering off into unknown territory.
Will he find his way back?
Are you lost forever?
Rain falls down,
Washing away the confusion.
Where have you been
the last hour of my life?
What is real, and what is not?
I continue on my journey.
Now it is my turn to
withdraw the knife
and bleed on the crowd.

CR SO

Ann Christine Tabaka lives in Delaware. She is a published poet and artist. She loves gardening and cooking. Chris lives with her husband and two cats. Her most recent credits are The Paragon Journal, The Literary Hatchet, Metaworker, Raven Cage Ezine, RavensPerch, Anapest Journal, Mused, Indiana Voice Journal, Halcyon Days Magazine, The Society of Classical Poets, and BSU's Celestial Musings Anthology' Poems Inspired by the Night Sky.'

PRIMARY SCHOOL PRAYERS / QUESTIONS I ASK MY DOCTOR - HANNAH SMITH-YEN

Primary School Prayers

1. Our Lord, who art in heaven
Jesus rose on the fifth day stained red
He ascended, he looks down
We soak the soil in blood,
Gild our dead and wait for absolution.

2. Hallowed be thy name
Six six six are the letters in your name
Let them ruin you
Let them touch you where you're soft softest
Let them speak your name like a sacred word
In an old language that sounds like
The rasp of dry wood against silk

3. Thy kingdom come
So if we look past the sinews
The gristle tendons /meat/ of it
The salty blood, the red between my teeth
The metal on my tongue
The bone ache, the prayers etched onto my ribs
This is all yours, right?

4. Thy will be done
you'll always sound like a zipper going down
like an oil slick's song
but maybe to you, it's more like a suitcase closing
i wish you could hear what i hear

5. On earth as it is in Heaven
peel away the skin
so that you bloom rose-red
dripping down your chin
greeting Persephone with the colour of her damnation
or salvation, whichever way you look at it

the right way

Questions I Ask my Doctor

but like, look.
can i excise it?
will my body still be stained
with clouding memories, low and heavy?
does the thought of touching sicken you, too?
will i ever be clean? can i shower again?
can running water wash away his touch, or is it too deep inside me?
spreading out across my meat and bones, a thick coating on my veins
is it wrapped around my heart like fat, yellow and glistening?
is it soft and warm behind my ribcage?
can you excise it from my body?
with scalpels that cut away at the fat, the grime, the bone-deep dirt
erasing the fingerprint impressions on my hips
cut it all away and i can start anew,
clear of scars and whisper-flashes of skin against skin
and skin against cloth and skin against teeth
can you go deeper, where it burrows inside of me?
a dark stain creeping across my body
signalling that i am no longer holy and pure
touch is not a prayer, it is a penance
can you make sure you get it all, doctor?
even in the hollows of my collarbones, where kisses rest,
and the dips between my ribs
clean his ashes from my lips, clean him out
or are there parts of me you cannot reach?
the hidden alcoves where i
keep his sweet nothings locked away
can i excise it?

℞   ℘

Hannah Smith-Yen was born in Guisborough and grew up around the world. She is currently a final year anthropology student at University College London, writing a dissertation on professional wrestling. You can find more of her work at hannahsmithyen.tumblr.com.

BONES / CHUM SCHOOL / BLASTING CAPS / PLOTS / IT IS NOT ENOUGH TO BE FUCKED, THEY WANT YOU KNOW IT AS WELL - RYAN QUINN FLANAGAN

Bones

There were no bones in the train yard
there were no bones even though that
is where they said they would be
there were plenty of stones, discarded bottles,
garbage bags of clothing littering the tracks
and I climbed up into a heavily graffitied side car
suddenly able to see the ghost of my breath
a few rats climbing over each other like children
in the playground,
but there were no bones at all
except the ones in my body,
wrenching my ankle real good
I jumped back down out
of the car.

Chum School

She went to chum school
because it was free.

The shark people thought
the kids who could not afford summer camp
should have a place to go.

And their parents should have a way
to be rid of their children for the summer
as well.

And they made the kids fill the buckets with chum.
Taught them how to throw it, and what it consisted of.
And you got to see sharks, to feed them.

And when the summer was over you got a certificate
and a little blue badge that signified you were
a graduate of chum school.
She no longer has the little blue badge,
but she looks out the certificate
and shows me.

She is still proud.
I can see it in her face.

A forty-two year old woman
who can't keep a man,
but knows how to feed
the sharks.

Blasting Caps

A
bomb
goes
off

and
everyone
panics

like
love
with
shrapnel

for
kisses,

no
survivors.

Plots

He asked if I knew
of any good plots

and I told him
the cemetery was
full of them

and since he was trying
to be a writer

and not
an undertaker

he failed to see
the humour.

It Is Not Enough to be Fucked,
they Want You Know it as Well

Arterial blood
you get to know the colour,
Keats on his deathbed
after his time in medical school;
it is not enough to be fucked,
they want you know it as well.
Like an aging carriage horse passing
the glue factory.

ଔ ନ

Ryan Quinn Flanagan is a Canadian-born author residing in Elliot Lake, Ontario, Canada with his other half and mounds of snow. His work can be found both in print and online in such places as: Evergreen Review, The New York Quarterly, Word Riot, In Between Hangovers, Red Fez, and The Oklahoma Review. His website can be found at: http://ryanquinnflanagan.yolasite.com/

"Listen," Delores said. "After breakfast, I was thinking we could go pick out that cemetery plot we spoke about."

"But why?" Gil said, looking up from the Sunday paper. "I mean, why now? We're active, we're healthy—"

"And we've also been to three funerals in the last eight months. What makes you think we're gonna be around forever? Our friends are dropping just as fast as your stock portfolio."

"But we're different," Gil said. "Remember last week? We were thinking about training for that marathon?"

"Gil, that was you. You see a guy in the paper cross the finish line, and all of a sudden you have the ability of an Olympic athlete. You're seventy-four. You're not gonna be here forever."

"Yeah, well neither are you."

"That's right, Gil. Neither will I."

Delores was in the kitchen preparing breakfast for the two of them: eggs and bacon with a side of toast for Gil, and sliced fruit with a bowl of oatmeal for her. Of course, Gil had to make things extra difficult by the way he liked his eggs over easy and his bacon done well. But then again, Delores would be the first one to admit that she wasn't exactly the Barefoot Contessa.

"Let me understand something," Gil said. "You want us to go and pick out the place where we're gonna die?"

"Not where we're going to die, Gil, where we're going to go after we die."

"You mean the ground."

"Or, maybe even above it, because I was actually thinking a mausoleum could be nice."

"My mother always used to say that those were for gentiles or celebrities. And guess what—we're neither."

"Listen, I'm not the one who told you to get that tattoo. Now none of the Jewish cemeteries will take us, so our options are limited."

"Oh, so, you're putting that on me?"

"There's no one else to put it on."

Gil didn't respond.

"I'm just asking you to keep an open mind, all right? Is that so much to ask?"

The eggs were ready and her oatmeal was ready, but the bacon looked like it still needed more time. No wonder they won't let us in, Delores thought.

She brought Gil's eggs to the table and told him to get started. In the meantime, she went back to the kitchen and sliced a banana for her oatmeal.

Gil sat at the kitchen table and began eating his breakfast. "How much do one of these things cost anyway?"

"From what I understand, they're pretty affordable."

"That's what you said about the sofa," Gil said, walking to the fridge to get some orange juice. He opened the door and said, "I want a nice casket. Nothing too fancy, but you know, something with taste."

"Since when do you care if something has taste? You have no taste."

"I have taste. Sure I do. Who says I don't have any taste?"

Delores flipped the bacon over in the frying pan and decided it was ready—perhaps not the way Gil liked it, but she didn't care, it would have to do.

Gil poured two glasses of orange juice for them and sat down at the table.

Delores brought over the bacon, and Gil took a piece right from the tray she served it on. But that was okay, since he didn't seem to mind the way it was only properly cooked and not burnt to a crisp.

She said, "So, after we eat, we'll head over to the cemetery?"

"Oh, c'mon, what about the game?"

"It's only ten-thirty. Besides, the place is right around the corner. It'll be quick. I promise."

"All right, fine. I'll go," he said, but only because I love you."

"Gil, shut up and eat your breakfast."

When they got to the front office of the Sayonara Memorial Gardens they were greeted by a young, hip-looking salesman who Delores had been in contact with over the phone. He wore dark sunglasses and had his hair slicked back with gel. They introduced themselves and walked towards the grounds of the cemetery.

"You guys are gonna love what we have to offer," the salesman said.

"We've got some great specials going on now, too."

Delores said, "You actually sold a plot to friends of ours a few weeks ago—the Flickers."

"Oh, they are a lovely couple. I don't know if they mentioned it, but they actually ended up buying this big, walk-in mausoleum for their entire family. And it's funny, because not too long ago mausoleums were totally passé. I'm not sure why, but they seem to be coming back in a big way—can't get rid of 'em fast enough."

"That might be nice, Gil," Delores said, nudging her husband of forty-five years.

"Eternity with your brother? Forget it. Could you imagine? The guy would never shut up about all those bargains he got at the flea market."

They came around a bend and made their first stop at an ordinary side-by-side plot for married couples. Each grave was marked by a simple plaque in the ground. It had their names and marked the dates of when they lived and died. There were a lot of them, too, almost an overwhelming amount. They ran in rows, one after the other, after the other.

"This is our standard offering," the salesman said. "A modest plot for a modest price."

There weren't many trees around, and shade was hard to come by. Delores figured this was part of the reason why there weren't many flowers left on top of any of the graves or any people around visiting. She moved her gaze around and began to feel uneasy. The grass wasn't nearly as green here as it was by the entrance. She found it all to be sort of barren.

"Gil, what do you think?"

He looked at his watch and said, "Seems fine to me."

Delores said, "I just don't think anyone would want to visit us here. That's the whole point, isn't it?"

"It certainly is," the salesman said. "And if it were up to me? Let me tell ya, I wouldn't be caught dead in one of those things. Let's move on, shall we?"

They walked over a small garden bridge and entered a much better manicured area of the cemetery. Unlike the other side, there were plenty of visitors here, moving about, paying respect to loved ones, leaving various mementos atop people they used to know. There were also plenty of big, sprawling trees that provided the area with much-needed shade. However, despite the improved surroundings, neither Gil nor Delores seemed to be swayed by what they saw. Gil continued thinking about the game he was about to miss, and Delores started to think about what it was like to be dead.

"So now that we're in a better neighborhood," the salesman said, "how are we liking things?" When neither of them responded, the salesman said, "How 'bout you follow me, I think I've got something might like."

They walked towards a large, marble columbarium made up of different compartments that held the remains of the structure's many occupants. Each niche had the deceased's name engraved on its front, and most of the compartments had an assortment of flowers left in the vases that were attached to the wall.

Out of nowhere, Gil came alive when he noticed a name that looked familiar. He moved towards the marble and ran his fingers across the plaque.

"Alas, poor Borowitz! I knew him, Delores; a fellow of infinite cheapness, for he never once offered to pick up a check. He burned me at lunch thousands of times, and now look at him, how he'll never again enjoy a free pastrami on rye!"

"That's terrible," the salesman said. "I'm so sorry for your loss."

Delores looked at the plaques and thought about the nothingness that awaited her. She couldn't get herself to believe that one day she'd be confined to a box, with a complete loss of her senses, nothing left but her cold, bare bones.

"I don't know," she said. "It doesn't seem like there's enough room here. You know how I get in tight spaces."

"My thoughts exactly," the salesman said. "How about we take a look at one of our private, walk-in mausoleums, similar to the one your friends bought."

During the walk to the mausoleums, Delores noticed a burial in progress where she watched a grieving woman weep while members of her family sprinkled handfuls of dirt on top of a casket before it was lowered into the ground. Delores felt for the woman and the people around her, as they were being forced to say goodbye to someone they loved. It was a haunting image, reminding her that one day she too would be in the very same position, the one who was covered in dirt, forced to cut ties with the living.

They approached a classical-style mausoleum that was white and made of granite. It was distinguished, with its large, Doric columns and its pediment roof. In front of it there was a garden area with benches where family members could sit and reflect on the dead.

"All right," the salesman said, "so this is it, the Big Kahuna. It sleeps six, with the option to add two more."

The inside was big and open. On the four walls there were six plaques, each of which was covered by a niche for the casket that was inside. Beside each plaque was a vase and a bouquet of fresh cut flowers, much nicer than the ones outside. The most unusual aspect of the mausoleum, however, was a flat screen TV, accompanied with a plush viewing area.

"Are you kidding?" Gil said. "A television? This is great."

"It's ridiculous is what it is."

The salesman said, "The entertainment center was an addition requested by the customer who happens to be the son of a former football player who wanted to come here and watch highlights of his father's games and be by his side."

"You know," Gil said, "I dabbled in a bit of football myself. Now I kick myself because I know if I would've stuck with it I could've been a huge star. Then who knows, maybe my kids would be coming to visit me in a place like this."

"How many children do you have?"

"Two daughters, and five grandchildren."

"My goodness," the salesman said. "That's wonderful. They'd love to visit you here."

"You know what I like most about this place?" Gil said. "Gives you the sense that there's a way out, you know, if you happen to wake up one day."

"That's a good point," the salesman said. "I never thought about it that way."

"Hey, hon?" Delores said. "What's it like to say something dumb every five seconds?"

Gil looked to the salesman and said, "You think I could check out some footage of the guy's old man? I'd like to see how I'd stack up to him."

"Certainly," the salesman said. "That's what it's here for."

Delores watched him turn on the TV and asked him how much a place like this cost.

"Well, I have the details of all the pricing in my office. I'd love to go back and look over some of the great specials we're running."

"How much is it?" Delores said. "I know you know. Just tell me."

He looked away, and said, "Fifty-thousand."

"Fifty grand," Gil said. "Are you kidding me?"

"I know it seems like a lot, but you can actually take out a mortgage—a quick one, you know, if you don't have the thirty years."

Delores was enraged at his attitude and the blatant disrespect he had for her and people in her position. She charged out of the mausoleum, took a few steps, and tried cooling herself down, but her attention was immediately drawn to the weeping woman whose head faced the ground as her family said their last goodbyes to the dead. It struck Delores that regardless of how well she ate, or how hard she exercised, or how much she accomplished, she would have no choice but to face death. The lack of permanence in life made her stomach reel. She struggled to come to terms with the fact that she lived in a world where nothing lasted forever.

Gil came out of the mausoleum and said to her, "You know, I have to admit, you were right once again. At first I thought you were crazy about wanting one of these things, but now that I've seen it, I absolutely want one, too."

Delores stared across the graves and reflected on the insignificant amount of time she'd spent being alive. She thought about the billions of years that stood before her, and the billions more that would continue after she was gone.

"Did you hear me?" Gil said. "I wanna buy a mausoleum for us. I don't care how much it costs. The only thing that matters is that we're together forever."

Delores brought her attention to Gil and wondered if he ever even once took a moment to consider the implications of what it meant to die, to vanish and never be heard from again.

"I know what you're thinking," Gil said, "it's expensive. But maybe it's time I cash in on those stocks, or at least what's left of them."

"Have you lost your mind? Those are our savings—money we have a responsibility to leave for the girls. Besides, all we need is something simple where they can find us.

Maybe we'll just end up getting cremated, because, really, what difference does it make?"

Gil said, "What about the TV?"

"We're not getting the TV."

"But why not?

"Gil—please."

The salesman came out of the mausoleum and said, "I was thinking we could go back to my office, hammer out a deal—I've got some popcorn waiting for us—and then who knows, maybe once it's all done we can open up a bottle of champagne and celebrate."

"C'mon, Gil. We're leaving."

The salesman said, "Woah, woah, woah. Stop the clock. There's gotta be something I can do. How about a Sayonara Memorial t-shirt, or a complementary ride in the company hearse—"

Delores thanked him for his time and said goodbye. She started walking towards the car with Gil trailing a few paces behind, taking one more look at the mausoleum.

He looked down at his watch, picked up his step, and said, "You know, if we hurry, I think we can make it home in time to catch the rest of the game!"

CR SO

Brett Kaplan lives and writes in South Florida. He received his MFA from Florida International University where he recently completed his thesis, a collection of short stories entitled, Existential Bebop. His work can be found in Subtle Fiction, Adeliade, and The Scarlet Leaf Review.

REMNANTS - AYAZ DARYL NIELSEN

last journal entry,
found with remnants
of my missing
uncle's skeleton:
'well, we've proven
silver bullets
do not work'

—-

an abandoned house
ashes in the coal furnace
shards of human bone

—-

in my haunted house
sugar-skull crew as renters
banshee among them

ᏍᏈ ᏍᎤ

*Ayaz Daryl Nielsen, veteran, hospice nurse, ex-roughneck (as on oil rigs)
lives in Longmont, Colorado, USA. Editor of bear creek haiku (30+ years/140+
issues) with poetry published worldwide (and deeply appreciated), he also is
online at: bear creek haiku poetry, poems and info*

BONES - ALAN BALTER

We have 206 bones in our skeletal system
Far too many to completely list 'em
But here are a few for your edification
In case you missed 'em in your education

Tibia, fibia, femur, and sternum
Are four of the larger if you'd care to learn 'em
But malleus, incus and stapes I fear
Are the smallest you have, so they fit in your ear

You have a funny bone called the "humerus"
You've only got two, so they aren't very numerous
Your ribs, on the contrary number twenty-four
Adam gave one away, still he had plenty more

Enclosing your brain is the hardest bone you've got
Known as the "cranium" more often than not
And "mandible" is the medical name for "jaw"
You rely on it mostly when it's time to gnaw

Your phalanges are your fingers and toes
Both may be places where a ring goes
And down around your knees are your patellas
You scraped them a lot when you were young fellas

Your vertebrae make up your spine; you've got 'em
Cervical, thoracic, and then lumbar near your bottom
They're separated by small discs in between
But should one slip, the pain can be mean

Of course, there are others that are well-known
Like the radius, ulna, and coccyx bone
Sit them all down in a comfortable seat
And at a fancy restaurant, say "Bone Appetit!"

ଔ ଓ

Alan Balter is a retired university professor who had a wonderful career, spanning 35 years, at Chicago State University where he prepared teachers for children with special needs. In retirement, he has published three novels, a half dozen personal essays, and a book entitled Poems for My Grandchildren and Everyone Else's. He lives in Northbrook, Illinois with his wife Barbara, also a retired teacher, and they enjoy extensive travel and 14 grandchildren.

The time had come. She felt a shift in her bones as they answered the call for her to rise. From the depths of the ocean, buried deep in the sediment of which she had become one, her bones collected like particles of metal drawn to a magnet. Piece by piece, she was whole once again.

She rose, conjured to the surface by a force unknown, yet welcomed. It was time. She looked right and then left in the murky water of blues and greens. She wasn't alone.

The closer she traveled to the top, she felt something below her feet. Wooden planks had collected as had her bones. One by one, thousands came together to lift her. With a whoosh, she was above the surface and back to a world where breath was needed to survive. She straightened, stood tall as she had many, many years ago. She wiggled her toes. Enjoying that she could once again. She looked about her as she pulled tangled seaweed from her fingers and plucked fish from her ribs, which she threw back home with a plop, to where they belonged; to where they could breathe. Sails hoisted, releasing cascades of water, which splashed on the deck at her feet. She recognized this ship. One she remembered quite well. Only this time was different. Much different.

She walked to the bow. Placing her hands along its familiar edge, she looked out, the rushed air drying her bones. There were more ships following behind. They were a fleet with majestic sails which saluted honorably. Far in the distance along the horizon of the setting sun, another ship materialized from the depths as had hers. A sound startled her. A hand gripped the edge. She reached below and pulled the soul up; another collection of bones called to duty. He climbed aboard. A collared chain hung about his neck, a restraint no longer needed. He nodded to her as he walked and joined the others, his watery footsteps marking his presence.

She returned to those who were waiting for her.

There, they stood. A legion of bones, hundreds huddled at the ready, free of chains, yet bonded by experience. Silence mothered them, holding their stories like a newborn baby swaddled in ocean blue...stories that had been stunted and now would grow, as people are meant to.

"My people," she said. "We have been called. Our ancestors want to know who we are. It is time. We've not been forgotten. We are an army of history. We hold secrets others yearn to know."

"Secrets?" A warrior stepped forth. "This is not about secrets, my Queen. We want more. We want a revolution."

"A revolution of what?" she asked.

"Must you ask? You are here for a reason, the same reason as I and he and she and she," he said pointing to the hundreds who continued to gather and board the ship, wet with purpose.

"I cannot deny that my bones do not share your plight. Have you thought of the power of our existence? Our history is our ammunition, to right wrongs done."

He responded, "You cannot be serious."

"If you do not like this ship, there are many behind us; each with a different purpose. I'm certain one will fit your needs of revenge." She climbed high upon a throne of piled barrels. "This ship, my ship is to strengthen our people. To fill in missing pieces so that they might feel whole once again, as others do from other lands who have written word to support their existence. Our people have called for us, to pull from what these waters have held for far too long. To fill in what has been erased. They want to know! Can you not see the value in this?"

"A value greater than vengeance?" His bones rattled with rage.

"To me, it is the greatest. But please, join another ship. For we must all do our part. Retaliation has its place, this is true."

She knew he was free of flesh that had been tortured, but he was not free of memory and it was cut deep into his bones. His thoughts had not misguided him. They simply were not her own.

"Please, brothers and sisters. Do as you must. We are all needed."

Men and women jumped ship. Some dove deep into the water and rose with shards of more recent shipwrecks and mangled metal from missing airplanes to become shafts and swords for their battles to come. Their haunting would be fierce and cruel in their retribution.

She turned to her people. There were still many. Yet, they were from too many places, each with a different language. Excited words of all shapes and sounds spilled from them chaotically. Arms outstretched, she said, "I command you, please. Speak with your minds, your souls, your hearts, so that I can understand you."

A woman rose her arm, the hand that should have been there was missing. "My daughter, she was taken to Brazil. I am from Cameroon."

"We will go. We will go there," she said.

"I was taken from the arms of my mother. In Mali."

"We will go. We will go there."

"My two sons, please," called a man with a skull jagged and halved. "They tell me one went to West Indies, the other to New Orleans. We are from Cote d'Ivoire."

"We will go. We will go there."

As night fell, she listened to each story that came pouring out of them. Her own, which had never left her, came swirling to the front of her eyes; vivid once again. Given away by her father, in exchange for a handful of gold and silver, she had never suffered in life until that day. Her father had stood before the strangers, a proud man of their village. He had stood before them, a king with many daughters, but only one who was worthy of such an honor trade. He had pushed her forward. Spoke of her grace and her fortitude and his pride of his #1 daughter; a queen to be. "She is the best. She is wise. Take her," he had said. And they did. As she was led away by men with skin the color of a yam, she held her head high and called on her worth. She had walked behind those men when she should have walked in front. They behind her. Soon, she was joined by others and more and more and more until she was a spec amongst them; each with differences she lost count to observe. Her status tarnished; her worth unrecognizable and unappreciated and unknown. When they stopped, having arrived at a destination unfamiliar, she was pulled from the crowd by a man with eyes green like a blade of grass fresh after rain and hair black and as curly as her dog's tail. "Ah, finally. Someone with sense has seen me." Sense was not the right word, she'd soon discovered. She felt quite worthless once bid upon by men who spoke a pointy language hard like bark splintered from the tree in a storm. Their skin, untouched by any god, looked like the cloudy river, angry after being disturbed in sleep by cows crossing. As she was shouted at and poked with sticks and touched in ways she had never been touched, she wished she'd been born last. She spoke to her bones, "Please hold me. I cannot."

A vessel as large as the forest carried her obedient bones and so many others from her land. Over the rising and setting of many suns, they all became maggots to a slaughtered wildebeest the lions were too full to finish eating. They squirmed amongst one another to find solace in their infested existence. Sounds, words, screams, floated around her day and night, night and day, as she, a maggot too, squirmed. Until one day, freed from a chain for a moment she didn't understand, she stood. She stood in the night, when the moon was full. It showed her the way. A path lit with silver. She ran. She thought nothing except of flying like the birds that followed them so freely. She reached the edge of the ship and jumped. The water welcomed her, soothed her burning skin, soaked her parched lips and took fingers to her eyes to close them so that she could finally rest.

She opened her eyes. The full moon, bright once again, revealed a glimmered path on the ancient water. She followed. She lead.

CR   BO

Peppur (aka The Hot One) Chambers *is an international writer/actor/producer. She's a published author of "Harlem's Awakening" (1888 Center/Black Hill Press) which has also been developed and performed as a one-woman show of the same title. She has created and co-written an award-winning webseries, "The Brown Betties Guide: How To Look For Love in All The Wrong Places"; and is the creator of the sultry, sassy, sophisticated Brown Betties™ who are featured in her long-running dinner-theater show, "Harlem's Night: A Cabaret Story" and "Harlem's Awakening." Peppur has written several plays, one of which, "Dick & Jayne Get A Life", played in the Hollywood and Prague Fringe Festivals.*

Peppur has contributed to Circle + Bloom, Prague Pulse Magazine, Bridge/Gate Magazines, Humor Mill Magazine, LA Beat, and The Firm FM radio show where she did a weekly, relationship-advice segment, "Keep It Spicy". She taught journalism at Prague College and is the co-creator her theater production company, CATNIP (Contemporary Theatre Now in Prague). A Midwestern Girl at heart, she is looking for her next adventure. www.peppurchambers.com

Sticks and Stones

There's an odd place in an alternate dimension,
where all wars are fought with skeletons.

These subjects of osteology lie dormant until conscription,
well preserved in the interim.

Adults only, minors never get to be
heroic revenants, noble bones.

Once wakened, they are fully conscious of their purpose,
realizing that the burden and horrors of war
have been put on their ossified cages only.

They, without souls, but not without honor,
the fleshed never harmed as these bony frames battle
with bow and arrow, sticks and stones, knife and spear.

All this,
for the same reasons inhabitants
destroy themselves on other worlds.

Tower of Bones

A parade seen
from the perspective
above the clavicles of a king among men;
or lengthy fields of bluebonnets,
or guitarists on stage.

He counted train cars aloud to me as they passed.

Now as I stand at ground level
and watch his funeral procession go by,
I long to once more
climb that tower of bones,
to view the majesty

of this life's moment
while perched atop my father's shoulders.

CR   SO

Linda Imbler is the author of the published poetry collection "Big Questions, Little Sleep." She is a Kansas-based Pushcart Nominee. Her work has appeared in numerous national and international journals. Linda's creative process and a current, complete listing of sites, which have or will publish her work can be found at lindaspoetryblog.blogspot.com.

RHAPSODY IN BONE - STEPHANIE L. HARPER

Beneath the frozen fathoms of the sea,
a maiden's body swells in rhapsody;
her father made her sustenance for fish
and creatures yet unseen by human eyes,
who feed until the carrion is spent.

The maiden's bones roll over with the tide,
entwined with deep-sea coral colonies,
and where her eyes were, now are dwellings kept
by denizens who have no need of light
beneath the frozen fathoms of the sea.

Though water's currents quell the dolphins' calls,
the doleful cries her fecund corpse intones
uncoil the sodden hearts of others' souls,
while hers, forsaken, flounders in the dark.
A maiden's body belts a rhapsody,

because her father threw her from a cliff:
Butt-hurt that she'd flat-out refused to stroke
his ego (teeny-peeny sack, he was,
of whims that changed as often as the winds),
her father made her sustenance for fish,

yet could not stop his daughter's sunken bones
from breathing sirens' cantos on the waves
and luring hunters to her icy grave—
that home to lonely spirits of the depths,
and creatures yet unseen by human eyes!

A hunter plunks his line into the sea,
where deep below, a bony treasury
still bears the stench of murder's milky dregs,
a tangy lunch for urchins clinging fast,
who feed until the carrion is spent.

Upon the swaying surf the hunter waits
with hero's grit, 'til suddenly, a lurch—
he's hooked the skeleton woman's rib! *This catch*

---

has heft suggesting banquets fit for kings,
who feed until the carrion is spent!

Oy veh! He hoists her bones onto his skiff
and shits his britches fearing he's been cursed
by Death, herself, arisen from the depths—
her salt-worn bones a host for writhing eels,
and creatures yet unseen by human eyes!

Try as he may to toss her back, he finds
her long front teeth affixed—and can't deny
this woman he's revived deserves to live:
those naked, tangled limbs, her smooth, bald head...
Her father made her sustenance for fish,

yet could not stop his daughter's sunken bones
from going viral with their exposés—
though water tries to quash the dolphins' calls—
for songs of fuckhead fathers make us sick,
when maidens' bodies swell in rhapsody!

Though many hunters know the songs of bones,
scarce few boast true cajones, fewer still
behold the face of Death with steadfast gaze,
and grow to love and keep all she became
beneath the frozen fathoms of the sea.

ଓ ଓ

Stephanie L. Harper *grew up in California, attended college in Iowa and* *Germany, completed her graduate studies and gave birth to her first child in* *Wisconsin, and lives with her husband and children in Oregon. She is the* *author of the chapbook,* THIS BEING DONE *(Finishing Line Press, June 2018),* *and her poems appear or are forthcoming in* Slippery Elm, Figroot, *Califragile, Harbinger Asylum, The Ibis Head Review, and* *elsewhere. Visit Stephanie online at slharperpoetry.com.* *Order Stephanie's new book: https://www.finishinglinepress.com*

IF YOU COUNTED SKELETONS / ANOTHER DEAD NIGHT - JOHN PATRICK ROBBINS

If You Counted Skeletons

I had far too many old stories laying around .
Much like dead bodies and old vices I hid them from sight buried in the clutter.
It was a tomb without riches.
But every danger was real one wrong step and that was it.
Everything here lingered like some far past it's prime bar.
It was a nightmare without end.
And simply called it home.
I built it over time and poor life choices.
It was my master piece on full display to everyone and not a single soul.
I made friends from ghosts and ignored every knock upon the door.
My thoughts and failures hung in the corners with the cobwebs.
Everything had a place in the chaos.
And still you would need a road map to find a exit in all this debris.
If you counted old skeletons in the closet you would probably call this place a morgue rather than a apartment.
But then again I think the morgue smelled far better.

Another Dead Night

To say you worked the graveyard shift at the morgue was a hilarious statement in itself.
But the sad part for me was that this was true.
I waited for the dead like some night clerk at seedy motel.
I knew the close to life's book.
And saw the start off point to what would be the greatest diet some would ever know.
"Hey Philis, you look like a bag of bones literally. What diet are you on?"
"It's called death, bitch!

You had to keep a sense humor when they were bringing in the dead like Domino's delivered pizzas.
You saw it all.
And after awhile you became blind to the scene.

It really took something fucked up to shock you.
The kids scraped up off the sidewalk were the worst.
No matter how you started we were destined for the slab.
More bones to the yard fuel to the flames.
Everyone had to die and it seems some chose to do so more so on these nights than others.
We had five altogether.
Three from a car wreck.
One suicide.
Another just old and forgotten and partridge and a pear tree.
Though I hated the holidays I once saw a guy dressed as Elvis, course he was a impersonator.
I always hated a fraud.

Then there was a night I saw a ghost.
It was in the paperwork first she spoke to me.
I saw the name and at first it didn't click.
Julia E. Loveless.
Another overdose.
I unzipped the bag and looked at my past.
It was her.
I left her there sat at my desk mixed a drink wasn't worried about the stiffs snitching on me.
I thought back to when that empty shell once knew life.
When I wasn't so fucked up and dead inside as the stiffs that kept me company.
I poured the rest of the flask in the glass.
I remember how she used to watch me mix a drink as she sat on the couch cigarette in hand.
Blanket across her naked body.
"You know from the way you mix those, You're going to put yourself in a early grave baby."
"Look who's talking, smoking a cigarette with a bad heart," I replied, handing her a drink of her own.
"True, but you need to slow down."
"Yeah, Jules, but what fun would that be sweetheart?"
I remembered those nights often together when the word was ours and the nights were filled with passion and life.
I remember her beside me asleep dead to the world.
And now its seems she was dead to all.
I took a hit from that same flask she had given me.
The bourbon hit my stomach heavy and burnt like fire.

Yeah it was going to kill me one night but it definitely wasn't tonight.
It been awhile since we had parted ways seems she must have missed me.
I can't say she was dying to see me but here she was.
And the sad part is even in death she looked far better than I did alive.
Course she always had her looks.
But least I was breathing.
Some skeletons never stay in the closet some simply open the door and slap you in the face.
I saw a ghost tonight she had haunted my thoughts haunted for awhile.
It took alot to shock someone like me.
Sometimes it best to seal the whole room and barricade the door.
And leave the old skeletons to there own Halloween cast scene.
Every night was dead here.

℞ ℬ

John Patrick Robbins' *work is often inspired by the people he hears around him. These two writes reflect a man far beyond jaded.*

MARY ANNE - JOY SPAHR

The first time Mary Anne murdered a man, she puked all over the blue and yellow plaid apron that used to be her mother's. She tried to wash out the stains, but the skirt was eternally soiled and she had to bury it with the body. The first time she cut into a man's throat and released the volcano of warm, thick blood, her hands shook. She struggled to keep the blade on task as it wobbled and clung to muscle and flesh. It was almost Autumn, that first time. The ground was soft and there was a cool breeze after the sun deserted its subjects. She was careful, even then, to make sure she left enough room in between the grave and the hole. She had read that if the fertilizer comes too close too soon, it can overwhelm the sapling and kill the baby tree before it ever takes root. She wrapped the body in an old blanket that she found in the garage and the bottom of the tree in an ice-cold towel. Both sat for two nights while she picked the perfect spot and prepared the ground. When she was ready to plant them, she used her father's rusty old furniture dolly to carry them to their new homes. Strapping the corpse in was surprisingly easy. She'd expected him to fold into a heap of farting jelly like he did right after he died, but he was as solid as the frozen tree roots and once she buckled and pulled tight the nylon belts, he gave up with little fight. She was pretty sure she'd broken a bone somewhere because she heard a crack when she kicked the wheels back and began to cart him across the faded brick sidewalk that encircled her little green house.

Getting the tree in the ground was a lot more challenging. The video she'd watched suggested mixing store bought soil with ground and instructed her to make sure that once laid down, the thick green and brown tentacles were arranged as to not strangle the life out of their brothers and sisters. She had dug the hole just a little too deep and had reach in past her elbows to sort out the mess. When she finally had both new life and dead man sufficiently planted, she closed the ground with purpose and pride, like a surgeon closing a wound. She cared for that first tree as if it was her first born. She'd lay a blanket over the unmarked grave and kneel in front of her offspring. Pruning and tending and humming it a song. She'd heard music was the trick- showing the little tree love. She'd ask it outright to bear her fruit and talk to it about the delicious things she'd bake with its harvest. She felt like a mother and a grandmother at the same time.

As time went on, she became less squeamish about the murders. She'd learned to do it in the yard, at night so no one could drive by and see and she wouldn't have to haul them so far. She'd meet them at her stand and sell them gorgeous ripe apples. She only offered Fuji and Red Delicious. She said the Granny Smiths were for baking, not eating. She liked to watch the sweet juice run down their chins as they took their last bites. Her apples were known to be the biggest and the sweetest. Everyone wanted to know her secret. She told some of them about the singing.

The men would come to see her. Many of them would drive by first with their families or their girlfriends. They would notice her modestly arranged little stand, painted white and lined with red gingham napkins she'd sewn herself. She would catch and then hold their eyes as they rubbernecked. She knew what they were thinking. She saw the want in them as they caught a glimpse of her muscular legs backlit by the sun and visible through her strapless cotton dresses. She could tell they were imagining tasting her pink lips while they were telling their passengers they had a craving for some fresh fruit. Sometimes they'd lose control for a moment as they passed, letting their tires slip into the country mud before correcting themselves.

When they came back in the evening, they'd alternate compliments and questions and always ask for a sample so they could linger while they ate. She'd wince as their teeth broke the skin. It pissed her off, but she'd smile politely, fingers crossed behind her back, and invite them to see the trees. They'd follow her like obedient children. In the beginning, she hit some of them with a shovel or let them think she was open to their advances and stabbed them hard right above the belt line as they learned in close. But she'd learned that bringing them down first before she finished them off was less efficient than it sounds. The best and cleanest way was to take them to the spot where she'd be planting her next bud and as they bent down to admire her work, bring the knife quick and clean across their Adam's apple. She missed out on watching the light go out of their eyes, but she'd hear them gurgle "why" and that was enough to satiate her.

It's important to note, because it's important to Mary Anne, that she was never a victim. No stepfathers or hairy uncles snuck into her room and fiddled with her innocence while her mother lay drunk on the living room sofa. No god fearing relatives locked her in a closet to pray or beat her with kitchen tools. Her parents didn't get murdered at a bodega in front of her or burn up in a fire that she started. Her father taught her how to tend the land and left her this house. Her mother taught her the precision and the art of baking the perfect pie. She had pets and friends and took dance class in town. She got fairly good grades and went to community college for a year and half. No boy in particular broke her heart and no girls called her names or refused to let her come to their sleepovers.

It was interesting to her that the men would ask her why. How should she know? Was she the one who left a wife and kids back at some overpriced bed and breakfast, waiting in a stranger's old house with a stack of chewed up board games and spotty WiFi? If they'd told where they were going, someone would surely have come looking, but they never did. The guilt of what they wanted outweighing their self-preservation. Of course, no one, man or woman, ever really saw her as a threat, so it was easy to let their guards down. And they did, finally, after the initial begging with their eyes and clawing at their throats trying to scoop the blood back in with their fingers, they all let down their guard. Eventually, they all became as quiet and still as branches on a windless day.

As her land became more and more productive, she became more efficient. She tried hiring machinery, but to be economical, she'd have to pay for six or seven holes at a time and leaving them until she had the perfect ingredients to plant was bad for the baby trees, so she invested in a portable trencher and an electric digger. No one questioned her purchases because her apples had become famous throughout the town and the next one over. Sometimes, she'd hire the young boy who lived a half mile down the road to come help her get things started. She made it a point, as much as she could, to lay blankets on the graves and sing soft music to her trees.

The first time she'd killed a man, she got sick. Each time after, as she simultaneously took and spawned a life, she became stronger and surer of herself. Her arms were like trunks that could hold up the world. Her hair blew in the wind in concert with the leaves, and her skin was smooth and glistened in the rain like dew on the apple blossoms. She drew life from her private forest and she kept it well fed.

And as her trees grew old, so did she. Her dark curls turned brittle and grey and her moist lips became surrounded by what her mother had called "smile lines." She had a better chance of seducing a man with the sweet smell of apples and cinnamon cooling in her windowsill than by bearing her sun damaged shoulders. The once fiery reds and iridescent greens that had lit up the grove were faded yellows and pinks. Their juice, once so tart, your cheeks would pucker up at the first bite, or so sweet, you had to close your eyes and drink it in like a baby vampire, was bland and grainy. She tried singing more often. She offered birds and bunnies and other garden pests, but nothing could bring back the luster and lust that had marked these trees as Mary Anne's. She became week and her core was cut with rings from the inside out. She spent most of her time on the front porch of her little green house drinking store-bought cider and remembering the satisfaction of planting her orchard.

She died sometime in late October. No one noticed for quite a while. The locals had stopped calling on her for fresh fruit and hot pies. Tourist who drove by the country road could barely see the old wooden cart now overgrown with weeds and brush. When they found her, after a winter thaw, her body had melted into the dead leaves next to a large grey tree. The dirt covered bones and grey matted curls looked like discarded branches and rotten roots. The ground was too cold for them to bury her there, so she was sent to the crematorium, her ashes spread in that same spot in the Spring. Some years later, a hipster real estate developer bought the property from the probate court. He had plans to turn it into a quaint little restaurant and hotel for city folk who wanted to unplug. He brought in his own construction crew, refusing to let a single job go to a local for fear his corner cutting might get called out. Unfortunately, he never got a chance to earn back his investment once the digging began and Mary Anne's secrets were uprooted at last.

CR   BO

Joy Spahr is a full time mom, part time student. She enjoys making up silly stories to tell her 4 year old son and writing stories that he's not allowed to read for a few more years.

She has worked as an assistant editor for The Gateway Review and had work published in the Mid Rivers Review. She is currently pursuing a creative writing certificate at St. Charles College.

PURITY OF NATURE / DIVINE PAPER / AN OLD SILENT POND - DEEPTI MITTAL

Purity of Nature

Blue color in the sky,
Birds are chirping in the light,
Talk merrily and speak feebly ,
Sun is blooming in its complete beauty,
Blue water in the sea,
Silence in the moon light,
Little stars are twinkling in midnight,
Hills and mountains are nearby,
Chilled, breeze weather absorbs the air,
Sound of stream of flowing water river,
Glossy Blue color Peacock are dancing,
Rodent with bushy tail squirrels are playing,
Long curved ivory tusks elephants are sleeping,
Bees are going to their hives with a sweet hum,
Frogs are jumping in the water,
Deer are running in the forest,
Jungle King is roaring in Blue light,
Early Dusk Saints are hymning,
Temple bells are ringing,
Fragrance and Sweetness of flowers are everywhere,
Blue waves in the silent water,

Sea breeze is blowing towards land,
Sailor is doing his seamanship,
Waves are flowing towards seashore,
Fishes are beaten by sea green water,
With leaves and branches trees are standing,
Surrounded by bush and shrub,
Colorful rainbow in the sky,
An arch of prismatic colors in the light,
Shower of rain covers the ground,
Rain worm comes up in rainwater,
Brighten in the Blue sky

Divine Paper

A Divine messenger, an angel,
Ink absorbs the pen,
Words, alphabets are seeing everywhere,
Animates your imagination,
Cover the inner thoughts,
Stroke the letter made by pen of brush,

Pop up and shape the sound character,
Pertaining to anecdote in many angles,
Full of high spirit and energy,
Power comes to every line in the paper,
Life is in itself is floating have wings to both sides,
Feather has been attached to Fountain pen,
Printed sheet containing news,
Constructed Life is seeing New Moon,
Pillars support the canvass,
Turn of pages touches the rhythm,
Transparency collides to the vision,
Sound comes at the end of every line,
Positive aura give shape to the life,
Pen and paper become bright apples,
Rich content fertile the seeds,
Enigma, puzzle opens the new curtain,
Geometric friction sparkle the fire,
Holy, virtuous manner hop on the ride,
Science of moral landed the paper,
Worship of Angel comes as an harmony,
Structured Bond soluble as a Divine,
Paragraph, passage, Book becomes the parcel,

Melts into the solution of vocab,
Missiles of words in rapid succession,
Capable to emit pages of Lava,
Sacred messenger, a Paper

An Old Silent Pond

The color and scent of the wisteria
Seems far away.

O snail
Climb Mount Fuji,
But slowly, slowly!
Trusting the Buddha, good and bad,
I bid farewell
To the departing year.
Everything I touch
with tenderness, alas,
pricks like a bramble.

I want to sleep
Swat the flies
Softly, please.
For love and for hate
I swat a fly and offer it
to an ant.
Night; and once again,
the while I wait for you, cold wind
turns into rain.
The summer river:

although there is a bridge, my horse
goes through the water.
A lightning flash:
between the forest trees
I have seen water.
Plum flower temple:
Voices rise
From the foothills
The crow has flown away:
swaying in the evening sun,
a lively tree.

Cherry blossoms bloom
Rumbly showers from the sky
Peace out, winter gloom!
Where did the snow go?
Who cares, it's warm weather time!
Start the Spring parties!
Moms forever loved
Always there for everyone
Send your thanks her way

Inkers love the Spring
More BBQs and pot lucks!
We get our grub on

Hidden eggs around
Kids are on the hunt all day
Easter bunny hop!

Oh whaaat? Spring is here?
Does that mean it's t-shirt time?
Get ready for sun!

ଓ   ଝ

Deepti Mittal is a poet, essayist and conservationist.

SEEING SHAPES - ELIZABETH HOYLE

Can one be ignorant of the shapes
that make them up?
All my life, I've lived
in a zoo of shapes
complex and simple
and I've known the labyrinth
that lies just deep below
my epidermis, yet I haven't
taken the time to explore
my own shapes.
Legs hipwidth apart, palms out, head up.
The mirror reflects my anatomical position
and the more and more I stare,
the more and more I see circles.
The small ones that compose my palms,
the ones I wish were smaller
that make up my bottom,
the half circles of my heels
that find their closure in the curves
of my insteps.
The barely-seen circles of my hip bones
that lead upward
to the sideways ovals of ribs
underneath my protruding breasts.
The circles don't stop there.
They travel up my shoulders,
down my knees, around the ends of my toes,
fingers, elbows.
My face, my nostrils, my eyes, my ears,
all these are made of so many, so big, so small, so ugly, so beautiful
circles.
And circles, by their nature,
are a microcosm of eternity.

ଓ ଛ

*Elizabeth Hoyle is a writer whose work has been featured Oddball Magazine,
DoveTales: An International Journal of the Arts, and The Wayfarer, as well as
in other online and print publications. She was born and raised in the*

mountains of southern West Virginia, where she lives still. She makes her online home at https://entwinedinpages.wordpress.com

Betsy found a dead animal curled up among a pile of sheets in the basement. She figured it had crawled in through the rectangular window that sat above the washer/dryer set. Large enough for a small human, like herself, or a sizable animal.

At first she wasn't sure what lay within the sheets, but felt the bulge of body when she wrapped her arms around the cotton. She recoiled. Then the obvious signs of decay sunk into her senses. The offensive smell. The crack of window open to winter's air. The mess of sheets she hadn't touched for months.

The room itself was accustomed to decay, to be honest. She and her husband, Sean, had purchased the place excited to have an old home. Stories of the war, possibilities of ghosts, a multitude of past's secrets warped into the walls.

But they hadn't put forth any work to the downside of owning an old home, so the broken windows - like this one - remained broken.

The dog clawed at the door at the top of the stairs, but she feared he'd dig his nose into the mess of sheets, too eager. She shoveled the animal and the sheet into a trash bag, moved it all outside, and that was that. She would have asked Sean to help, but he was at work.

"The window in the basement is cracked open - broken - and I can't figure out how to fix it."

Sean asked a number of possibilities each starting with "Have you tried" to which she nodded her head, yes, yes, yes. They stood over the kitchen island while he ate cold lasagna out of the pan, a work meeting pushing into the evening. She stood with one foot folded over the other, trying to keep them warm. She wanted to run upstairs and grab socks, but she remained, her elbows on the island, looking up to Sean.

He pushed his glasses up the crook of his nose and put the lasagna down. "That was really good, by the way. I was famished."

She mumbled thanks. "Could you come down now? I just don't like the idea of it open. Someone could fit in it, really."

He agreed to follow her but replied he was more worried about the foundation of the house than interlopers. "We're so nestled off the road. Who would saunter back here? And for what?" He reasoned the odds were in their favor.

Descending the stairs, Betsy heard a rustling from where a makeshift closet stood in the corner – perhaps a former generation had stored wine there? – but it didn't seem functional now. The door swung on rusty hinges. It held cobwebs and maybe an old broom someone left behind. Betsy heard the little door clatter and she raced to see if something had dodged into it as a hiding place.

"See?" She heard Sean behind her. "Animals looking for warmth. This winter has been something else. Dan from work? You remember him? He says this will be the longest, roughest winter we've seen."

"Well, all the more reason to fix the window, Sean. We can't afford to heat the house if the heat is leaving the house."

He climbed atop the dryer. The length of his body wedged in the space, his backend stuck toward her face, as he jumbled the lock and rocked the window.

Betsy stood below shoving a screwdriver toward Sean. "It's the paint, I think. Too many coats on the lock and so it won't twist into place. Do you think you could pry it?"

He grabbed at the screwdriver. She felt winter on his fingers. He drove the tool into the lock. Bits of paint chips ricocheted in the air. "My hands are nearly frozen, Betsy, and this damn thing isn't budging. Can I look at this tomorrow? When there's at least some sunlight streaming in?" She was disappointed, but he had positioned the window so it appeared closed before she could say no.

Hanging over their shared sink, toothbrushes rubbing in and out of their mouths, Betsy eyed Sean in the mirror. He had taken off his glasses and she followed the hanging lines under his eyes. The skin tucked and bellowed and she thought of curtains on a window. When he had aged, she wasn't certain. They had lived here only four years. Four winters, she thought, which had been considerably timid. But his work had been increasingly demanding. Long nights and meetings and conference calls and spreadsheets of numbers she didn't pretend to understand.

He rinsed his brush and let it clank into the glass. "I'll have to go in for a little bit tomorrow. Dan has this out of town client he insists I meet. Lunch meeting, actually."

"But it's Saturday."

"Nature of the beast." He shrugged and left the bathroom. She heard the bedsprings compete with his weight.

She stood in the bathroom, the tile warmed, a little circle of heat generating from her. She thought of another day alone in the house, as it had been lately. She understood the working days and had committed to a 9-5, her office positioned in the sunroom toward the back of the house where she worked on freelance writing, various editing jobs, etc. But then the long nights and now empty weekends.

By the time she situated herself beside Sean in the bed, his nose rustled deep under a snore. A winter landscape unfolded through the window and her brain ticked into the movie The Shining. She pictured Sean's face protruding through a wall of their house as Jack Nicholson does in the film. "All work and no play" taunted her as she drifted into sleep where she found herself following the snowy labyrinth, her feet worked into frostbite.

She opened the dryer and relished in its warmth. The day had dipped closer to zero than not, despite the sun bursting in through their windows. In walking the dog, Pete, she recalled her nightmare and wiggled her toes in exaggeration. But Pete loved the snow. He dove his snout into the white curves of unnatural landscape where the wind had whipped drifts of snow. Back at the house she had to pry off pieces of frozen clumps in his fur. Miniature icicles. He resembled the abominable snowman. Her hands submerged in hot clothes was a welcomed opposition.

And then a skitter-scatter. Hard nails on cold concrete.

She heard the critter but couldn't see the critter. She followed sounds around the basement and talked at it under her breath. Where are you? Where are you hiding? What do you want from me? The basement wrapped its arms in defense hugging each corner. Her antagonist. Each menacing, dusted, dingy square inch of it.

She ascended the stairs in defeat bearing the weight of the laundry.

"Perhaps work is too slow for you right now." Sean equated all life's problems against work. His father had been the same, of course, and she knew she was somehow likely falling into her own mother's habits.

"Sean, I have enough work, that's not the problem. If I'm bored – and that's your insinuation – perhaps it's because my husband is never home." She hadn't intended to take on an argument today.

He rolled his eyes and she assumed he was weighing her paycheck against his. Their bills tallied in his head with numbers carried into neat, little columns. "Betsy. Dear. Love-of-my-life." Each placated name pushed at her temper. "This is a growing business. Do you want a comfortable life? Do you want to keep working from home? It's a sacrifice now for our future." She wondered what connotations surrounded the word 'our' in his head.

"Look, Sean, it's whatever, okay? I know you're committed to long hours right now. But then you go and minimize the problems I have here. I'll just call someone out to the house to fix the window since we can't do it ourselves. It's the dead of winter and I don't need that window open to the world."

This resolved the window issue, but Betsy found two more dead animals at the end of the same week. They had clustered into the back closet area. She found them after Pete pushed into the basement and growled at the corner. Not only that, but they had stolen pieces of dirty laundry to situate themselves.

She left the mess for Sean.

She took Pete with her outside and walked the perimeter of the house. Was there another point of entry? Snow had swooped up along most of the house's edges. She assumed a critter's path would be obvious to spot, but the wind – even now as she and Pete stood dumbfounded – relentlessly thundered in all directions. Her hair whipped into a frenzy and splashed against her face.

It was Tuesday and nearing 8:00 PM. Sean had committed to another night meeting. She tugged at Pete and they meandered toward the street. It was so mind-numbing cold, she couldn't fathom why any animal hadn't hunkered down into its own natural shelter. She thought she might find them out on the street waiting for her to go back inside. Waiting for her to turn her back so they could scurry up the driveway and into the basement.

Halfway to the street – the driveway lasting half a mile – she realized she should have brought a flashlight but reasoned Pete would sniff out an animal, really.

She was so consumed with her search – her head beating against itself and the wind – she hadn't noticed the car parked on the road in front of their house. Its lights were off but it cast a steady flow of exhaust. Only when Pete tugged toward it did she look up and into its windows. Two men, perhaps Sean and his partner, sat in the front. She could only see forms, dark lumps of bodies, no pronounced details. She watched as they embraced for what felt longer than a standard hug. And why would work partners hug, anyway?

The passenger door opened and Pete barked an aggressive warning until he realized it was Sean.

"Betsy? What are you doing out here? You'll freeze to death." His words forced a flash of her nightmare into memory. All work and no play, her mind reminded her, but then she thought she had had it all wrong. The hugging forms, two shadows of human clung together, hung in her mind but not as a tangible idea.

"Where's your car?"

He turned toward the street as if he had forgotten the answer. "Oh, yea." His words took off with the wind. "Dan brought me home."

"Okay." She scratched at her scalp and pushed the flowing strands of hair behind her ears. Why hadn't she put on a hat? Pete tugged toward the house, restless and cold. "But why?"

"Car troubles." And then that shoulder shrug. Nature of the beast. Placated names. It is what it is. He walked up the drive and past her, then turned back, "You coming inside? It's freezing out here. Honestly. What were you doing anyway?" He didn't wait for an answer, assuming she'd follow him and explain once inside the house. Instead she stood looking toward the street. A fresh wave of snow began to descend, some of it caught in the street lights. She focused on the lines in the street from Dan's tires. She stared into them as if they could talk. As if they would argue against or for what her simple mind worked itself around. The long hours. The extended lunches. The new suits.

Then across the street burrowed below a pine tree, a set of yellow eyes matched hers. She couldn't discern the animal but watched the outline of its body slinking below the tree line, its eyes on her, waiting for her to return to the house.

 C&3 &0

Katie Strine tolerates life through literature and dark beer. She lives in the east suburbs of Cleveland with her family - husband, son and dog - who accompany her on oddball adventures. Her work has been published in The Writing Disorder, The Wayne Literary Review and Visitant. Stay in touch via LinkedIn and Facebook.

INNOCENCE - CARL SCHARWATH

Art should have been her savior, but in the end her delicate life was consumed by creativity. When Aria's father died her world began to emerge into a new realm. She had felt this new presentment: all one had to do is witness the transformation of her home. Once clean and ordered, Aria began to hoard. Unopened mail, catalogs, empty boxes, clothes and a compulsive shoppers treasures soon littered the floor and furniture. The vista began to close in like storm clouds filling in the blue of a morning sky. Then the storms and lightening came, a constant pain in her feet that was only relieved with painkillers. This was not a gentle medicine, but a prescribed poison that filled her with toxins and turned her blood into pharmaceutical rivers.

Aria's only sin was her innocence and her past life was filled with hope and challenges. She had a boyfriend of 13 years who she adored and loved. His support was one of trust and loyalty. Many times he challenged her to break from the shell of shyness and insecurities to share her passions with others. Unfortunately there was always an excuse of either not being quite ready or her need to create more art and needing the time to sort through each piece. Her lover, a dedicated runner even took the time to teach Aria his passion. They started slow together, just like their tender relationship until 1 year later Aria proudly completed her first half-marathon. He knew about the pain pills and wanted her to be free from this devil in a plastic bottle and thought exercise was the real prescription.

The trusted boyfriend knew the skeleton in his lover's closet, every single bone an intricate part of her psyche held in a non-judgmental silence. Aria reminded me of that time in life when you patiently waited for other people to tell you whether or not you were OK, and trusted them, as if there could be no other way to find out. The boyfriend unfortunately had his own skeleton in the closet; he was married. Their relationship weathered this awkward situation with simply perfected love between two souls searching for an answer together.

All seemed to have changed suddenly and without warning. The only empty space in her home was the bed. The sheets seemed to encase and protect her until noon, however each new day only welcomed Aria to prolonged boredom and hopelessness. With so much free time, the former artist discovered a long-lost passion. Art was her obsession and the art that answered her passion was collage art. Countless magazines and catalogs supplied the images while her fingers painstakingly applied them to a one-inch square canvas. Over time at least seventy images filled tiny easels and were spread throughout the rooms. Hundred of eyes stared at her, perfected models seemed to mock and surrealistic backgrounds would not welcome her into this tiny world that she created.

Suddenly and slowly a new change happened like the start of a snowfall, with flakes dancing schizophrenically seeking an empty spot on the ground to cover. Night terrors and sleepwalking, a side effect from the medicine would hamper her only chance for peace. This adverse and unintended consequence interrupted her delta sleep with confusion and arousal. Aria heard voices from the other rooms, the eyes of the collages followed her knowingly, the mouths moved slightly as she navigated each step timidly. Upon awakening some of the collages appeared to change places throughout the rooms. Her memory of sleepwalking was clouded, the flashbacks and voices could have only been a dream? The movement of the art a physiological trick of the mind? Tired and distressed her only focus was to create more collages.

The apartment was now totally closing in on Aria. The floors were completely covered with unopened mail and slick, slippery, glossy magazines. She could no longer venture out unless it was to fill a prescription that invoked a fictitious euphoria and an invisible crutch to save her from anxiety.

Most nights her sleepwalking and frequent bathroom trips were blessed by some invisible hand or memory motor skills. She navigated the littered landscape and delicately avoided brushing against any collages that seemed perched like tiny, lonely headstones awaiting a visit. The visit would come again after a heavy dose of pharmaceuticals and a toxic mix of depression and fear. The dream turned realistic and her dark eyes kept staring as she explored the darkness. She felt her soul tearing away from each bone of her skeleton as if giving up on a blemished life. Her pupils had grown bigger and bigger until they transformed into huge black lakes of fear. Each step felt different this time, each step methodical in a growing feeling of vertigo. Her balance like the exit from a carnival ride caused a fall against the art table. Aria barely awake felt sleep and the blood rushing from her head. The blood flowed over an unfinished collage mixing pigment with humanity and the final creation.

CR SO

Carl Scharwath has appeared globally with 100+ journals selecting his poetry, short stories, essays or art photography. Two poetry books 'Journey To Become Forgotten' (Kind of a Hurricane Press) and 'Abandoned' (ScarsTv) have been published. Carl is the art editor for Minute Magazine, a dedicated runner and 2nd degree black-belt in Taekwondo.

RITUAL OF RAPE - AHJA FOX

I find a female deer pelvis
swathed in grapevines, tendrils
weaving in and out of two
eye-like sockets, dressing the ossein
in traditional costume.

A crown to the fawn who's speckled back will
lose vibrancy and curvature before I
reach acceptance.
Puckered cheeks and gravity-stricken nail beds—
cracks to the surface of living.

The bone mirrors its owner's face, something fans
from the top. I want to pull needles through
the telephone hooks
of its sides.
I want to stitch it to my jaw, walk falsely
among the demons that roam trees, listening
for the still heartbeat.

Snap the bridge
where the sacrum would have trailed
when the curious buck approached her.

Tuck the finger one points out guilt with
and the finger one screams fuck with
under the pinched DNA, right in the ridge
of the pubic arch.

Release the bone dust.
A history of getting pressed
into a bow-legged stance
because the spine cannot face what is behind.

I question if demons mark their chest
with the dust of the earth and remember
that all wear their victims (trachea noosed tight).

CR ꙅꙩ

Ahja Fox *resides in Aurora, Colorado with her artist husband with whom she creates multimedia pieces. She describes her love for words as 'suicide by writing and reading'. You can find her work published or forthcoming in Rigorous, The Perch, Progenitor, Taxicab Magazine, and more. Stay up-to-date on her reading/performance schedule and publications by following her on Instagram and Twitter at aefoxx.*

OF PLUMBING AND NIGHTMARES - BRETT STOUT

I'm sitting in the beat up white work van with my co-worker Marvin next to some vacant generic strip mall out in some North Atlanta suburb at five in the a.m. It's fucking freezing and coal black outside. I sit and smoke cigarettes and drink my crappy and cheap gas station coffee while Marvin snorts a line of speed to get him going and then puts in his dentures that were resting on the van console. We should be inside working, but the boss isn't here this early, so fuck it and fuck him. I need a few more minutes to wake up and procrastinate, and then it's back to the concrete. The concrete has been killing me for these last three days. It's my job to take the heavy electric saw and cut the concrete into huge blocks. Then, once I'm done cutting them into rectangular blocks, I have to lug these chunks of concrete weighing over fifty pounds each up twenty steps and around the corner to the giant green dumpster. My back is killing me, my hands are chaffed and still bleeding from yesterday and my entire skeleton is numb from the freezing fucking cold. I continue to sit in the van smoking cigarettes and drinking cheap and crappy gas station coffee while feeling Social Security instead of twenty.

CR ßO

Brett Stout is a 38-year-old artist and writer. He is a high school dropout and former construction worker turned college graduate and Paramedic. He creates controversial art while breathing toxic paint fumes from a small cramped apartment referred to as "the nerd lab" in Myrtle Beach , SC. His artwork has appeared in a wide range of various media from small webzines like the Paradise Review to the University of Oklahoma Medical School Journal.

NO ESCAPE / EVERYTHING / BLACK / THE POLISH GIRL / SILENCE / THE DOOR / START STOP / THE TRUTH / AMBIVALENCE / THE CIRCLE / UNTITLED / TRUE LOVE / A STRANGE KETTLE OF FISH - MARC CARVER

No Escape

I stared into the Pissaro painting
as I sat there
I thought if I looked for long enough
I might be able to walk past those pink flowers
touch my hand lightly along their tips
walk past the people on the path
then walk around the corner
and disappear into those woods.

After awhile I could even smell the flowers
as people kept walking in front of the painting
and taking pictures of it.

But I knew the painting would not let this tired old pile of bones in
it could not be that easy
there was no escape.

Everything

Welcome
to the cleverest idiot who ever lived
I am clever
because I know what you want
and an idiot because I give it to you
so come on
tell me what you want
and I will tell you
what you really want
altogether
everything

Black

As I looked at the church
I saw all the people
black ties and suits
another gone
there must have been twenty
and as I went around the corner
there were more and more
must have been forty
and it hadn't even started yet.
I started to think it could be some local celebrity.

It got me to thinking about my funeral
there would not be many there
if any.
I would be quite surprised if my wife and son
would go
but I don't care
I will be dead.

The Polish Girl

The polish girl smiles at me
as she passes with her new born baby.
Her Polish man used to be a bit of a player.
Then they got caught on that beach in north Africa
Terrorists wanting death.

So now
he has settled down
and she has made life

Even in a strange way
Good can come
from terror

Silence

I wait for silence to fill every part of the room
the corners
the floor

even silent mist comes down from the ceiling
but still
I see those eager eyes
hungry eyes
wanting to believe
to know there is more than Netflix and sky movies in life
more than going to work to pay the bills
more than growing old and dying
but I can't possibly tell you what it is
so instead
I say silent

The Door

I looked at him
he looked angry but it wasn't with me
even though he said it was.
He had let something slip
the first probably
in his life.
He had kept it a secret for over thirty years
it took me another ten years to find the key
and open the door.
The strange thing is
the knowing didn't help me at all.
It is his birthday today
and all I can feel for him
is sorrow.

Start Stop

When do you ever start
when do you ever begin
has my life started or has it finished.
If it did start I can't truly say when it began.
I guess you have to start
so you are able to finish.
But if I never start
then surely it can never finish
what a terrible thought

The Truth

I like it
when there is not a sound
complete silence
so all you have left
is those thoughts
in your head
I don't know where they come from
I don't care much either
but they are the truth
I know that

Ambivalence

The man stands at the bar
he tries to talk to everyone who comes to the bar
but most ignore him
I don't know how long he has been there
but I am guessing a while
he goes to the toilet three times in ten minutes
again he looks around for a friend
he is not young
not young enough to make friends
but old enough
for everyone to walk past him
me
I know better
that is why I sit by myself
with my beer
and no one

The Circle

I wrote a poem once
it was a long time ago
I guess that makes me a poet
but I have a strange feeling I was a poet
a long time before that.

The wind is strong today
and if I tore this poem from the pad it would fly and fly
I would never see it again
just like my first poem about that big fish and my pain
long
long
gone.

untitled

people come and they go
not many stay
the ones you want to stay
are always the ones to leave
You can sit with the stillness
until it almost makes you crazy.
And still they come and go
days turn into months and months years
seasons pick up speed
grow and grow like doubts in your mind.
they all mean something
they all mean everything
everything and nothing

True Love

I want to walk out into the world
like a beaming beacon of love
everyone I looked at
and everybody I touched
would feel and become true love like me.
Oh
what a world that would be.

A Strange Kettle of Fish

All that I am
is a couple of legs and arms
stuck onto a trunk
with a head whipped on top

What a strange creature
I surely look like
wondering about
not knowing which way to go.
People must look at me and think
What is that

⊗   ⊗

Marc Carver *has published ten collections of poetry but to him the most important thing is to get an email from someone he does not know that says they enjoy his work.*

AFTER THE ARMISTICE - CHRISTOPHER GREER

We are entwined together in this field,
Exhausted bones caressed by Mother Earth.
Kudzu creeps, crawling across us at will,
Entangled finality by the firth.
We relax unhindered in supple soil,
Waking no longer when morning-time breaks,
Nor rising to run when twilight is roiled—
Lightning lurks closely and thunderheads quake.
We tell no secrets, expel no more vows,
Lie silently stationed, restful repose.
While the weary continue to carouse,
The contented begin to decompose.
Our commended spirits finally freed,
We waste away clinging to victory.

ଔ   ଓ

Christopher Greer *is an educator and writer who lives in Alpharetta, GA. His work has appeared in, or is forthcoming from, Canary, Inwood Indiana, Visitant, and other publications. He holds a Master of Science from Purdue University.*

HAM HOCKS - ERIEL FAUSER

I left a pot of hocks and greens to boil in a crockpot as I packed up my dorm room. It was my Papa Lee's recipe: drain the marrow, save the fat, hold the salt, add a pepper. Golden. The key to hocks is the broth: the fat must dissolve enough into the bouillon before melting down the marrow. You have to monitor the pot to ensure the many pieces remain distinct. If the hocks become the greens become the pepper, the meal's no good.

Halfway through boxing up my book collection, my mom called to tell me my cousin Kenny had died. Cancer. When she hung up, I grabbed a fresh roll of packing tape and continued packing up my dorm. There wasn't much else I could do. My parents were six hours from campus; the hospital Kenny died in was eight. I only had so long to fill those boxes with my things.

cancer (n.) the disease caused by an uncontrolled division of abnormal cells in a part of the body; from the Greek "karkinos": a giant crab that assisted Hydra in its battle against Hercules; one of Herc's Twelve Labors

The family nicknamed Kenny Herc after his twelfth round of chemo. I humored him with the word etymology and whatnot about cancer and crabs and how it all tied together. He didn't get it, but he laughed enough to adjust the nasal cannula pumping oxygen into his body, which agitated the flow meter and summoned a plump nurse into his bedroom to shoo me away.

The last time I saw Kenny, I was on a 3-day shower strike in preparation for my LSAT and he was hooked up to his last dose of CHOP; he was barely coherent so I can't count it. The last time I saw Kenny outside of a hospital was when we were fifteen. It was the last time he and I were in Barrett Station together.

He was sitting shotgun in a Caddy with a baby pig in his lap. The passenger door was cracked so he could stretch his long, brown legs across Momo Rene's driveway. His shaved head brushed against the roof of the Caddy while his tumor pulsed behind his ear. It had shrunk over the years but — in spite of the chemo, the surgeries, and the diet — Kenny was still dying.

"Hey Bart," his mouth wrapped around every syllable as it spilled from his mouth. "How's it going?"

I chucked my SAT manual into the backseat, then crawled in. "Whose pig?"

My other cousin, Dre slid into the driver's seat. "Like em? I stole it from a Jew. Name's Otis."

"The Jew?"

"No, stupid," Dre snorted. "The pig. I named him Otis."

"I thought Jews didn't mess with pigs?" I said.

"Aw, you know they don't read the same Bible as Catholics."

Kenny rubbed Otis' belly, then asked: "Why we got a Jewish pig?"

"Cousin Chouke needs it. Kinda like a gift. We're celebratin his homecoming."

I rolled my eyes. "From prison?"

Last time I saw Cousin Chouke was at Dre's eighth birthday. We had finished the birthday song and were cutting into a buttercream cake when the doorbell rang. Sheriff had Chouke in custody for cutting the heads off Miss Shirley's chickens. All my uncles, my aunts, and even Papa Lee left to scrounge up bail money. My parents took me home without getting my slice of cake to-go.

I hated Chouke ever since.

"He's blood," insisted Dre. "Besides, he's offered to help us out," He went on, backing the Caddy out of Momo's driveway with a grin carved into his plump face. "Today, we get rid of Papa Lee's curse. For good."

"Aw hell," Kenny groaned.

I pressed my head into the window. "We're getting too old for this shit."

The family curse started with Papa Lee. He quit his job as showrunner to St. Martin's Church so he could focus on family. Too dependent on Papa Lee, the congregation crumbled – no more seasonal fairs, gumbo cook-offs, or after-Sunday-Sunday school.

Everything went to shit.

The town lost faith.

Church attendance went down.

Employment plummeted.

The water supply was contaminated.

God cursed Papa Lee for abandoning his people and, as punishment, killed off a member of the family each year.

Every summer after Papa Lee's death, my cousins and I made an attempt to remove the curse. It started five years ago with cousin Travi – the summer he burned down St. Martin's in the name of the family curse. The first of many failed attempts.

Dre parked the Caddy outside the Baptist Church. It was bigger than the Catholic Church. Bloated too. The windows reeked of the Gospel, overflowed with the Holy Ghost, and fed the dying grass beyond the pane with warm holy water.

"Why're we here?"

"We need money." Dre answered Kenny as he counted a wad of cash: $177.00.

My fingers curled around the door handle. "What do we need that kind of money for?"

"It's the price for Chouke's services."

"What services?"

"The curse riddin' services."

I followed Dre out of the car. "The hell is Chouke doing?"

He shushed me. "We're on holy ground."

"Fuck that," I grabbed the neck of his shirt. "Chouke's bad news, Dre."

Kenny zipped Otis into his hoodie, then added: "My mom says he killed someone."

Dre shrugged. "He's blood."

I released Dre's shirt from my grip. "You sound like Travi."

"Is that bad?"

I didn't know.

"I'll explain everything after we get the money."

Otis squirmed and wheezed inside Kenny's hoodie. "I don't think the Baptists are gonna give us any charity," he said.

"You know Baptists got dough," said Dre.

"All that money goes to God."

Dre smiled his fat-boy grin. "Exactly."

We spread out.

Kenny stood in back. Dre took the left, me the right.

We sat through a reading from the Book of Ezra, witnessed six Baptists catch the Holy Ghost, and clapped our hands to a rhythmic rendition of "Holy, Holy, Holy" before the donation basket was released.

Trembling, I tucked my hands beneath my thighs and watched the basket bounce from Baptist to Baptist, each emptying their clutches and coat pockets into the wooden weavings.

I stole a glance at Dre; with his bounty secured, he slipped from the aisle.

A round-faced girl, probably twelve or thirteen, dropped a ten with a star and heart drawn over Hamilton's face into the basket, then passed it to the man next to her. He dropped a blank check with a Christ watermark on top of her bill then handed it to me.

I yanked my hands from beneath my thighs and knocked it to the ground. Paper scattered beneath the benches.

Sliding from the bench, I dropped to my knees and started digging. I grabbed everything green beneath me. Crushed it in my hand. Stuffed it into my bra. I scooped up the remaining envelopes and bills, piled them into the basket, and then looked up.

Glaring at me like I was some sinful roadside attraction, that round-faced girl had both eyes on me.

I stood with the basket in shaky hands. The rest of the Baptists had risen to their feet to "amen" through the closing prayer. That little girl was the only person who could see me: a Catholic phantom here to disturb the peace.

I reached into my bra and removed the first bit of paper: a twenty-dollar bill. I placed it on top of the remaining envelopes and then dropped the basket into her lap. Her glare softened; she looked like she was going to cry or that she was thinking the very words, "I'm gonna pray for you".

We didn't talk about the money.

Dre drove down Oak Avenue until we were back on Lynchburg, pulling over every so often to let Kenny vomit on the sidewalk. A combination of Dre's junk food and the chemo made Kenny sicker by the hour. Dre and I stood on either side of him, listening to him yak, meal after meal.

We didn't talk about that either.

We sat on the hood of the Caddy outside Big E's mini-mart. Kenny fed Otis a strip of jerky while I squeezed Kool-Aid in his mouth after each piece. Dre handed him hot chips to nibble on and I gave him more Kool-Aid. Otis was one of us.

"Quit feedin' him that jerky," I told Kenny.

"Why?"

I snatched the greased bag from his hand before he could force another slab into Otis' snout. "This is pork jerky, dummy."

"So?"

"That's forced cannibalism."

"Aw shit," Dre quit counting the money to check over his shoulder. "That's a felony."

"What do you know about it, fatass?" said Kenny.

"This one guy cousin Boo used to work with – his fiance's best friend's boss once fed a live chicken fried chicken, and you know what happened? Cops put him in prison for life."

"You're lyin'," I said.

"Right hand to the man."

Kenny tossed the jerky beneath the Caddy.

"Whatever man." I laughed. "I'm sure the cops are gonna be more pissed about us stealing Otis than feeding him one of his uncles."

Dre stuffed the money into his pocket. "You won't be sayin that when you're sharing a cell with Travi."

Kenny chuckled. I didn't.

"Kenny," I started to say, "How much longer is your treatment?"

He tugged on Otis's ears and counted to himself. "Momma says I should be done soon but I don't feel any different."

"Man, fuck cancer!" Dre spat.

"That sucks," I added, stupidly. I didn't know any other way to respond to something like that. I still don't.

"How'd you do on the SAT?" Kenny asked me.

"1420 outta 1600. I'm retaking it in a month."

Kenny nodded. "I wish I could graduate already."

I smiled, though I wasn't set on the idea of graduating at fifteen. Kenny was ready to get away from his mom's watchful eye and tearful hospital stays, away from his organic diet and morning PT with his dad. My mom just wanted me as far away from Barrett as possible.

I would've traded places with Kenny – his cancer for my degree. That way, Kenny could be free from the curse and I could spend the little time I had left fighting it.

Dre took a swig from his cream soda. "School ain't for me. Money is."

"I wish I could go to school," Kenny said, drawing circles around the mouth of his soda can with a fingertip. "It's always just my momma and me and-" he took in a breath, "She reminds me every day that I'm gonna die. I hate feeling like that."

Dre let his soda can slide from his hand. It bounced once then emptied itself into a foamy puddle of whiteness. Otis stepped into the puddle and licked up the dirty cream.

Dre leaned in close. "Nobody's gonna die. The curse ends tonight."

I wrapped an arm around Kenny's shoulders. "We're doing this for the family. For you, Kenny."

He smiled as he dragged the sleeve of his shirt across his cheeks.

"It's gonna work, Herc." Dre promised, emphasizing the Herc, the nickname we only ever used to reassure Kenny of his strength. "I stole a pig from a Jew and Bart looted a Baptist church. Shit, it has to work."

I forced myself to laugh. "If not, Dre and I will be sharing a space in hell together."

"You and I are goin' to hell anyway."

Kenny smiled wider, laughing even. "Alright," he reached down to curl his finger around Otis' tail. "I wish we hung out more, guys. I miss ya'll."

Dre snorted. "Whatever, Elephant Man."

We waited until the sun sank behind the Catholic Church before we climbed back in the Caddy.

Dre drove down Lynchburg towards FM 1942. He followed the freeway from the feeder – seat belts on, speedometer just under the limit. We rode for a good half hour before a motel sign came into view. Dre parked in the lot, killed the engine, and then we climbed out. With Otis tucked beneath Kenny's arm and the banded bills in Dre's pocket, we marched on.

"He's in there," Dre said, pointing to room number 5. He peered in the window first, hesitating as we listened to cars weave in and out of the motel lot.

We knocked on Number 5.

Kenny dropped into a squat, moaning with his hands clasped behind his head.

"Not gonna puke again, are you?" I asked him with my hand on his back.

Kenny groaned. "Think it was that jerky."

I watched Kenny coax his stomach as Dre continued to knock. Otis circled Kenny's hunched body. His blotchy face raised up, eyes on me: a patch of black covered his beady eye, but the rest of him was all pink. Otis dipped his snout towards the gravel at our feet, wheezing softly into our soles. When he lifted his tiny head, those beady eyes found me. To this day, I swear he was smiling at me.

The door opened.

Chouke was massive. Long ways and sideways. Sunken bloodshot eyes, a crooked nose, hollow cheeks, and a mouth of broken teeth. He wore nothing but a pair of tattered, green cargo pants. His body was bony, covered in scar tissue and tattoos. His hair was long and thin, balding at the scalp and braided down to his waist.

He terrified me. I thought of running back to the Caddy and driving home, beyond Barrett and away from the curse.

When he stepped into the soft light above his door, he said one thing: "You got the money?"

Dre nodded and stammered a "yessir" as he fished the baggie from his pocket. "Three hundred. Like you said."

Chouke counted the bills in his hands then pulled the door open.

I followed Dre through with my head turned back towards Kenny. He had tears in his eyes and Otis squeezed against his chest.

The four of us sat on the edge of the motel bed as Chouke paced. We listened to the heavy bottoms of his boots thump against the chipped floorboards and the hem of his cargos brush over the prickly threads of the rug. When he finished packing, he pulled a t-shirt over his head and threw a duffle over his shoulder.

His eyes then fixed on Otis. "Give em here," he said.

Kenny hugged Otis tighter.

I reached for Otis and closed my fingers around Kenny's wrist. "We have to give him back later. The pig. He belongs..."

My voice trailed off as I watched the rage build in Chouke's face. I clenched my teeth and watched his hands, waiting for him to strike me or punch a hole into the wall because I dared to talk back.

Kenny began to cry beside me.

"No, we don't." Dre said, yanking at Otis' tail. "It's your pig, Chouke. We took 'em for you."

"It's not his pig," I snapped, barely a whisper. "Dre said you needed it for the ritual so we thought you could use him for that and then we could return him. Right, Dre?"

Dre didn't reply.

Chouke flashed a smirk—so quickly I thought I'd imagined it. "Sure," he said. "I only need a little blood."

My own blood went cold at the sound. I swallowed and nodded, trying to bleach any image of a bloody Otis from my mind.

We piled on the bed of Chouke's truck while he drove us back into Barrett. He parked in a ditch then led us through the ravine. We followed him, shoulder to shoulder, keeping Kenny in the middle. Chouke dragged his feet until we reached the bayou at the base of Papa Lee's old hill. It was fenced off after Travi's fire took down St. Martins. Chouke found a hole in the fence, pulled aside the wiring, and then waved inward.

We climbed through.

At the top, Chouke told us to sit in the grass and wait, so we did. He doused his body in a white powder.

"Gimme the pig," said Chouke. A chalky hand extended into our circle.

Kenny clung to Otis. "You'll give him back right?"

Chouke demanded a second time. Kenny gave in.

"He promised," I told Kenny. "He'll give him back to us."

Dre shook his head.

Chouke squeezed Otis beneath his armpit. Otis squirmed and squealed. Chouke clapped his hands, causing the powder to break from his skin and fill the air with white clouds.

On our knees with our arms around one another, we waited.

Chouke squatted down to dig through his duffle. He removed a long, blunt blade and a silver bowl from the bag.

"No." Kenny lunged forward, but Dre and I pulled him back in. We knew what was next.

I turned my head into Kenny's shoulder and listened as Otis squealed himself into an eternal silence. I gagged as the sound of his fuzzy, pink flesh splitting filled my ears, followed by the echo of blood dinging against the bottom that silver bowl. The smell of rust filled our circle.

Kenny cried. Otis was dead.

Dre's bottom lip trembled inward, the dimple in his chin vibrated above the many folds of his neck. "I'm sorry," he cried. "I'm so, so sorry."

Chouke tossed Otis' body down the hill and howled. Speckles of his blood painted the dying earth beneath us and the skin of our faces.

Chouke moved toward us. "Stand up!" he panted. "Give me your hands."

Dre dragged us to our feet. We vibrated with fear.

Chouke took my hand from my own pocket and drew the blade across it in one clean slice. I screamed as tears spilled from my eyes and my hand filled with Otis' blood and my own.

"You all need to be cleansed." He grabbed Kenny's hand and sliced it open as quickly as he did mine. "Bleed out the curse," he said before slicing open Dre's. "Bleed!"

Dre swatted the blade from Chouke's hand. "Run!" he tumbled headfirst downhill.

I dragged Kenny upright and slid after Dre.

We rolled over jagged rocks and ant dunes, snake pits and wet, red dirt until we crashed into the wire fence.

Kenny wheezed beside me, clutching his stomach.

Dre scrambled. "Move!" he pulled at our elbows. "Go! Go! Go!"

Hobbling behind Kenny and Dre, I made myself look back. Chouke's ashy body glowed at the top of Papa Lee's hill, watching us. Laughing at us.

We never saw Chouke chase us. Still, we ran until we reached the stoplight separating Barrett from the highway. That was when Kenny started vomiting again.

"Are you kidding me? Now?" Dre galloped onward.

Kenny hurled up the remaining bits of junk food, trying to catch it in his palms so he could keep running. He tried to stand, but slipped in the gravel.

"Slow down, Dre." I knelt beside Kenny and rubbed his back. "Chouke isn't following us."

Kenny spat into his vomit pool. "You – sure?"

I nodded. "This whole thing was bullshit."

"The ritual worked," Dre swore it.

"How did it work if we didn't even finish it?"

Kenny began to speak, barely a grumble at our feet. "Did you know he was gonna kill Otis?"

Dre's hands loosened at his side, hanging limply. The red glare of the stoplight above us illuminated the grimace on his face.

"Not really," he said. "I didn't know Chouke was gonna kill 'em. I mean, I had an idea that something was gonna happen – but I wasn't sure."

Kenny fell silent until the red glare above us flashed green. The moment it did, he leapt to his feet and smashed into Dre. Their bodies collided, but Kenny was too weak to tackle Dre. He fell into the gravel, but scurried back to his feet to swing his frail fists into Dre's face.

"You evil son-of-a-bitch! I hate you! I hate you so much!"

Dre toppled over and slid against the asphalt. "C'mon Herc! It was a – a misinterpretation!"

I tried to secure Kenny's arms within my own.

"None of this would've happened if you weren't obsessed with the curse!"

Dre's plump hands strangled the rocks beneath him. He mashed his lips together, staring down FM 1942. "I'm sorry, okay?" he mumbled. "I just – I just like having you guys around."

"Shut up, Dre." Kenny whimpered. "You used us. Just like you used Otis."

"I just wanted to get rid of the curse."

"There is no curse." I threw my hands to the sky. "We're not doing this anymore, Dre. It's over."

The last thing Kenny said to Dre came just before the Caddy was parked back in Momo Rene's garage: "I'm never coming back to Barrett again."

And he kept that promise.

The timer on my crock-pot dinged itself to sleep. I sealed the final box of my things and slid it into a corner.

I knew Otis was done for the moment he looked at me outside Number 5. I'm as much a murderer as Dre is. A part of me has always believed Kenny knew that too, that he held me to same disdain he did Dre and Travi – even Chouke.

I pulled a glass bowl from my kitchen pantry and spooned the dark broth into it, followed by the soggy strips of green and a hock.

When I sat at my empty table, I couldn't lift the spoon. The greens sunk to the bottom of the broth, which was now a murky gray-green. Meat from the hock peeled away, shredded itself, then sunk to the bottom of the bowl. Lumps of pig fat collected along the rim. The broth was ruined—hardly edible. The many pieces to the stew were now indistinguishable. Overcooked bits of green latched to the bubbles of lard while the shallots and the garlic dissolved into the murkiness, leaving nothing visible but a bare bone in my bowl.

CR ∞

Eriel B. M. Fauser grew up in the candy-painted city of Houston, Texas. Her girlhood was split between the bayou and the suburbs, where she garners most of her writing inspiration. She received her BA in English with minors in Creative Work and Global Business from the University of Houston. She is currently pursuing an MFA in Writing from the New Writer's Project at the University of Texas at Austin, where she also serves on the board of the graduate literary journal, Bat City Review. Her work can be found in Glass Mountain, The Aletheia, Edible Houston, Cold Creek Review, and on her computer.

JOHN HENRY'S LAST - RICHARD BOWER

John Henry dreamed the night before the steam hammer
competition. Since childhood, he'd had a premonition of
dying with his hammer in his hand, and every schoolchild
from Alabama to Ohio knew how that turned true. He beat
the steam engine, punching railroad ties and hammering
through rock faster than mere machine, at the cost of his heart.
But this night, he dreamed of fields filled with wheat
aside mountains and forests swathed with pristine, apple
orchards. He traded hammer for plow and furrowed the ground.
Smoke signals puffed across the ocean sky, delivering
his happiness to the sun.

His father, a slave who starved; himself, a freeman who starved,
John Henry stole bread and had been sentenced to the chain
gang in his youth. His freedom earned swinging a railroad
hammer. For food and land, he swung for his life again;
until salted sweat beaded from his sun-darkened skin.

Pollyanne, his good wife, washed the worn clothes, patched
holes, and watched the railroad lead to another turn, another
tunnel, another pass. Everyone loved her as she looked
westward. John felt her presence guiding his hammer–swinging
rhythmic, persistent, and leveed. The throbbing in his temple
paced even with the hammer strokes upon the railroad line,
extending its manifest of people west, carrying wheat
from the plains east.

The dark morning of his challenge, John Henry woke. His eyes
opened, night surrounding his cot as he lay stomach down,
cheek on its side. A flawless skeleton stood beside his bed–
eyeless sockets, no flesh to carry, calcitic white bones. John
Henry's muscled arms immobilized, no kick in his legs.
Tranquilized by sleep, his mind connected only to itself,
so he waited for his muscles to behave.

The skeleton nodded its head downward at his prone position,
as if sharing a secret. After a moment unfolding hours, John Henry
gained control and swept his arm out through the untouchable

hip bone. His swing wild, uncontrolled, the skeleton faded. Smiling.

 લ   ૭

Richard Bower writes, runs, and teaches in Central New York. He is glad skeletons stay under the skin and fears the day they'd look to be seen. He has been published previously in Postcard Shorts and has flash forthcoming from Storyland Literary Review. https://about.me/richard_bower

COUNTING EVERY RIB - KATHARINE VALENTINO

At a table at a beachfront open-air restaurant in Puerto Vallarta, Mexico, my date and I are approached by a Chihuahua who is even tinier than he would be if you couldn't count all his ribs. I think the poor fellow must be hungry, and this is distressing enough. But then I see nearby a much larger dog, a Doberman-mix who is nothing more than dull eyes and dry skin over bones. The Doberman, I conclude, is starving.

Are there degrees of starvation? "Six degrees of starvation?" Let's see: Hungry, starving, dead. That's three. Maybe snackish could be No. 1 and hungry No. 2. Then what? Famished? No, too much like a Beverly Hills teenager. Dead is certainly No. 6, though.

Now that I think of it, it's "six degrees of separation," not starvation. Well, dead is about as separate as it gets. Separate. Distant. Some distance from these mutts would be good right now. Not in miles, though; I'm trying to have a vacation here, and I'm not going to give it up just because of ... somebody starving, What must it feel like to be almost dead and watch others dine?

Such distress when we've come to the beach just to eat a lot and have a good time!

A third dog nears our table. This one is a terrier who looks as though he crawled into a dustbin last week and just crawled out again. Is he more or less starved than the other two? Now, I'm feeling guilty about having ordered my tacos al pastor. Three of them, there on my plate, arranged nicely, marinated meat topped off by sweet pineapple on fresh corn tortillas, salsa on the side. Delicious! But how can I eat while surrounded by such need?

We have two dogs with us at our feet—two well fed and well-cared for dogs who are now looking for what we who eat well call "treats." So, five dogs now surround our table.

I look around me at the other diners. The majority of them are Mexican families. They are on holiday on the last day of the Mexican Semana Santa (Easter Week), and they are having a good time. Children are cavorting here and there. Bebés are being passed from madres to padres to abuelas to amigos at other tables. Señoritas are changing from salty bikinis to more demure attire under cover of beach towels. A young papá is proudly showing off a tattoo of his baby son—an almost perfect likeness, we agree, when he shows us a picture of the boy. At a table near the kitchen, a guy with a paunch and an air of authority suddenly falls asleep, his head narrowly missing his meal. Nobody is paying any attention to the dogs except me.

So, OK. I hand a morsel of chicken from my first taco to a suddenly animated Chihuahua, who moves forward next to my Lilly Dog. To be fair, I give Lilly a bite, too, and I hand a bite to my dinner companion to give to his Lucy Dog who is on the other side of the table. With that, the Doberman moves forward very, very politely and sits himself between Lilly and the Chihuahua. Lilly moves over a little so everyone has enough room. She doesn't seem threatened by a dog who might intimidate her after a hundred big dinners between those bones and that skin.

The Doberman gets another bite. Now, the terrier moves closer and gets her first bite of chicken. I watch as she becomes in that moment considerably more alert.

I take a bite of taco and then give each waiting dog a bite, then take another bite myself. And so it goes until my meal is finished, at which point I offer my plate of crumbs and some leftover tortillas to the Doberman. He's the biggest and therefore most in need. I hold the plate for him. I feel so loving. I am so engrossed in this scene where I am a benefactor doing my part to make the world a better place, a la the Sixties. We all thought then that we would make the entire world a better place. Now it's come down to a few mouthfuls for three dogs.

Still holding the plate for the Doberman, I glance up at my date. I'm expecting approval, but the expression on his face... At the next table, there's a boy, maybe 7 or 8, pointing at me. His face is full of provincial pique, and he's yanking on his mother's skirt. His mother is staring at my date with her eyebrows raised. Clearly, he should do something about this situation. Other diners at surrounding tables seem to agree; they're all staring at me.

I've been told that Mexicans consider stray dogs to be "animales unicos" or "only animals," more like wild pests than pets. It wasn't uncommon for them to treat strays poorly as a result. Obviously, they don't approve of my feeding dogs at the table.

"Well," my date says, leaning forward to pat my shoulder, "it's kind of neat to be the weirdest thing these amigos have seen all day."

He turns toward our audience, and now with a genuine smile and a chuckle, says, "She loves dogs.'"

He's right. I do.

Katharine Valentino worked for 25 years at menial jobs before acquiring a BA degree in journalism from Indiana University in Bloomington. For the next 20 years, she worked at slightly more interesting jobs and occasionally was even allowed to write some technical thing or another. Now retired from full-time work, she stays busy as the owner of Setting Forth (https://settingforth.pub/). She writes creative nonfiction, edits everything from user guides to poetry, and publishes some of the books she edits.

THE SHE SKELETON - RACHID BENHARROUSSE

The extraterrestrial beauty,
the shining, golden bones;
the envious sun bowing
to SHE!

SHE is the skeleton,
the meta-gorgeous whiteness.
I didn't touch SHE.
My flesh would only
wound SHE with ugliness.

But! ugliness died
in her finite, dead ugly flesh.
All hail the immortality, the grace
of SHE skeleton!

ଓ ଛ

Rachid Benharrousse is a poet, writer, columnist, and an English Literature Major. His works have appeared in Sasa Post and Juice Books and forthcoming in other magazines! He has won the first place in a national short-story competition and he loves skeletons, especially of cows!

BONES - GEOFF KOURY

buried
secret
lonely

smooth
fresh
white

gnawed
splintered
hollowed

licked
tossed
piled

ଔ ଙ

Geoff Koury *lives outside of Washington D.C. and facilitates a monthly poetry workshop. He enjoys riding electric unicycles.*

DÁNSZENTMIKLÓS - CSILLA MATHE

Flecks of white on red
peeling shards of paint slathered on an oxidized, green copper gate
and the weathered engraved plate, which heralds the humble abode
of my Timár grandfather.
I suppose it matches the name carved into his tombstone we have yet
to see
that is just over one year old.

We did not make time to visit the dead this year
when our time with the living grows so short.

Our only living link to the 1920s
lay like a skeleton with aching joints, over which paper-like skin is
stretched
lined like a notepad with fading etchings of a novel she can no longer
tell
and we pray to God she will wake each morning
if only to stir so her poor dingy mutt can feast like a queen
and be rubbed with the love only a peasant girl's hands could give,
with dirt painted under fingernails like French tips.

She is 85 years old and asks me if I am her sister,
how we came here,
and if I have siblings,
when my sister is sitting in the same room behind me on the sofa bed.

We point to the photos caked in a layer of dust
like the confectioner's sugar on the flaky pastries she baked for us
four years ago.
She didn't plan for it to be this way she says
tears strangling the ends of her vocal chords.
"Ne öregedjetek meg."
"Do not grow old," she tells us.

I remember hating it there,
bathing in a tub with hard-water rings like brown tattoos in a once-
white basin
squatting by a spider spinning its doily-like web beneath the soap

---

117

dish
and washing the artist and her handiwork down the drain with only
half a mind to momentarily admire nature's greatness.
Only half a mind because I'd rather not bathe with spider webs
hanging inches from my face.

I awoke the last day:
the reason I came was to see this wilting grandmother,
whether senile or sane
and bring her some happiness
Scraped from a jar, like hardened honey.
All this time, I had spent my days pitying the joy I left outside the
withered gate
beyond the expanses of farmland
somewhere coasting above the clouds, heavy with the burden of rain
Feeling I left my heart somewhere in American suburbia.

I wonder if this may be the last day I ever wake in this dusty bed
within walls built of straw and mud
in the place my grandmother raised my mother
The small cottage house on the land which ripened fire-fleshed
apricots
dripping with morning dew.
Where my grandfather's grapes were cultivated for weak red wine
where brown hens lay a pretty speckled egg a day
while a spring kitten napped on the splintered stairs leading up to the
attic.
An attic where salamis were once strung from the ceiling.
where a land once fertile now is dry like sand
and where maybe one day many years from now we may visit to find
the name plate removed
the gate repaired
a stranger living on the land that broke us
but was ours.

CR   ഇ

Csilla Mathe is a Rutgers University graduate and is happily teaching English in New Jersey. She is still giggling that her publishing cherry was popped by "Boned" and is currently seeking hiking buddies for a Mount Kilimanjaro trek.

CAPUCHIN CRYPT, ROME, ITALY. - DANNY MCLAREN

there are bones everywhere.
they line the walls, the ceilings, mark the path you walk on the floor.
arcs above every doorway,
chandeliers made up of pieces of fallen brothers.

to be immortalized like this is frightening.
yet, oddly comforting.
clergy of centuries past will never leave this holy place.
an ever-growing council of souls to watch over you, to guide you.
the feeling of eyes that have long since rotted away peering down at
you.

they will always be in good company here.
kindly old caretakers and members of the church still remain.
and new faces pass by, staring in awe,
in fear,
in curiosity.

it's okay, a voice behind you whispers, it's not supposed to be scary.
death isn't to be feared, after all.
these men who you look up at now are no longer afraid.
life moves quickly, of course, but once it is done you will join them.
maybe not here, maybe not on these walls, but somewhere.

there's a guest book on your way out.
you leave your regards to the dead.

ʘ ⁊

Danny McLaren is a queer writer, photographer, and musician from Toronto. They are currently an undergraduate student majoring in gender studies, with an interest in equity, inclusivity, and diversity-related work, and they let these themes guide much of their work as an artist. They are an editor and co-founder of an arts and culture magazine called Alien Pub.
Twitter: https://twitter.com/dannymclrn
Alien Pub's Twitter: https://twitter.com/alienpubmag

KNAVE / BAR FLY - JOAN MCNERNEY

Knave

Full of himself flaunting
his black leather jacket
covered with silver studs.
Bling hangs from his bulging neck.
Flashy zircons, deep cologne,
tattoos, piercings, purple hair.
Puffed up, he struts across alleys.
Headlight eyes scoping
each corner searching prey.
Pushing down anything
in his way. Sniffing rear
doors, sniffing out death.
His hands move like claws
through shadows with
crooked nails buffed blue.
Lugging a bag of tricks loaded
with brass knuckles, chains,
zip guns, switchblade knives.
Opening his cavern mouth,
smacking wide lips, he drains
a cool cocktail of ruby red blood.

Bar Fly

At Jewel Box Tavern
lights are always dim
so you can't look closely.
Wearing stiletto heels, she
traipses along followed by
billows of cheap perfume.
Dressed in a second skin of
electric blue velveteen
covered with silver glitz.
She looks for a mark, some
clown who carries thick wads
of cash and a stash of coke.

Tapping the shoulder of
the willing joker with her long
lacquered fingernails.
First she must meet him
in the back alley to pay up
with her pound of flesh.
Showing its age, her face
is coated by pastes, crèmes,
thick rouge, blazing red lipstick.
Her brown eyes encrusted with
liners, mascara and shadow
revealed a certain sadness,
Secreted in the dark and dank
women's room, she snorts
that magical white powder.
Nothing matters now.
There is no despair
only this embrace of bliss.

                                      ☙ ❧

Joan McNerney's poetry has been included in numerous literary zines such as Moonlight Dreamers of Yellow Haze, Seven Circle Press, Dinner with the Muse, Blueline, Halcyon Days *and included in* Bright Hills Press, Kind of A Hurricane Press *and* Poppy Road Review *anthologies. She has been nominated four times for Best of the Net.*

CRANIO - SALVATORE DIFALCO

After work, Ruggerio Puma decided to stop for a drink at Johnny's Ball, a sports bar located near his midtown flat. He'd been to Johnny's Ball once before, had disliked the Buffalo wings and found the draught beer warm as piss; but he needed to wind down before he went home, and convenience trumped misgiving on this occasion.

Ruggerio wrote copy for a thriving advertising agency, but was struggling. Ideas that used to flutter into his head like flash cards now had to be coaxed, coddled, poked and prodded out. He'd even taken the advice of Anthony, the head writer, and tried smoking weed to get the juices flowing, but only wound up drifting off into his own silly associations, or conceived of suggestions too outlandish or stupid to be of any use. Some days, no matter how hard he tried, he had nothing. Today had been such a day. His team had been brainstorming a promotional pitch for a new Advil product. All he could think of during their session was how much his head ached and that he could sure use an Advil. When he made this known to his colleagues, they ridiculed him.

"Aw, did ya hear that guys? Poor Reggie's head hurts."

"Want me to rub it better, pal?"

"There's an ice-pack in the freezer. Donato used to ice his corns with it."

"No wonder his head hurts, it's huge."

"Yeah, quite the melon."

"I'd get that checked out."

Everyone had a good laugh at his expense. And then, unabashedly, they turned their back-and-forth about his whining into an actual pitch for the product, featuring a man with an oversized head complaining to a doctor that it weighed a ton. Advil could reduce the size and weight of the sufferer's head. So went the pitch. Max, the staff illustrator, went so far as to sketch panels of a man holding his pumpkin-sized head while a superhero, dressed as a giant box of the new Advil product, delivered him from the affliction.

Ruggerio sat at the bar and ordered a double bourbon. The bartender had a shaved, perfectly round head and sleeve tattoos with skull-and-bone designs on both arms. He also had a metal nub jutting out of his lower lip, which made Ruggerio wonder if it was merely cosmetic or pertained to the bartender's sexual predilections.

"I'm Tank, your affable bartender, haha. And how are you this evening?"

"Hi, Tank. Ruggerio. Friends call me Reggie. I'm okay."

"Just okay?"

"Been a long day, you know."

"I hear you." Tank licked his lips and frowned. "Ruggerio?"

"My family's Sicilian. Ruggerio's common there. It actually translates to Roger. From the Normans. They were there way back when."

"Hm. Interesting. You don't like being called Roger?"

"Never took. Everyone's always called me Reggie. Even my mother—God rest her soul—called me Reggie."

"Ah, sorry. She passed when?"

"Been a few years. Cheers."

Ruggerio sipped the bourbon. It felt good going down, spreading warmth through his chest and shoulders and causing his nerves to stop jangling. He thought of his poor mother who had died of complications from dementia. Not a pleasant way to go out. She'd spent five years hallucinating animals and little people, and didn't recognize her own son for the last two years.

Tank moved off to serve another customer. On the flat screen mounted over the liquor bottles, Barry Bonds, the contentious former baseball slugger, spoke to a sports journalist. Ruggerio couldn't tell if it was a new interview, but Barry looked slimmed down from his latter playing days. He'd started out as a lean, base-stealing contact hitter with some pop. Then, over the years, had transmogrified into an upper-deck jacking monster. Maybe the interview had something to do with the Hall of Fame. Ruggerio figured Barry belonged there, even if he'd been juicing. Everyone was juicing back then.

He overheard two guys in suits, at a table just behind him, talking about Barry Bonds in terms of his head size.

"Looks almost normal now. Remember how big it got?"

"Fuck yeah. He must have been doing horse roids."

"Haha, yeah. They say his head size increased from, like, a seven to an eight and a half."

"Is that big?"

"Buddy, that's huge. Upper three percentile."

"How do you know that shit?"

"I know, I know."

"Yeah, his head was huge by the end. Like one of those Earth globes."

"It's smaller now."

"Heads can shrink?"

"I guess. Not sure. It's still pretty big though."

Tank asked Ruggerio if he wanted another drink, but a nascent headache ticked his right eye. Another drink might birth it. Headaches had been plaguing him for the last month or so. Bad ones. They'd become an oppressive constant. Before that, he had rarely experienced a headache that an aspirin or a strong espresso couldn't nip.

"Think I'm good," he said, rubbing his right temple.

Tank stared at Ruggerio's head while he dried a pint glass with a cloth. It was this stare which started the wheels turning in Ruggerio's mind. What was the guy staring at? Did his head look that unusual? Was it really as big as his colleagues had insinuated?

"You might be dehydrated," Tank said, filling the pint glass he'd been handling with water from a frosty pitcher. "Drink this. It'll help. If I don't drink enough water when I'm in here I get dry." He rubbed his forearms as if to demonstrate. "And sometimes I get headaches."

"Thanks."

Ruggerio drank some water, but it didn't go down well, almost making him gag.

"You okay?" Tank asked.

"I—I think I'm just going to split. Thanks for the drink."

"No problem."

Ruggerio paid and slid off his stool. When he turned away from the bar the duo in suits were staring. More specifically, they were staring at his head. He stopped and glared at them until they averted their eyes. What, they're mocking my head size now? he thought, hastening to the exit. Jesus.

As he stepped into the warmish evening air, he reached up his hands and grasped his head. A passing group of young women in reds and blacks ogled him, whispering, then laughed out loud when they were safely down the street. Ruggerio ignored their merriment and squeezed his head. Was it possible? he thought. Was it possible that his head was growing, or had grown in the past few months?

As he walked home he tried summoning his hat size. Truth was, other than toques and adjustable ball caps, he'd never been fitted for a hat. If eight was huge, what size was his head? Then he recalled his college football days at Western. He had played tight end for the varsity team, and as far as he could recall had worn a size seven helmet. That wasn't huge.

When he got home, he immediately went to the bathroom and studied his head, turning it this way and that and straining his eyes to size it up. Yeah, it was definitely not a seven now. What the fuck had happened? He'd dabbled with steroids back in college, but only briefly, and except for a vicious case of acne vulgaris had never experienced any side-effects. Seemed unlikely steroids were the culprit.

He searched the Internet for information about abnormal skull growth—a mistake. The condition, generally known as macrocephaly, was caused by any of a multitude of rare disorders. He read about maladies like hyperostosis frontalis interna (a thickening of the frontal skull bone), fibrous dysplasia, Sotos syndrome (distinguished by cerebral gigantism), Adams-Oliver syndrome, Crouzon disease, Cowden disease, Noonan syndrome, melorheostosis, and something called cardiofaciocutaneous syndrome...

Ruggerio's headache intensified. He took an aspirin, but after a few minutes found himself kneeling at the toilet, puking his guts out. His head continued pounding. He went to the kitchen and opened the refrigerator. He pulled a bag of peas out of the freezer compartment and retreated to his bedroom. He threw himself on the bed, slapped the bag of peas over his right eye, and tried to still his mind.

It had been a bad day. Chalk it up to that. All this business about his head. Absurd. There were the headaches, true. And he didn't feel right, hadn't in months. But stress could trigger headaches. Stress was a quiet killer. Stress killed the body, spirit and mind. His creative failure at work and feelings of inadequacy had manifested themselves with headaches. Of course: his brain needed a break. He'd been hammering away for years trying to spin silk from shit, that is to say trying to sell shit to people, shit they probably didn't need. Maybe all he needed was a vacation where he didn't have to think about anything. He'd always wanted to go on a hot-air balloon ride. It seemed like the serenest thing a person could do. He just imagined himself floating slowly and soundlessly over the landscape, not a thought in his head, not a care in the world.

He opened his eyes to daylight. The headache had broken. He felt relieved and oddly refreshed from his dense, dreamless sleep.

Running late for work, he washed up hastily in the bathroom. He made a cup of coffee in his Keurig and drank it while he dressed. Last thing he wanted to do was be late for work. He'd learned his lesson about complaining to those vultures. If he showed up late, he'd only draw more attention to himself, and thus more ridicule.

When he got to work, everyone was already in a meeting that had been called that morning. Had he read his emails, he would have known about it. When he entered the conference room, the big boss,

Stuart Mangold, wearing a beige linen suit with a red-and-white polka dot bow-tie, was addressing other members of the creative team. He didn't pause or acknowledge Ruggerio as he took a seat at the big table. His colleagues weren't so oblivious, grabbing their heads and making agonized faces as Ruggerio forced a smile and tried to catch the boss's drift.

"As I was saying," Stuart Mangold intoned in his rather high-pitched voice, "it's come to my attention that someone's been stealing toilet paper. We're not talking a roll or two here. Someone has pilfered several large boxes with a month's supply of toilet paper, for the whole building. That's a lot of toilet paper, people. That's a ton of toilet paper. Security's working to discover the thief or thieves, but they suspect an inside job." Stuart stopped talking and with thinned eyes looked at every member of the creative team. When his eyes fell on Ruggerio, he smiled. "Nice you can join us, Mr. Puma. I see you have recovered from your headache. You look hale. No more headaches with Super Advil in the house, huh?" Everyone tittered. "Well, glad you could make it, albeit tardily, which can be forgiven if it is due to your headache." More titters. "But tell me this, Reggie, during your episode—and I want you to answer frankly with no fear of repercussion—during your episode, did you happen to haul off some boxes of toilet paper? I'm not accusing you, I'm just asking."

Ruggerio looked around the table at his smirking colleagues. They were making sport of him? If so, it was intolerable.

"I know nothing of any toilet paper."

"Of course not," Stuart said, winking at the others. "Okay then. As a result of this theft, and to punish the perpetrator, we'll not be providing toilet paper for the balance of October. Let's say we'll reinstate toilet paper on Halloween. How's does that sound?"

A collective groan issued from the creative team. The meeting was adjourned. Ruggerio quickly slipped off to his cubicle. He didn't want to engage with anyone. He fired up his computer and started looking randomly at some websites. One of them featured the red crabs of Christmas Island. An accompanying article considered the mysterious statues of Easter Island. Someone tapped him on the shoulder.

He swiveled around in his chair. It was Stuart Mangold.

"Beavering away, eh?"

"Uh, yeah."

"Is everything okay? I mean, you look okay. But I'm turning sixty—that's right, sixty—next week and I can fairly say I know when someone's not right. Are you not right, Reggie? Tell papa everything."

"Look, Mr. Mangold, I'm in a bit of a slump."

"Problems with the lady?"

"I'm single. It's not that."

"Then what is it?"

"It's . . . it's my head."

"It's your—"

Stuart burst out laughing. He laughed hard, snorting and slapping his thigh. Then, in the midst of his merriment, he pointed at Ruggerio and said, "Good one. Good one, man. I'd heard you were quite the wit. Well-timed. Haha. Brilliant!" He pulled out a handkerchief and wiped his eyes. "I love this job," he said, walking off. "I really do."

Ruggerio sat back in his chair and sighed. These people were a bunch of fucking idiots. Of course, he'd known this for a long time. From the outset, actually. When he couldn't get any traction with his journalism career, he turned to advertising. He figured it would be an easy gig, and it was, for the most part. Except for all the idiots you had to deal with and all the shit you had to eat, buckets of it. His head was pounding. He rested his elbows on his desk and let his head fall into his open hands.

Fuck, it felt heavy. Like a fucking cannonball. This was ridiculous. He considered making a doctor's appointment. He even went to dial the number, then remembered that Dr. Allega could be a real asshole. A few years ago, after a bad break-up with his fiancee Giannamaria, he'd gone in to see him for depression, and though Dr. Allega did refer him to a psychiatrist—who prescribed some antidepressants that left Ruggerio dazed and dry-mouthed for weeks—he mocked him for succumbing to, as he termed it, pussy-whipping. Another time, when Ruggerio went to see him for some rectal bleeding, Dr. Allega insinuated that he'd been the victim of rough anal intercourse. "No loob for the strap-on?" he recalled him quipping. No, he wasn't going to call Dr. Allega. He'd be all over him about an enlarging head.

At lunch, Ruggerio ditched the crew, who were headed to Swiss Chalet for a feast, and went for a walk. He wanted to find out exactly how big his head was—he needed it measured—and searched for a haberdashery, but these days such establishments are few and far between. He did land upon a tailor, and thought he could get his head sized there, but when he proposed this to the wizened, ancient tailor, he turned him out of the shop and told him never to come back. Such a violent reaction. The old tailor must have had some history with a corrupt hat-maker.

When Ruggerio passed an old-fashioned woman's dress-shop, which also sold woman's finery and hats, he ventured inside and approached the saleslady, a matronly woman with enormous bosoms and a florid complexion. Her name-tag read: AGNES.

"How may I help you?" she asked with a vaguely British accent.

"I know this may sound strange," Ruggerio said, " but I need my head sized."

"For a hat?"

He thought about it. If he admitted he was merely concerned that his head was growing, she might get spooked.

"Yes," he said at last. "I need to know my hat size. It's for a wedding."

"Ah, I see, top hat. Yes. Lovely. All the rage this season. I can certainly measure your head, if you wish."

A black-shawled old woman rifling through marked-down dresses regarded Ruggerio with a stern gaze. She seemed to be measuring his head with her beady little eyes. He was going to say something, but stopped himself when Agnes returned with a tape measure.

"Okay," she said, "arms at sides. Remain still. Let's see how big this pumpkin really is."

Ruggerio reared his head.

"What is it?" Agnes asked, oblivious to her slight.

"Nothing," he said, swallowing. "Go on, please."

After some fumbling and looping and readjusting, Agnes declared that she had successfully sized Ruggerio's head.

He waited for her to voice the number, but she hesitated, as if trying to intensify the drama of its disclosure. The old lady leaned in, sucking her dentures, also keen to hear the result.

"Well?" Ruggerio barked, at the limits of his patience.

"Now now, sir. I'm doing you a favour. Your head size—ta-da—is just over eight."

"Jesus."

"I doubt Jesus' head was that big, sir."

"Man, eight is really big."

"Yes," Agnes said. "XXX grande, as they say."

"I'm embarrassed."

"Poff, no need be. My old Unks Aberfoyle wore an eight-and-half derby back in the day. He used four pillows in his bed to support that noggin. Me and my cousins used to call him Unky Dumpty. He did die from a fall, poor man. Broke that massive skull wide open. All the brains—"

"Okay, I get the picture, ma'am."

"That's the thanks ya get," the old woman piped-in. "So ya got a big old head, wah wah. Wah wah. You donks are so entitled. Wah wah, I got a big head. Go buy a big hat for that big fat head now and see how it goes."

"Ah, don't listen to her," Agnes said, tapping her temple. "Dementia."

"I've not got dementia, you little hussy."

"I'd best be on my way," Ruggerio said, and he exited before further damage could be inflicted on his crumpled ego.

As he walked back to his office, he kept catching sight of himself in glass storefronts and windshields. It was true, he had a gigantic head. A Mardi Gras float came to mind, one of those ambulant Krewe du Vieux jobs. Eight plus, eight plus, that was fucked up. He had to call Dr. Allega. Even if the guy mocked him, he had to see him. He had to find out what the fuck this was. He felt so heavy walking, that is to say, his head felt incredibly heavy as he tottered back to his office. People stared. Children pointed. The fucking horror! At his office he avoided all eye contact and skulked into his cubicle. He rested his head on his desk. That felt wonderful. Then he heard his name and started.

Iggy, one of the IT guys, loomed by his cubicle like a titillated scarecrow.

"What do you want?" Ruggerio said. He wasn't in the mood for shenanigans.

"Dude," Iggy said. "Having a bad hair day?"

"What? Bad hair? What the fuck is it, Iggy? Don't have time for your shit."

"Eight plus," he said, nodding.

"What did you say?"

"Eight plus, bro. We know. We know."

"What is this?"

"Look," Iggy said. "We feel for you. The IT department, that is. We commiserate. Now there's a good word. I've heard you use it before."

Ruggerio wasn't sure what was going on, but he had a feeling someone had planted an electronic bug or something on him. There was no bottom to their cruelty. He passed his hands down his shirt-front and patted his pants. He checked under and around his desk.

"You'd never find it, if we did," Iggy said. "But we didn't have to. You know, Kenneth, that little twit in the mailroom? His mother owns that dress-shop you visited at lunch. Yeah, uh-huh. News travels fast these days. I mean, eight plus—Jesus. You gotta get hats made custom."

Ruggerio stood up. He wasn't a big man, but he had a big temper, and had been known to uncage it on occasion. He stepped toward Iggy, who took a step back.

"If you think I'm gonna let you make me a laughingstock," Ruggerio said, "you're mistaken. If you've let the cat out of the bag—"

"It was already let out of the bag, as you put it. I'm just giving you a heads up."

With that Iggy darted off, cackling. Great, Ruggerio thought. Just great. Now he surely would be a laughingstock, if he wasn't already. He spent the rest of the afternoon ducking everyone or in the men's room splashing cold water on his face and fighting off panic anxiety. His head ached, needless to say. And his jaw ached, that was new.

When he finally left work he took the back stairs to avoid any confrontations. He stopped at Johnny's Ball for a drink. Tank manned the bar. A friendly face was always heartening. But when Ruggerio took a stool at the bar, Tank didn't seem to recall him. Not only that, but the amiable vibes from the evening before had been replaced by a sour countenance and a prickly, even menacing energy.

"What's your poison?" he asked with lidded eyes.

"I'll have a bourbon, Tank."

"Only friends call me Tank. Who are you to call me Tank?"

"No offense. I was here yesterday. You introduced yourself as Tank."

"I fucking highly doubt that."

"Hey man, what's your problem? I can leave if you don't feel like serving me."

"Don't be so fucking sensitive."

Someone from a booth asked them to pipe down.

"Shut the fuck up, Rudy!" Tank shouted at the complaining party.

"Fucking tool."

"Yeah," Ruggerio said under breath.

Tank stared at him for a full minute before he turned to get the drink.

What the fuck was wrong with the guy? Was he on drugs? Ruggerio's head felt hot and huge. He rested his forehead on the cool zinc of the bar counter. Ah, relief.

"Don't lean on the zinc," Tank said. "You'll get face grease all over it."

"Face grease, right."

Ruggerio downed the bourbon in one go. He didn't feel like hanging around.

"Leaving so soon?" Tank sneered.

"I don't know what's crawled up your ass, but I'm not into it."

Ruggerio turned around and headed for the exit. On the way he passed a table with a silver-haired man in a navy blazer and a young woman dressed in red. They were laughing, not unusual on its own, but when the woman pointed to Ruggerio and bent over in a spasm of hilarity, he knew he was the object of their ridicule.

He hurried out. Streetlights flared, horns blared, voices rushed at him in a buzzy sonic wave. Everything seemed too bright and loud. He had trouble walking. His equilibrium was off. He found himself grabbing at parking meters and street signs to stay upright. His neck muscles strained to keep his head erect, and the minute he let them slacken, it tipped to one side. It was as frightening as it was absurd.

He made it home, barely. He let himself into his flat and fell on his sofa, supporting his head on the arm-rest. Jesus, what if he had Sotos syndrome? The phrase cerebral gigantism filled him with dread. Fibrous dysplasia was equally disquieting. Why was this happening to him? His family had no history of such a thing, at least not to his knowledge. An Uncle Ignazio, who'd lived in Buffalo and ran a numbers operation back in the 1960s, was a huge man, reputedly weighing over 400 pounds. But Ruggerio didn't know if he had an enormous head to go along with his prodigious girth.

This was fucked up. His skull plates seemed to be expanding at that very moment to accommodate the growth. But was his brain actually swelling up or were the bones thickening?

He pressed his fingers to his skull. It hurt to touch it. Eight plus, he thought. Eight plus.

He started weeping uncontrollably. Tears streamed sideways down his horizontal face.

He couldn't sit up. His head felt cemented to the sofa's armrest. He tried again to lift it but couldn't. His panic only made things worse. He knocked over a lamp. The loud crash brought him back to his senses. As fucked up as this situation was, he had to remain calm. With his head firmly planted on the armrest, he counted to 10 and regulated his breathing.

Finally, with a violent twist, he rolled off the sofa, only to land hard on the floor. His head hit the floor tiles like an anvil. He couldn't lift it. He could only worm himself along the tiles, his forehead rubbing a path through the dust.

He wriggled and writhed his way to his bedroom and then to the side of his bed. By lifting his buttocks and straightening his legs, then grabbing his head securely with both hands and heaving it up, simultaneously with his torso, he was able to hurl himself onto his bed. His head plunged into the pillow, depressing the mattress below it.

Exhausted mentally and physically, Ruggerio soon fell asleep. He dreamed he rode a scarlet hot-air balloon into the blue heavens. He felt weightless and free floating over the quilted landscape of greens, yellows and browns. Then he looked up and saw that the scarlet balloon was actually in flames and that he was falling. He was falling to earth in a languid blur. Falling, falling. He wasn't afraid.

CR SO

Salvatore Difalco *is the author of 4 books. His short fiction has appeared in many print and online formats. He splits his time between Toronto and Palermo, Sicily. website:* http://saldifalco.weebly.com

NAPOLEON'S PENIS / NOT MY COUSIN MAGDA SAYS GOODNIGHT TO THE CHILDREN / MOMMY BABY, DADDY MAYBE / POOR RICHARD / MIX TAPE AFTER AN INJURY - MICHAEL SALCMAN

Napoleon's Penis

If history's written by the victors, as some historians say,
its dislocations are caused by priests and valets,

those inadequate functionaries who attend to the great
while robbing the body or stealing coins from the plate.

Take Bonaparte (himself a practitioner of grand theft)
buried in the Pantheon when not much was left,

his servant Antommarchi stole both stomach and heart
while a priest sawed away at a more intimate part;

Vignali administered the Emperor's last rites
and amputated his penis the very same night.

His member ended in a jar on an urologist's desk
but measured against Rasputin's didn't live up to the test.

And I pray Francis Xavier, a missionary from Spain
had no experience of post-mortem pain

when his arm was deposited in a reliquary in Rome
and the hand divided between two other homes.

Without the Inquisition, Galileo would find it truly bizarre
that the thumb he once held up to measure a star

was detached at his death and a fifth lumbar bone excised—
as if his proof were disproved and his knowledge despised.

And lest we forget, poets are no more immune
not practiced in practicality when not singing a tune,

poor Shelley entrusted his heart to a friend
but no one received it when he failed to mark "send".

Not My Cousin Magda Says Goodnight to the Children

He was the Minister of Fear, she the hopeless seeker
of reincarnation; like my cousin Magda
Mrs. Goebels knew Mengele, loved her children.

They were given Wagnerian names—
Hildegard, Helga, Helmut, Hedwig, Heidrun, Holdine;
they wore nightclothes in their bunks and ribbons in their hair.

Helmut was nine and wore braces:
he may have heard the shot that killed their god,
thought the Red Army cannons meant rain and thunder.

Hilde, Joseph's "little mouse," was only eleven,
Holde was eight, Hedda shy of seven and Heide four.
When they followed their mother upstairs, some were smiling.

In the Red Army photo it's easy to count the bodies
lying outside the Vorbunker—five girls and a boy
their bones clumped and charred at the side of their mother.

Hopped up on speed Joseph first destroyed the dogs,
then injected his kids with morphine and cyanide.
Twelve years old, Helga must have struggled—

the Russians found bruises on her body. Almost done
he shot Magda, his center of calm and saw her frozen smile
one last time fixed on the rubble outside of their window.

Mommy Baby, Daddy Maybe

Like some 19th century phrenologist counting bumps
on a head, you're looking for a clue
as to who might be your daughter's father—
the stern Italian psychiatrist you married
or a one night stand like me.

You suspect art's in the genes
(and a little craziness too)
not to mention her pubic hair,
which you unblushingly describe,
during our last dinner of the 60's,

as ethnically black and curly,
looking for the hidden Jew
like a crypto-Nazi might
toweling off in a gym
checking the love pies of Waspy girls.

It makes me stop my fork in mid-air,
holding the linguini hostage,
to hear you sound like a Camp Kommandant
examining prisoners' dicks.

Back in the day we boned around a lot—
hence the continent of genes,
brown eyes and olive skin
in your own contaminated pool.

We might have been cousins long ago.
Does anyone's line run true?
When the head of your granddaughter crowns next year
and its hair seems more like mine don't call me.

Poor Richard

In a parking lot in Leicester Shakespeare might have said
fortune buckled on his back.
Thus history avenges murderous kings
and the rest: eats away the clay
of battlefield and bedroom, dry heaves
and phlegm our common cement.

Greatly reviled for black rage and a spavined back,
Richard bravely fought hand to hand
at Bosworth until his soul had fled, cleaved by a halberd.
Always unlucky his corpse was taken for safety to an abbey
later burned and sacked. God laughs.
Five centuries pass before a twisted spine and DNA

erupt in a car park. Mocked even at rest
Poor Richard discovers humility, fortune's final jest.

Mix Tape After An Injury

Words go before everything: the low winter sun
coruscates a line of houses and steeples,
factories and boat sheds, writes silvery grays,
re-pointed bricks, green metal siding
crinkled with age, and ice chips cracking in a breeze
rising off the water in a sulcus of my occipital brain.

My left ankle gives way bending beneath a branch
as it did when I was five. Crumpled on uneven ground,
I fold up and gather myself for the long slide
butt first up the stairs
to my cave, a wolf injured by a trap
who blunders into further confinement.

By day I lie in bed unwashed and unshaven,
embalmed by silence, pretzels at hand and a cat
who stays away for hours, put off
no doubt by the fetor of decay
and the sound of politics on the radio.
I don't have the blues, just the blahs.

By night my ancient bladder insists I crutch
bed to toilet and back in the dark,
waking my wife as I pirouette out of control,
decades of age gained in a few hours,
new knowledge of why some prefer death
to helplessness.

Don't think I'm overcome with despair and rage:
there's time enough to read books and be freed
by whimsy. One day I shall rise from my sepulcher
in resurrection—a cartoon of ultimate freedom.
No cartoon my cat eats little bits of steak,
pasta and popcorn. I am entertained.

Daylight leans forward into darkness—
America forecloses on Kodak and Wonder Bread,
on Oldsmobile and Beth Steel.
I get spammed by CME asking if I'm comfortable
with lower extremity dislocations—
only with high ankle sprains I reply.

Time slows lying in bed alone—
in the brain the hours wait the mind out
and shadows fall like premonitions,
chains of circumstance weighing me down:
sixty-five in this awful time, a djinn without a master,
a minim of bright red blood on my knee.

଼ ଼

Michael Salcman *is a former chairman of neurosurgery at the University of Maryland and president of the Contemporary Museum in Baltimore. Poems appear in* Arts & Letters, Hopkins Review, Hudson Review, New Letters *and* Poet Lore. *Books include* The Clock Made of Confetti, *nominated for* The Poets' Prize, The Enemy of Good is Better, Poetry in Medicine, *his popular anthology of classic and contemporary poems on doctors, patients, illness & healing (Persea Books, 2015), and* A Prague Spring, Before & After, *winner of the 2015 Sinclair Poetry Prize from Evening Street Press (2016).*

PLASTIC SURGERY - TAMARA MC

Liposuction:
1. Stomach: lower, upper, waist, mons ... (sp?)
2. Back: flanks
3. Legs: knees (around tops, sides), (calves?), inner thighs, outer thighs, love handles, front things, back thighs
4. Neck: lower, around jawbones

Nose job:
1. Straighten nose: off-center
2. Bump off top
3. Smaller at bridge
4. Smaller bulge
5. Slightly upward
6. Height and width removed

Breasts:
1. Reduction
2. One breast bigger (right): make them the same size
3. Lift (as high as possible). Remove as much skin as possible.
4. Implant (small, I'm thinking 300). I'd prefer them taut and separate.
5. Do we have to go under muscle?
6. Reduce nipple size

Fat Injections:
1. Cheek bones
2. Monkey lines, [Restylane now, still have them]
3. Frown lines on forehead (?), [tell him I have them, just Botox now]
4. Lips (lower and upper) Angelina Jolie (Haha)

Laser:
1. FX on face, chest, and neck?
a. Dark spots?
b. Soft little lines around eyes, when I smile

Questions:
1.) How long healing time?
2.) Before I can go out?
3.) Regime for taking care of myself? Breasts massage? Creams face?

4.) Stockings? How long?
5.) Exercise?
6.) Walk? Weight lift in arms?
7.) What should I tell boys?
8.) How much weight lose?
9.) Follow up surgeries?

ᘓ   ᘔ

Dr. Tamara MC is an Applied Linguist who focuses on issues related to language, culture, and identity in the Middle East and beyond. She has taught ESL/EFL for over twenty years and was a full-time faculty member at the University of Arizona. A published poet, she has studied Poetry and Nonfiction in the MFA program at Columbia University in New York City. She is the recipient of several residencies/workshops including The Iowa Writers' Workshop, Bread Loaf, Ragdale, and Sewanee.

"Well," I whispered to Lou, "he did have a drop-dead drop shot."

"Very funny, Jake," he whispered back.

Lou is Louis M. Gordon, a Detective Sergeant-Supervisor in the New York City Police Department. Thirty years ago, he was a student in my senior English Honors class. "Mr. Jacobs," I was, in those days. My actual name is Jerome (no middle initial) Jacobs, nickname, Jake, not Jerry. Lou and I go way back.

The late James "Jumbo" Thurston had dropped dead of a heart attack while gardening. The Minister had run through his tropes: American dream (immigrant from South Africa), family man (married, one child), work (highly successful), fitness (committed squash player), irony of death (so young), blah blah blah.

Lou claims I taught him both to write and to stop horsing around. He once said that, if not for me, he might have wound up a dead junkie or an insurance salesman. From time to time, he still has me eyeball a few things he has to write, like evidence reports.

Even so, he was doing me a big favor by accompanying me to the funeral. Lou ranks high enough in the NYPD that he must have a perfect grasp of the calculus of the IOU or, as people in public life say, "I *owe* you."

Like most of the other men present, we were wearing dark lightweight suits and "tasteful" ties. We were marooned, for the moment, on a little island in the middle of the lavish country-club reception that followed the cremation. This was all taking place in Great Neck, a posh north-shore suburb just across the New York City line.

Or, as Jumbo would put it, "Location, location. Always go to the T, Jacobs! Prime real estate." And he would suit the action to the word, slamming his hip into me so hard that I would find myself two feet to the right of the T, whereupon he would feather a drop-dead drop shot into the front left corner, which, run as I might, I could not retrieve. Jumbo was, in short, a prick, which was related to my reason for having asked Lou Gordon to accompany me to today's obsequies for the deceased (or, as Mark Twain put it, "orgies for the diseased.")

After introducing ourselves to the Widow Thurston, who looked more worried than sorrowful (was she toting up putative bequests?), Lou and I were back on our island. I was uncomfortably aware that I was making him waste half a day during a week in which he was busy with, among other things, a horrific drive-by shooting in the Bronx, which was attracting all kinds of unwelcome attention, including mayoral.

Consummate gentleman that he is, Lou had already relieved me of this burden. "Not to worry, Jake, I don't mind getting out of the kitchen for a few hours. If God is watching, by the time I get back, my guys may have someone in custody." He had not even asked why I had invited him.

In forty years of teaching, maybe I had discussed too many books with too many students. When you're trying to fill up one of those long classes that can't seem to catch fire, you find yourself falling into what I call "the post-post school of lit crit" –i.e., anything goes. Let's say a student who seldom speaks, pipes up with an idea on the approximate level of fake news: "Wordsworth really loved nature, right, Mr. J.?" If truth were the game, I would have disabused him/her of the notion that fairness requires equal time for all views, a notion dear to many adolescent minds.

Ergo, this habit of multiple truths (let's be polite) may have been an indirect reason for Lou's presence. To get to the point, I could not entirely swallow the accepted truth about Jumbo's death. After reading the notice in the *Times* the other day ("massive cardiac infarction"), one of my first reactions was to suspect foul play. So I decided to seek a second opinion.

Speaking of multiple truths, there may also be a second opinion regarding my morbid hypothesis. Since, over the years in which we had played squash, I had resisted many urges to hurry this man toward his afterlife, could I have been I projecting my own "deep and dark desires" (*Macbeth*)? For example, at the end of an especially contentious game a few months ago, I had stalked off the court muttering imprecations that may have included, "Fuck you! Drop dead, you fucking son-of-a-bitch!"

"Tsk, tsk, temper!" he taunted.

Jumbo's victory in that particular game had had the earmarks of a hostile takeover, which was among his off-court endeavors as an M & A specialist. The game still sticks in my craw. Even now, I can smell the cigarette smoke on the ginger-haired little bastard's breath.

To get back to the facts, as reported by our National Paper of Record, and fleshed out by gossip, on a hot and humid Saturday afternoon in July, after two hours of morning squash, followed by a heavy lunch, this fit man of fifty-six was felled by a massive heart attack. Like Marlon Brando in *The Godfather* (Part One), Jumbo Thurston dropped dead in his own garden.

On the drive back to the city, since Lou still hadn't asked, I decided to take the initiative. Because he was scrupulous about not using NYPD vehicles for personal travel, I was driving. Realizing how silly and trite my suspicions sounded (even to myself), I broached them indirectly, under the guise of revisiting the Minister's remarks. I also assumed the facetious tone left over from my teaching days, which ended in retirement six years ago.

"I wonder if you caught the undertone of the eulogy."

"'Undertone'? What?" Lou had been lost in his own thoughts. "Well, wasn't the 'undertone,' as you call it, what it always is, a bunch of cliché's papering over the dead guy's faults? You already told me you never liked him."

"Not to put too fine a point on it, he was a prick."

As we approached the merger with the Van Wyck, we got stuck in traffic, which always happens on the Long Island "Distressway." One minute you're sailing along, the next, it's stop and go –and stop. When I had asked Lou about this on the way out, he had made one of his dry ripostes.

"Why ask me? I never drew traffic duty."

"If you don't mind, Lou," I said now, "I'll explain why I called him that, by going back to the eulogy."

"Why not? I bet this will be like one of your crazy lit. crit. riffs. I always enjoyed those, Jake."

"Let's take it point by point."

"'Respect the text.'"

"Yup. Here we go." The traffic had eased, but that was not what I meant. "Number One: 'family first.' Yeah, right, husband, father, Indian chief! I don't think so. When we played squash all those times, he would brag about how many hours he also logged at 'the grind,' his job."

'You're talking to a cop, Jake. Do you know what our divorce rates are like? And do you know the principal cause?" Lou said this knowing that I knew he was an exception. Jessica, his first, and only, wife, is a lawyer who works with the homeless, and they have two normal (whatever that means) daughters, both in their teens.

I kept hammering at Point Number One. "Plus, most Saturday mornings, he would take the train in for..."

"Okay, okay, I get the idea. You know, if you had one flaw as a teacher, Jake, it was that, when you were on a roll, you couldn't stop. Actually, I think you once acknowledged as much, when we were reading *Othello*. Remember? In the middle of one of your monologues, the passing bell rang. We had been discussing the drinking scene where Iago causes chaos. A bell rings, and he says something like, 'Time flies when you're having fun.' You ended class by repeating that line."

Instead of providing the exact quotation, I said, "You always had a good memory, Lou. Point Number Two: '... universally respected by colleagues...' Actually, over the years, Jumbo often bragged about that. Early on, he was a financial advisor to 'Preferred Clients,' which meant, as I recall, ten million and up."

Lou interrupted. "Jess and I keep our own fortune, which is closer to ten thou, in an Index fund. That's because we read that, in the long run..."

I finished his sentence. "...financial advisers seldom beat the market. But they always collect 'the vig.' "

"You said, 'Early on,' Jake. After that?" Lou was obviously interested in money. Who isn't?

"I think he became a take-over specialist. But he never went into the details. Since he was normally such a braggart, I always assumed he worked along the border of legality –or south of the border."

Lou nodded. "Jess talks a lot about that sort of thing. One reason she left a lucrative practice of corporate law was the stench of dirty money. But get to the point, Jake. We're close to the tunnel. So far, not many surprises. I'm afraid this may not be one of your better efforts."

"Lou, Lou! My feelings are hurt." He shrugged. Then, we hit another traffic jam, a big one this time. At least, the gods were not tired of listening.

"Point Number Three is where this gets really good. Remember when the Minister waxed elephant about the American dream, about how Jumbo, 'a native of South Africa, arrived on our shores two decades ago'? Well, never mind the inaccuracy of that statement: he was certainly never a 'native,' either before or after the advent of majority rule in 1994, the year before he cleared out. There's something else. Another guy I play with, at a different club, a grad student in Philosophy from Johannesburg... As I'm sure you know, they call the place "Jo'burg."

"Or 'Joeys,' " Lou added. "I was there for a conference in 2012. Good steak."

"Anyway, this guy told me a story that was all over their press in the 90's. Guess what?"

"I remember that ploy, Jake, a hoary, but goodie. In the middle of a lecture, you would direct a question to the student who was paying least attention. Remember the time you did it –I think we were studying *Huck Finn*—to Harvey Grunewald, when he was sleeping? We all howled.

"Did you ever hear what happened to Harvey?" I asked. "I haven't seen him at any of the reunions. Speak, Memory! Didn't he drop out in the middle of senior year?"

"Actually, he was caught shoplifting, for the third time, and it turned out he had a serious drug problem. His parents shipped him off to a private clinic in Texas. The Headmaster called a special meeting with our class, and fed us a bullshit story about how the family had moved."

"Hmm. I wonder why he never told *us* that story." I welcomed this excursus into crimes and misdemeanors.

Lou must have read my mind. "Where is this going, Jake?" By now, we were inching through the tunnel.

"Bear with me a minute more. I promise, you'll know by the time we get to your office." Which was in the complex just north of City Hall, about ten minutes beyond the tunnel.

"Fine. South Africa?"

"In the early nineties, when petty crime in Jo'berg was spinning out of control, three or four young thugs tried to mug an upstanding citizen named J.J. Thurston. He pulled out a handgun and shot two of them. One died, the other was paralyzed from the waist down. The courts ruled 'Self-Defense.' "

At that point, Lou's light bulb flashed. (More literally, we had just emerged on the Manhattan side of the tunnel.) "Oh, no, don't tell me! Not that tired old crap about how 'he didn't die of natural causes.' Ah ha! So that's why you asked *me* to go to the funeral with you. Come on, Jake, why not get a..." And, instead of completing the insult, he blew out a long breath. Why had it taken him so long? Maybe because he had been resisting the idea that his dear old teacher was capable of such inanity.

"Okay, okay," I conceded. "I won't bore you with the rest."

We drove on in silence. When we arrived at Headquarters, I pulled over, turned on the blinkers, thanked him, and started to apologize. He cut me off.

"Never mind, Jake," he said, "what are friends for?" Halfway out the door, he paused, and added, "Besides, as usual with you, the *obiter dicta* of that ridiculous *schtick* were very entertaining. As we all knew back in the day, you might not have always been a reliable narrator, but you told a hell of a story. Just like Huck, as someone –

Samantha Rodriguez, I believe it was—pointed out once, at the senior lunch table."

"Understood," I meekly replied.

Leaning down into the car for a fist bump, which revealed a small brown leather shoulder holster, Lou winked. "Suppose I call you as soon as I get the drive-by case under control. Lunch?"

"You're my hero, Detective." I turned left, headed south, and three minutes later, I was climbing the ramp to the Brooklyn Bridge.

When two months passed without a word, I began to wonder if I had put the kibosh on our friendship. Where, I wondered for the fiftieth time, was this foolishness coming from? Perhaps, like Don Quixote, the source was literary. Over the years, as a sort of brainwash for the heavier stuff I had taught, I had always been a big fan of mystery novels.

In at least a couple, corpses are dug up, and foul play is confirmed. Then, there's one in which the victim is injected with poison by means of an ingenious plastic syringe that leaves an imitation snakebite. In another, an old guy who has apparently been asleep behind a newspaper at his club turns out to be dead. (I think the solution depended on the time of death, but I can't remember what he died from.) And, in still another one, set either in a mansion or on an island, a hated figure is murdered, and the murderer turns out to be everybody. Murder by Committee.

Meanwhile, hours and even whole days passed, during which I pushed my suspicions to the back of my mind. No one can teach English for forty years without understanding how poisonous obsessions can be. So, possibly with more energy than usual, I kept up my routine as a retiree: I read, listened to records and CD's, watched nature programs on Public TV, and went, alone or with friends, to concerts, museums, art shows, and movies.

One of these friends was a retired colleague named Mary Robison who, like me, had been a teacher for several decades. ("Not 'Robinson,'" she would inform students at the beginning of the term, writing the correct spelling on the board.) A trim sixty-something (would that be a "sexagenarian"?), M.R.'s field was Biology. She is currently the driving force behind a consortium of Lower Manhattan community gardens.

Although Mary is a bit obsessive, for my taste, during the last couple of years, I have been, as they say, "seeing" her. (I realize the irony of calling someone else 'obsessive.') Ours is a relationship that chugs along at a low level. As far as I know, she has never been married. We both get what we need from the relationship, and I think she may be as glad as I am not to be asked for more.

I'll mention, in passing, that I don't believe in casual romances, especially for old widowers like me. According to one of my less prudent friends, most of the women you're likely to meet, at places like the Y, coffee shops, or even concerts, seem to be gold diggers, mentally ill, or both.

No more theatergoing for me, either. The few "classics" I attended before stopping, turned out to be anything but. Every single one was a mistake, transpositions of the originals that were designed to create "relevance," and that totally ignored the romantic side of the old plays in favor of the violent, cynical and disgusting. Why pay forty or fifty bucks to see the first half of another stinker?

And, of course, in the interests of fitness, sanity and fun, among my other activities, I kept on playing, yes, squash, two or three times a week. Here, of course, my "foul play" obsession leaked through my attempts to enjoy the game. For how could my partners have failed to mention the newly dead bully and cheat, James Jumbo Thurston?

"Anyone remember the match Jumbo and Jake played a couple of years ago?" The recollect-or was a motor-mouthed braggart and small-time movie producer named Marvin Bird, who must have bad-mouthed Jumbo to me behind his back twenty times when he was still among the living. No one bit, presumably because no one wanted to hear that story again. But Marvin is irrepressible.

"Jumbo was up, two games to nil, way ahead in the third. Then, suddenly, Jake was in the zone. Shot after shot, tremendous! Feathery drop shots, smashing rails, cross-courts, lobs that died in the back corner –plus, he was running the diagonal like a gazelle. Before you could blink, he had pulled even. And, once he won that game, in the next two, he blew Jumbo away. I think the final scores were 9-7, 9-1, 9-nil. Correct me if I'm wrong, but I think Jumbo smashed his racquet against the wall, and stalked off the court without saying a word. Remember that one, Jake?"

"I do, I do." And leaving it at that, we resumed play.

Several weeks after the funeral, I read in the paper that two teenaged suspects had been arraigned in the Bronx drive-by shootings. There was a photo of police spokesman, Detective Sergeant-Supervisor Louis M. Gordon, smiling grimly into the camera.

Three months after the funeral, and about a week after I had given up, Lou finally called. After the usual prelims, he suggested lunch the next day, at a glorified coffee shop near Headquarters: big menus, big portions, big prices, and a rogue's gallery of former Miss Subway's. As usual, I was free.

"I would have called sooner, Jake," he explained, "but I've been checking out a few things for you. I assume you're still wondering who killed Roger Rabbit?"

"It's been on the back burner," I admitted.

"I dug up some stuff that might be of interest," he said. "I'll tell you over lunch." Oh, boy!

After we had ordered, and our beverages of choice had arrived, Lou jiggled the ice in his iced coffee, and, without preamble, began to talk. Every so often, he referred to what I assumed were notes, on his smartphone. When his club sandwich came, he pushed it aside, so I also waited before cracking open my chicken potpie, which usually burns my mouth, anyway. To cool my heated imagination, I clutched my diet ginger ale. This is the gist of what he said:

"Motive, opportunity, means. You've read the books and seen the TV shows and movies, right, Jake? Let's take them in reverse order." He ticked off the points on his fingers. "Means: no way to autopsy a cremated body, and, when the local police went in, at my request, they found no material evidence: no suspicious fingerprints on a coffee cup, no footprints in the garden. Of course, they weren't looking too hard, since the death cert already indicated a 'fatal cardiac infarction.'

"Opportunity? Lots of that! Jumbo was alone in the house. His wife was playing soccer mom to their son, an only child. Which brings us to the important element: motive. *Everyone* had a motive to kill this guy, Jake. Not to put too fine a point on it, but, as you indicated, he was an outstanding piece of shit.

"Luckily, you're not my only connection at the sports club. A couple of my colleagues play racquetball on a court adjoining the squash courts. These guys are loud –I mean, really loud. But they had all heard Jumbo repeatedly go off on people. Apparently, 'sportsmanship' was not in his vocabulary. I'm sure you had first-hand experience." I nodded.

"As for the domestic angle, Jumbo's narcissism –shall we call it that, instead of tiptoeing around it?– probably did not include infidelity. In fact, he was loudly monogamous. If I may venture a comparison, he was something like all those swindlers who pride themselves on church or synagogue attendance.

"Let's follow the money. Naomi, his wife, nee' Entitlebaum (just kidding), is a greedy woman given to large expenditures on bling, and such, and, yes, Jumbo carried a hefty life insurance policy.

But she had no lovers, either (at least, none that I could find), and she already had a fat bank account of her own. Even so, when it comes to greed..." Lou shrugged, and consulted his phone.

"Work. As we've already said, Jumbo was a piece of shit: super-competitive, always looking for an edge, party to numerous dubious transactions. 'But,' you might object, 'isn't that the name of the game?' Still, we can't rule out an irate client who lost his shirt on one of Jumbo's bum stock tips, or an executive who worked all his life building up a business, only to be thrown out on his ass after a Jumbo takeover." Afraid to break the spell, I did not even sip my ginger ale. The potpie was no longer steaming.

"Okay. With all those possibilities, I could spend a year's budget, and tie up my whole staff, tracking them down. Could I justify that, Jake? Ha!" Lou finally came up for air, and took a few quick bites from his sandwich, before resuming the monologue. I doubt he had talked this much during the whole year he was my student.

"I've saved the most interesting part for last: the South African connection. Those three 'muggers' he shot? I exchanged a few e-mails with a 'tec' I met at the 2012 conference I mentioned after the funeral. Listen to this, Jake: Jumbo was working under cover for the South African Police, or SAP (unfortunate acronym). And the 'muggers' were actually militants who had sneaked back into the country from Zimbabwe.

"As you can imagine, the case was murky. The official line was 'shot while eluding detention for membership in the African National Congress,' which, at the time, was an outlawed, super-violent anti-apartheid group. Jumbo might have been stalking the three cadres, and they turned on him. Of course, none of that came out at the trial. Anyway..." Another deep breath, and a gulp of iced coffee.

"After the advent of majority rule, in 1994, when the ANC took power, he didn't stick around long enough to participate in what they called the 'Truth and Reconciliation' process, whereby many people buried the figurative hatchet, for acts they may have committed with real ones. The shooting gives us a bunch of new suspects to add to our already long list: fringe haters from the ANC, members of the victims' families. (As you may know, Jake, revenge is sanctioned in some of South Africa's indigenous cultures.)"

With that, Lou drew another breath, and turned his full attention to his sandwich. My chicken potpie was still untouched, and it crossed my mind to wonder whether the crust had kept it warm during the long monologue. Fork poised to find out, I could not resist one final question.

"So?"

"'So'?" Holding up his traffic-cop hand, Lou swallowed, gulped some more coffee, and wiped his mouth with the big pink linen napkin. " 'So,' you ask, 'what does it all add up to?' I was just getting to that." He looked me in the eye.

"Although the number of suspects is legion, the fact is, Jake, I think *you* killed Jumbo Thurston." Was he joking? "You killed him right in here." Ignoring my look of astonishment, Lou leaned across the table, tapped my forehead twice with his index finger, and returned to his sandwich.

CR   SO

Stories by **Ron Singer** *have appeared in many publications., He is also the author of ten books, including* Uhuru Revisited: Interviews with African Pro-Democracy Leaders *(2015),which is available in about 100 libraries across the U.S., and beyond. For details, please visit www.ronsinger.net.*

A CLOSET FULL - SAMANTHA MEEHAN

The skeletons in my closet keep trying to get out
They're scratching at the door
And sticking their bony fingers
Out through the slats
It isn't the ones that have
Been living here a while
As much as those newly acquired
Each one trying to slip out
And reveal me
The older skeletons yawn
And roll their eyes
"They'll learn"

 CR   ƧO

Samantha Meehan is a floral designer and a life-long Bostonian. She is passionate about creating things that make people feel- through flowers, poems, food and art. She hopes to finally clean out her closet and release her secret stockpile of poetry into the world.

MY BOYFRIEND'S BROTHER'S WEDDING
- M.D.G. HUGHES

Riley had a sinking suspicion that she was out two thousand dollars, plus a few irreplaceable items.

At least she was spending some quality time with Tom, as quality as time could be in a ditch waving away mosquitoes whilst searching for her lost lingerie and cocktail gown.

The taxi driver sat on the hood of his car in the breakdown lane. Chain smoking Marlboros and thinking about his meter clicking over dollars and cents of the easiest fare of his life.

Tom had agreed to undertake what he saw as a pointless task only after he had watched Riley tearfully scream at their coach driver for fifteen minutes when they had arrived in Portland.

Riley had gotten particularly irate when the driver had looked at his watch in the midst of her tirade, "Oh, I'm sorry am I keeping you?" Riley had asked, seething with rage. A rage that had only been vulcanized by the driver's response, "Yeah actually. I gotta go up to Seattle and back again before I quit tonight, so if you don't mind."

Riley had been left gasping in front of the station manager as the driver had walked away, lighting a cigarette before immediately stamping it out and getting back on the bus.

In a Hail Mary attempt to calm Riley before she popped a blood vessel Tom had offered to lend her his spare jeans and hoodie for the weekend, at least until they could get to the mall and replenish her lost items. At this Riley had turned her apoplectic fury in his direction.

"You know when you're traveling you have all your favorite jewelry, all your favorite clothes, all the things you want to wear all the time?" Riley had seethed to Tom when he'd implied he didn't see the big deal.

"Well that's the situation here, plus some very sentimental stuff that I had brought with me especially for your brother's wedding."

Riley's tone had conveyed to Tom that the loss of her things would be laid at his feet if he did not accompany her to recover them without another word.

* * *

Now they were both sweating and dirty hunting the stretch of highway where Riley was sure her suitcase had flown out of the greyhound's locker after a particularly violent lurch earlier in the day.

When they had arrived into Portland, Riley had stood patiently while all the other passengers, including Tom, received their bags from the driver. She thought it was odd that she had had to wait until the very end. That morning Riley had run to catch the bus before it pulled out of its bay in Seattle. Tom had been stood at the bottom of the steps asking the driver to just wait a few more minutes. The driver had begrudgingly agreed, taking the opportunity to sneak in one more cigarette before embarking on the four hour drive.

When Riley finally arrived the driver took her bag without a word and threw it into the baggage locker, slamming the door in frustration. Riley looked at Tom, abashed. Tom merely raised his eyebrows and tapped his watch.

* * *

Looking at his watch now in the light of the setting sun Tom studied Riley's behind as she picked her way through the undergrowth. He was impressed by her tenacity, but really hoped she was going to give in soon. Tom had to be at the wedding venue by nine the next morning, and hoped that the two of them could still have a fun night out on the town before hooking up in their hotel room.

As Tom stood by the highway letting his imagination steal his attention he snapped back to the task at hand when Riley swung around with a victorious cry.

Holding a small black leather case above her head Riley waved to Tom beckoning him closer.

"Babe! This is my toiletries bag, we're in the right place."

Tom was impressed. It had taken Riley a solid fifteen minutes to get the driver to admit that he had seen the locker fly open on this stretch of highway. A further five minutes for a manager to offer to compensate her two hundred and fifty dollars. At this paltry sum Riley had scoffed and pulled out her phone to call the cab that was now waiting for them a few yards back.

Riley took Tom's hand and pointed to the fence at the top of the steep highway embankment where her suitcase lent drunkenly, with its contents scattered around it.

Before Tom had time to react Riley was dragging him up the hill and handed him her case.

"Here, hold this, I'll grab all my stuff and we can get out of here."

Tom leant against the fence, watching the cars fly by on the highway below them, a steady stream of taillights in the dusk.

As Riley gathered up the last of her clothes and shoes and shoved them in the case she turned and looked through the fence into the woods beyond.

"Dammit, look babe, somehow a ton of my stuff went over the fence, will you climb over and get it for me?"

Tom looked at the high chain link fence. Checking his watch again he considered the possibility of grabbing a few more of Riley's things and still having time to make the rehearsal dinner and then a screw back at the hotel, verses the inevitable argument that would ensue if he refused to go over the fence.

"Sure thing hun," said Tom meekly, placing the suitcase down and grabbing the chain link.

With flecks of rust digging into his fingers Tom swung a leg over and paused at the top of the fence, looking down at Riley, who was smiling up at him. Tom checked the ground beneath him and jumped down, he let out a yelp of pain as his foot twisted on a root that had been covered by leaves and highway litter.

Grasping the fence Tom winced as he tried to put weight on his ankle. Turning to look at Riley Tom hoped for a glimmer of sympathy from his girlfriend. Instead, as soon as their eyes met she pointed to a shoe at the tree line.

"There's the other one of my heels babe, can you grab it?"

Shrugging, Tom stepped gingerly forward, testing his ankle before putting all his weight on it. As he limped under the overhanging trees he saw the suggestion of a trail in the undergrowth. Scattered along it was some of Riley's detritus. A hairdryer hung by its cord from a branch and the low sun reflected off the mirror of a powder case that had been propped up on a stump.

"Um, Riley?"

"Yeah?"

"There's a lot of your stuff in here, you think maybe you could come over so I don't miss anything?"

"You can't manage it?"

I probably could if you hadn't packed so much stuff, Tom thought to himself. To Riley he said, "I mean maybe, I just would hate to miss any of your things in the dark."

"Ok, let me run down and tell the cab driver what we're doing, I don't want to get stuck out here."

While Tom waited for Riley to get back he picked up the compact and put it in his pocket. Sitting on the stump he lifted his pant leg to have a look at his ankle. In the dim light under the trees he wasn't sure if the dappled color was bruising or just the shadows pressing in on him. Lifting his head to look for any more of Riley's things Tom looked deep into the woods. Spying at least four more things that could only be Riley's Tom turned back to the fence to see what was taking her so long.

Riley had to empty her wallet to persuade the cab driver to stay. He'd tried to weasel out of waiting for them with some story about how it was the end of his shift and he needed to get home to his wife and kids.

Riley had told him to stop complaining and stay there, turning her back on him and not seeing the middle finger he extended in her direction. Riley climbed the embankment and up over the fence, being careful to not jump on the root that had caught Tom out earlier.

Stepping up to her boyfriend Riley gave Tom a playful smack on the shoulder.

"Come on then, handsome, we better get a move on if we're still going to screw in the hotel room later."

Tom started, overjoyed that he and Riley were working towards the same goal. Standing to his feet he winced at the pain in his ankle. Even though he hadn't been able to see any bruising Tom knew that his ankle looked bigger than it should. Placing one hand on Riley's shoulder for support he pointed down the faint trail at the items he'd already seen. Both of them looked up at the orange sky, knowing they were short on time to find everything.

As they scooped up two blouses, some leggings, and a particularly lacy pair of panties they noticed more things further into the woods.

Tom was sweating now, the effort of limping along taking its toll.

"Please babe, haven't we got enough? Can't we come back tomorrow?"

"When Tom? When are we going to have the chance between setting up the venue, the ceremony, the dancing? We won't be done until after dark and then our tickets home are for first thing in the morning Sunday. So when?"

"Shh, what was that?" said Tom, staring between the mossy trunks.

"Nothing, probably a rabbit or a fox." said Riley. "Dusk is when all those animals are up and doing stuff."

"I don't know, it seemed pretty big."

"There's nothing big here babe, this is a forest inside a city, there is nothing to freak out about."

"Ok, fine, nothing bigger than a fox. But a rabid fox? That would. Mess. You. Up." said Tom wide eyed at the thought of a small woodland creature leaping out of the undergrowth snapping its foamy jaws at his neck.

"Come on, just a little longer, please babe, I haven't found any of my jewelry yet, and I had my mom's locket in my bag."

Tom hesitated, suddenly understanding Riley's behavior that had seemed so odd compared to her easygoing nature.

* * *

When Riley was five her dad had taken her out of town on a daddy-daughter camping trip. It had been the best weekend of Riley's young life. Cooking s'mores, catching fish, even shooting a rifle at empty bean cans.

When Riley and her dad had turned the corner into their neighborhood a low cloud of smoke and red glow had filled the windshield. By the time Riley and her dad turned onto their street Riley's dad had been praying the prayer of the desperate.

"Oh God, please God, no God, don't let it be God."

The fire chief's report had said that Riley's mom had fallen asleep on the couch and left an unlit burner on the gas stove running. The chief wrote that Mrs. Porter must have turned on a lamp and the small spark ignited the gas filled home. She died instantly.

Riley had almost nothing of her mother's. Everything that her mother had been and had was in that house. Except for the locket. For reasons unknown to Riley Riley's mom had stored a letter and a locket in a safety deposit box at the bank. When her mother's will was read both items were bequeathed to Riley and became her most treasured possessions.

* * *

Tom took a deep breath and pushed himself away from the tree he had leant against and took Riley by the hand.

"Ok, like thirty more minutes, and then it will be way too dark to even see where we're going, let alone find a necklace in the woods."

"Ok," Riley nodded, "thirty minutes. Although, the dark isn't really an issue is it?" Pulling her phone out of her pocket Riley swiped her thumb up to turn on the flash. Shining it in front of them she headed into the forest.

Tom grabbed a long stick that had fallen from one of the surrounding trees. Using it as a makeshift crutch he hobbled after Riley's bobbing light.

As dusk turned to full night the two of them were able to locate more and more of Riley's lost luggage. Tom wondered how it had gotten so far back between the trees along the trail. He shrugged and figured stuff could get thrown pretty far out of a bus doing eighty on a windy day.

After fifteen of their self-imposed thirty minute time limit Riley gave a cry of triumph as she spotted something glinting in a tree branch just out of reach.

"Babe, look, can you reach that?"

Tom stretched up and hooked a finger through a delicate gold chain. Gently tugging for fear of snapping the links and losing the pendant in the dark Tom felt the chain shift, but it wouldn't come free.

"It's hooked on something babe."

"Well, what if I sit on your shoulders and then I'd be tall enough to untangle it?"

Tom knelt, hoping that this was the locket so they could get back to the hotel. Any thought of getting laid was far from his mind now. Tom just wanted a shower, a sandwich, and a fistful of painkillers for his ankle.

Standing on his good leg and then gingerly putting weight on his injured ankle Tom raised Riley up until she was level with the mass of leaves in which the chain was entwined. He nearly fell as she recoiled violently and threw her weight backwards.

"What the hell Riley?"

"Get me down, get me down, get me down."

Sliding Riley off his back Tom put his hands on her shoulders to hold her steady.

"What's going on?"

"Well, it was definitely one of my necklaces."

"So why didn't you grab it? Too tangled?"

"Well, yes and no. It is tangled, but not accidentally. It's been put there on purpose."

"What? How do you know that?"

"Because it has been threaded through the eye sockets of a skull and that can't happen by accident."

"A human skull?" Tom was staring up at the hanging chain above him both intrigued and apprehensive.

"No, a bird skull."

"Oh, well, then get back on and you can grab it down."

"No!"

In the white light of her phone's flash Riley's eyes widened in horror at Tom's suggestion that she grab a dead bird's skull.

"Ok, Ok, I'll get it."

Reaching up with his makeshift walking stick Tom pushed through the leaves until he heard the click of wood on bone. Jerking the stick up into the tree and releasing it so his hands were free he caught the skull before it could hit the ground.

Tom undid the necklace from its grisly jewelry box. Dropping the chain into Riley's hand Tom held the skull up to get a closer look.

"I think it's an eagle skull," said Tom, "definitely a bird of prey," he continued, pressing the pad of his finger against the sharp hook of the beak. Carefully placing the skull at the base of the tree Tom decided he would pick it up on their way back, thinking it would make a good story later. Checking his watch as he stood Tom realized that their self-imposed limit was up.

"Ok babe, that's all she wrote. Let's go."

"Really?" said Riley, sticking out her bottom lip. "One, we haven't found my mom's locket. Two, you're not in any way interested in finding out who put my necklace through a bird skull?"

"One," said Tom, also counting on his fingers, "we are not going to find your mom's locket in the dark forest at night.

"And two. No. No I am not. Because there is zero chance that some kind of gentle forest dweller did it to help out. It was for sure done to freak us out, so let's freaking go."

Picking up his stick Tom turned to beat a limping retreat back to the fence and the highway. Tom pulled his own phone from his pocket to illuminate his way, Riley was still aiming her light deeper into the woods.

"Um, Riles, which way is it?" asked Tom, sweeping his light across the waist high undergrowth.

Riley spun around, looking for the trail they had followed into the woods. Before Riley could point it out to Tom her light shone off something to their left.

"Babe look, over there." Riley strode off deeper into the woods to investigate the reflection.

Tom hobbled after Riley, glancing to try and find any trace of the trail they had been on moments before.

Riley grasped her mother's locket in her hand as it swung in the cool night breeze. Tom came to a stop behind her and followed the chain up to where it disappeared among the pine needles.

"Is it in another skull?" asked Riley, unable to see above the branch the necklace was hung from.

"It's in something." said Tom, "it looks like metal though, it's shiny."

Tom reached out his hand, balancing on the toes of his good foot he could just brush his fingertips against the smooth surface of whatever was encasing the necklace. Pulling his fingers back quickly and stuffing them in his mouth Tom sucked in his breath sharply.

"Shit that's freezing."

Looking closely Tom saw that in the chill night air the metal sphere was starting to drip with a frosty condensation and that the pine needles around it looked like a Christmas card. Before he could lift his stick to knock the sphere and necklace out of the tree Riley pulled her hand back and shook it in startled pain.

"What the hell?"

Looking down she saw that the intense cold had burnt the filigree of her mother's locket onto her palm. Holding her hand out to Tom she illuminated it with her flashlight.

"Ok, so now we can leave?" said Tom.

"After we get my locket back, sure."

Before Tom had time to argue Riley grabbed the stick from him and swung it at the tree branch.

Riley's blow shattered the branch into frozen splinters that rained down on the two of them. Brushing at the frozen shards as they burnt through their clothes Tom and Riley moved backwards as the ground beneath them was coated in a thin layer of frost.

Tom and Riley looked desperately for the trail that would take them out of the forest and into the lights and warmth of the city.

"Where's the trail Tom?" Riley demanded.

"What do you mean 'where's the trail'? I told you a minute ago I didn't know the way, and then you just ran off over here," snapped Tom.

A loud groan silenced Riley before she could reply. Looking around them they both saw tree trunks being enveloped in ice and frost.

"I think, that maybe, we should just go." said Tom, lurching forward in the direction of the tree where they had found the eagle skull.

As he scooped to pick up the skull a tree behind them exploded knocking Tom and Riley into the carpet of pine needles. Scrabbling through the dirt and leaves to the other side of the wide tree trunk they sat panting as shards of frozen wood flew around them. Tom and Riley held each other as the tree they cowered behind shook with the force of multiple impacts.

Now the forest was full of the sound of cracking as more and more trees froze.

"We need to go. Now." said Tom, listening for the distant sounds of the highway.

"This way."

Riley accepted Tom's hand and stood, she looped his arm over her shoulders so that she could support Tom's weight as they hurried in what they hoped was the right direction.

Shivering and slipping on the frosty ground as the cold overtook them Tom and Riley saw headlights rushing past through the dark trees. Encouraged by the sight of civilization they picked up their pace. Tom slammed the end of his stick into the ground as hard as he could with each step, desperate to keep from falling on the increasingly treacherous terrain. When only a few feet separated them from the fence Tom and Riley began yelling down to get the attention of the cab driver.

"Start the car!"

"We need to go! Now!"

Riley leapt at the fence and screamed in anguish as the brittle metal shattered in her hands, she collapsed as shards of wire pierced her hands.

Tom took his stick and swung at the fence. Breaking a hole big enough for the two of them to walk through.

"Up you come babe," said Tom. He helped Riley stand by grasping her elbow. Both of them could see their breath now as the temperature continued to plummet.

"Tom, I'm really scared, what's happening?"

"I don't know sweetheart, but we're going now. It's going to be ok."

Sitting the two of them scooted down the slick embankment to where the cab had been.

"That bastard." said Tom. "He's left us out here. Oh babe, don't cry. We can walk, maybe even hitch a lift." Tom paused, taking in Riley's bleeding hands and the leaf mulch that covered the two of them. "Well, maybe not hitch, but we can get to town."

"Tom, what are you talking about? Just call someone, call your brother."

Tom smacked his hand to his forehead, reaching into his pocket he pulled out his phone.

The warm air from his pocket instantly condensed on the screen. As Tom taped the home button the suddenly brittle glass shattered under the pressure and the phone went dark.

Behind them an explosion of white light filled the woods. Cars driving by spun out as the ice covered the highway and drivers were blinded by the glow from the forest.

Tom and Riley began to run, Tom grunted when his injured foot hit the blacktop. Riley started sobbing at the growing pain in her hands.

As car upon car rammed into one another behind them the highway was illuminated by a fireball of exploding gas tanks.

Tom fell first, his ankle giving out and pitching him onto his outstretched hands. As he lay with his forehead on the cold road he urged Riley onwards, desperate for her to escape whatever was coming.

Riley turned, slipping and landing on her shredded hands she cried out, falling silent as her head cracked against the breakdown lane.

Tom crawled towards Riley's prone body. Wrapping himself around her to shield her from the cold his teeth chattered and his tears froze to his cheeks. In the light from the forest and the glow of the car fire Tom saw a small creature come walking down the embankment. Naked and not bothered by the cold, not even having to tread carefully on the slick slope, the creature came boldly towards them. The things feet were wide and two toed, with a claw on the back of its ankle that dug into the thickening ice.

A low buzz emanated from the things chest and with a twitch of a tentacle it beckoned to something out of sight.

Soon the side of the highway was inundated with a swarm of the creature. Each of them shied away from the heat of the fire, staying close to the ice encased fence until they could make their way down the slope to Tom and Riley.

Tom swept his hand around hoping to grab a stick, a rock, anything to ward off whatever the things were that shuffled his way. His walking stick was just out of reach and soon hidden by the legs of the creatures. Tom grabbed Riley's shoulder and pulled her along, pushing with his good leg.

Tom felt something under his hand. Wrapping his numb fingers around it he lifted it up to his face. A book of matches, nearly empty. The cab driver must have dropped it. Tom noted how the creatures had avoided the fire and wondered.

Shivering Tom managed to grip the match between his fingers and rip it from the book.

"Tom? Tom? What's going on?" Riley's eyelids fluttered as she floated up to consciousness. "Why is it so cold?"

Riley gave a small scream as hundreds of stalked eyes turn towards her voice. She gripped Tom and screamed again at the flash of agony from her hands.

"Tom, what–"

"Shh, here hold this." Tom tried to pass Riley the match book before realizing that her ruined hands would be no better at holding it than his shaking ones.

"Here, between your teeth."

Riley bit down on the edge of the book, Tom raised the paper match and drew it across the strike paper.

The light of the match barely showed in the incandescence from the forest, but the creatures saw it, and the creatures feared it.

As one the mass of claws and tentacles lurched backwards. The buzzing increased in volume and pitch becoming a high whine like a mass of huge mosquitoes.

Tom held out the match towards them, reveling as they slunk back from it, but very aware that he had maybe twenty seconds before the match burnt down to his fingers and the creatures renewed their chilling advance.

Taking the empty book of matches out of Riley's mouth Tom lit the corner furthest from where spit had dampened the cardboard. Remembering the compact in his pocket Tom flipped it open and pulled out the powder puff.

Having no idea if this would work he held the flame at arms length and blew the loose powder over the top of it. To Tom's elation the powder transformed into motes of fire and covered the nearest creatures. Everywhere a speck of burning powder touched their silvery flesh a fiery spider web spread.

Tom and Riley had to cover their ears as the creatures' mosquito whine ramped up to a deafening scream.

The two of them sat on the frozen ground and watched with horrified delight as the initial advance of tentacled beasts pushed back from the small cloud of fire. Every time one of the burning creatures brushed against another the fiery trail leapt from skin to skin. Soon the entire multitude was screaming and flailing their tentacled arms into the air. The things turned and retreated back up the embankment, crumbling to dust.

Standing carefully on the slick surface Tom helped Riley to her feet. Cradling her injured hands Riley looked over her shoulder at the dust blowing in the frigid breeze.

"Tom, what happened?"

"Babe, I do not know, can you walk?"

"I think so, what about you? Your ankle?"

"I'll make do –"

A scream of metal silenced Tom.

Pushing through the burning cars was a bus. It pulled to a stop beside them and the door slid open. A wave of climate controlled air swept over Tom and Riley as lurched towards the steps.

"Jes-us," said the bus driver, taking in Tom's skewed stance and Riley's ragged hands "uh, any luck finding your bag?"

"Very fucking funny," said Riley through gritted teeth.

"You two want a ride?" said the bus driver as the two of them hobbled up the steps. As Riley reached the top she heard Tom gasp behind her. Looking back Riley was just in time to see Tom's head wrapped in tentacles and his face blistering with cold.

Riley lunged for Tom to pull him into the sanctuary of the bus, her ruined hands failed to get any purchase and Tom slipped away into the darkness. Riley turned to the driver to beg him for help.

The driver held Riley's mother's locket up and used his free hand to pull the door closed.

"Was it worth it?" laughed the driver grimly.

Riley was encased in the metal confines of the bus. Over the hiss of the engine Riley heard a buzzing hum, and from behind each chair frost coated tentacles slithered into view.

☙ ❧

Matt D.C. Hughes hails from Fair Oak, England. He currently lives and writes in Portland Oregon. He is married with three children. This story was written because a co-worker lost her bag on a greyhound bus. Twitter: @mdchughes

DEAF FROG - J. DAVID LISS

I

"Tomorrow she'll release the video on You Tube. Have the Commissioner call the Mayor to ask them not to run it."

We were all shaken. We were all queasy. Getting that reaction from the Homicide Division took a special kind of crazy.

"How do you know she's going to send it to You Tube and not just to us? Can they stop it from running?"

"I don't know if they can stop it. Matty will know that. Tell Matty to write out in four simple sentences exactly what the Mayor will have to ask for. Never mind. I'll ask him."

"How do you know she'll send it to You Tube?"

"This kind of crazy likes to show off. If folks like us are ready to puke, think about how the civilians will react." I picked up my desk phone and called Mickey Moran, Deputy Commissioner for Public Affairs.

"It's Frank. Come downstairs. There's something you need to know about, maybe see, if you haven't had breakfast yet." Moran hung up. He didn't give me any shit, didn't call me Sherlock, didn't tell me to fuck myself, didn't give me his apocryphal warning not to speak with the media. He wasn't use to me calling him.

I called Matty. "The Mayor is going to have to call You Tube. It would be embarrassing for all of us if he did, and didn't know what he was talking about. Come to my office. Moran is coming too. We need to figure something out." There was no backtalk from Matty either. No, *Once again your job is down the toilet, Detective Scott, and only technology can save you.* I'd never asked Matty to come to my office before. He stinks, and after he leaves I was going to have to clean his chair and anything he touched with alcohol wipes. But what he and Moran needed to see had to be shown behind closed doors.

Finally, I called Dr. Goldberg, the forensic psychiatrist we worked with most closely. "Michael, please come to my office as soon as you can. Moran and Matty are on their way."

"You invited Matty to your office?"

"Yeah."

"I'll be right there."

Goldberg was smart. He picked up on clues, like a detective. I never call him by his first name. We Irish guys love to call Jews by their last names and they love doing the same to us. Just by calling him *Michael*, I knew I would get his attention.

Within 10 minutes everyone was in my office. Matty did stink. He does not wash frequently. In fact, his given name is Martin, not Mathew. We called him Matty because his hair was usually matted down with grease. If he wasn't a computer genius with a fan boy's love of detective work, we would never have let him into 1 Police Plaza. But the Department was able to hire one of the best technological minds in the City for the cost of a cop and a lot of kowtowing. So we dealt with the smell.

"I'm going to tell you all what I need you to do now, before showing you the video. I think that once you see it, it will be a while before you can focus, and we're not going to have time to spare. Take notes.

Matty, two things from you. I'll need you to write a very simple script for when the Mayor calls You Tube to tell them to stop this from being shown. I'm speculating that this woman will post it tomorrow and we need to stop it from being seen. Then, you need to figure out whatever you can about the woman who made it. We're going to need to find her. Maybe there's some way for you to trace it."

"Detective Scott, lucky for you I speak stupid detective, because what you just said does not translate into language. You can't stop something from being shown on You Tube preemptively. It has to be taken down after it's posted. And then it's too late. Too many people know how to download and repost video. Also, the Mayor would have to call Google, which is Alphabet, which owns You Tube. And I will not get involved with that pea-brain calling really smart people. My fingerprints will not be anywhere near the colossal embarrassment of that conversation, Francis."

"Shut up. Write down what I just told you to do." I'm usually very diplomatic with Matty. He was taken aback.

"Mickey, you're going to need to have two things going on. You're going to figure out how to spin this for the general public, but you're also going to need to prepare the rank and file in the precincts if it goes viral."

"Are you saying that I'm going to have to prepare an internal communications plan? What the hell is this?"

"Yes. Write that down — an internal communications plan. You're not going to want to think about this for a while, but you're going to have to move fast. You'll need to get something out there tonight. Tomorrow is too late. You won't have time for lunch or dinner, but you won't want it."

Moran scraped away in his notebook.

"Michael, you've got to help me figure this out."

All three stared at me. In my nine years on the Force, no one had ever heard me ask for help. For all the shit I took from the Commissioner, who hated my father the ex-governor; for all the praise I get from the Mayor and the papers for being New York's own version of Sherlock Holmes, the detective who figures out impossible cases; for all the politics that mixes with police work and makes the job ten times harder, I had worked with half the department and got along fine with everyone. But no one had ever heard me ask for help.

I clicked the play arrow on the big screen of my computer. The first thing you noticed about the woman who called herself Anna Prophet was the incongruity of her size and her scale. What I mean by that is if you saw her without the context of any other object, say photographed against a gray background, she would look beautiful and petite. Her red hair fell below her shoulder and had a Veronica Lake dip over one eye. But when you saw her next to other people, or common items like chairs and tables, you saw that she was a giant. She was at least 6'4"—and well muscled. You could see as she stood up from her chair how strong she was, because she moved as if gravity were for lesser beings and the only reason her feet stayed on the ground was because she willed them to.

The chair was a mid-century modern work of bent teakwood and black leather. She walked to the camera and I flinched because it felt like she was walking over to my face to punch it in – she was that threatening, even on video. She took up the whole field of view. She started to speak. Her rich, tenor voice sounded like a cello playing a dirge. Her articulation was a pleasure to hear if you loved the English language: British, elite – a slavering lioness reciting Shakespeare as her fangs ripped your jugular.

When she spoke, the depth of her silky voice was intensified by the precision of her language. "My name is Anna Prophet and don't be fooled by this accent, I'm a true New Yorker and I LOVE New York, as the commercials used to say. Of course, Anna Prophet is a made-up name. Anna was a New Testament prophet. I'm a new media prophet." She waved an extra-large hand at the camera. "Come along. There's something I want to show you."

She stepped back from the camera, which panned the entire room. It was a large space. At one end was a raised platform. On the platform was an operating table with an unconscious man strapped to it. Next to him was a man dressed as a doctor, surgical mask on. Also on the platform was a blonde woman strapped to a chair and gagged. On the other end of the room, there were about a dozen seats, all filled. I knew every one of the men in those seats and Mickey recognized most of them and guessed at the others — they were the crime bosses of New York and New Jersey.

She started speaking again, but now her British accent was gone. She spoke in unaccented American. "Enough with the accent.

"These gentlemen run the **Mafia**," Anna Prophet emphasized the word *Mafia* and made a bit of a face as she said it, then she chuckled. "The **Mafia**," she repeated, as if it were a punchline to a joke. "Here's why they've joined me." She held up a box. It was filled with fingers. "I kidnapped their first-born sons and daughters, cut off their left pinkies and kept them, cut off their right pinkies and sent them to their daddies.

"I really didn't have to kidnap their children to get their attention since I hacked into their business systems and found out a great deal concerning their assets. I could simply have threatened them with that information. But these are stubborn men who need to learn new ways.

"This is a classroom. I'm the professor. Soon the learning will begin. But before we continue, I do want to share with you these amusing clips from their home security systems, which I also hacked." There followed a two-minute clip of a number of the Mafioso using the toilet for different things. It was unkind, embarrassing.

"The **Dons**," she again stressed the word and chuckled. "They and their antagonists, the police, are out of touch. But I arranged this get-together to really stress something with them and with you, my fellow New Yorkers. To be powerful in today's world, one has to be bilingual, speaking both violence and technology. I'll proceed with the demonstration of what I mean in a moment, but first I'd like to share a joke with you.

"A scientist was pursuing an important experiment. He trained a frog to jump whenever he said the word *jump*. After the frog had mastered the trick, he amputated one of the frog's front legs and commanded *jump*. Awkwardly, the frog jumped on three legs. He then severed the other front leg and commanded, *jump*. The frog pushed off with his rear legs in what was more a roll than a jump. The scientist then amputated a rear leg and said *jump* and the frog manfully paddled with one leg but got nowhere. He then amputated the fourth leg and said *jump*, but the frog did not move forward at all. The scientist then wrote in his notebook, *When you amputate all of a frog's legs, it becomes deaf.*" Anna Prophet gave a little chuckle.

"Now to the experiment. On the operating table we have Big Vinnie Calabria, reputedly New York's most fearsome gangster. Yesterday, he went for a drive but his Mercedes lost control, hit a tree, and he was knocked unconscious. Actually, I took control of his car by hacking its control system and did that.

"He's sleeping because I've injected him with a heroin derivative that is so powerful, so addictive, that one dose makes you an irrecoverable junky. He has had two doses." Turning to the doctor, Anna Prophet continued. "Doctor, I don't want Vinnie's screams to disturb the audience, so wake him up by cutting out his tongue, about half way back. Your hands are shaking, doctor. I hope you don't make a mess of things, the way you messed your pants when I first asked you to join me here. Use the pliers and the scissors." She turned back to the camera. "It's so hard to get a surgeon to make a house call nowadays."

The camera swiveled back to the operating table and focused on Calabria's mouth. Hands shaking, the doctor grabbed his tongue with the pliers and cut it off with the scissors. Calabria woke screaming, choking on his own blood as it spilled down his throat. Losing his tongue didn't seem to lessen the volume of his screams.

Anna Prophet approached Calabria with a hypodermic. Speaking loudly to be heard over the screams, she said, "In this syringe is a diluted solution of my super heroin. It will be enough to blunt his pain and calm him down, but not enough to satisfy the craving." She injected the drug directly into Calabria's jugular. The Don stopped screaming. His eyes widened. He was tightly bound and couldn't move, but his ruined face turned toward the syringe like a flower turning toward the sun.

"Wouldn't you like more, Vinnie? I have plenty. In fact, look on the floor over there." The camera shifted. There was a half dozen full syringes lined up. "They're filled with your favorite thing, Vinnie, and I'm going to take off these straps in just a minute and let you take all of it." Calabria was straining at the straps on his hands and feet and torso, trying to roll off the table. "But first the experiment."

Anna Prophet took a pistol from a holster hidden in her clothing. It was a slender .22 caliber Ruger—a marksman's gun, not a thug's. Like a professor using a laser pointer, she aimed the slim gun at Calabria's elbows and pulled the trigger. They smashed to a pulp. Calabria screamed that wet scream. Anna Prophet shot his knees, then his hands, then his feet, until Calabria was a pulped tomato that could scream, but not talk. His boney kneecaps showed through the gaping holes in his legs.

Anna Prophet reloaded the gun and ordered the doctor to unstrap the gangster. The doctor's hands were shaking so badly he almost couldn't. But Anna Prophet gave the doctor a look that promised death — worse than death — and he pulled himself together and freed Calabria.

"It's all yours, Vinnie. Go and get it." Calabria fell off the table. He couldn't move. He flopped a little in the direction of the syringes, but couldn't move forward.

Anna Prophet faced the camera. "He really wants that heroin, but he isn't going for it. My conclusion: Vinnie Calabria is deaf. She turned to the other Dons in the room, some crying, some puking, some frozen with fear, some hardened with resolve. How about you gentlemen; can you hear me?" Now she yelled: "CAN YOU **HEAR** ME? How about you my fellow New Yorkers? Can you hear me?

"Oh, and you may be wondering, who is the woman strapped in the chair. The answer: I don't know. We took her this morning. Watch footage that we hacked from nearby store security cameras." Grainy images took over the screen. The scene was obviously Madison Avenue. The blonde woman was walking into a store when she was grabbed by three masked men and shoved into a car.

"I chose her because she's blonde and I knew it would show up well, even on the crappy security cameras."

Now the camera shifted to the gagged face of the woman. The gag was stained with puke, her face with tears. She was shaking. Anna Prophet walked behind her, put the gun to the back of her neck and pulled the trigger, splattering the front row of gangsters with blood and brains.

"I just wanted to show you that sometimes I will take someone off the street and kill her. Or him," she added. "One doesn't really need something as prosaic as **a reason**.

Then, gunmen stepped out from the perimeter of the room, one for each Don, and shot the gangsters in the head. They all fell forward, dead. Finally, Anna Prophet casually turned to the doctor, rapidly aimed the .22 and shot him through the eye. The only person still alive was Calabria, who almost certainly wished he were dead.

To end the video she went back to the elite British accent: "This is Anna Prophet, signing off."

The screen went dark.

Nobody spoke.

Then Dr. Goldberg said, "Frank, how did you get this video? Was it delivered to you personally?"

"No. One copy went to the Mayor; one went to the Commissioner. They spoke and brought me in."

"Thank God."

"Why?"

"She doesn't know you're on the case. Don't let that get out. Who knows?"

"No one yet. Only Homicide has seen this."

Goldberg turned to Mickey and gave an order. "No one knows that Frank has the case. We can't give her a name and face to define as the enemy. Understand?"

"Yes."

Matty was paralyzed. "Matty," I said. He moved, but did not answer. "Matty?" He looked at me but seemed lost. He was pale white. "**Matty,**" I snapped, "the street scene in the security cameras, that was Madison Avenue."

Matty came awake. "You're right. I can trace the store cameras from the location. I'll see if I can crack how the video was stolen and where it went."

"Good. Michael, I'll need a psychological profile. **Michael.**"

"You want a psychological profile? Let's start with some questions. Does she lack resources?" No one answered.

"This is not rhetorical. Does she lack resources?"

I answered, "Obviously not. She's got at least two dozen men under her control and huge technological sophistication."

"Then why did she steal video from store security cameras rather than taking clear pictures of her own? It would have looked a thousand times better on You Tube."

Matty answered. "It isn't hard to hack into store security networks. There's a hole you can send a truck into."

"You didn't answer my question. I asked why she would do it when she didn't have to."

I cut in, frightened now. "Matty, do not trace that video. Do not. That's an order."

Goldberg: "Good, you're seeing it, Frank."

Mickey now spoke. "Michael, Frank, what are you guys talking about? Why wouldn't we follow up on any clue at all?"

Matty said, "I know why. You think I can be traced. You think Prophet wants us to do the forensics because she'll hack us and find out who her enemy is. Frank, I am the best. You have no idea what I can do. She has no idea who she is dealing with."

Goldberg: "Do you want **her** to know she's dealing with **you,** Matty? What if she can figure that out? My brain started working on her psychological profile as I was watching the video. But you weren't seeing the potential computer pitfalls. Frank had to focus you on the idea that security videos could be a way of tracing her. You didn't think of that. Now, you aren't thinking about defense, only offense. With Anna Prophet, that may be a death sentence for all of us."

Moran: I don't know what to tell people. Shit, I'm afraid to issue a press release with my name on it.

Goldberg: "That's how you need to be thinking about this."

Me: "So we're all agreed she's so dangerous we need to play defense as well as offense. Matty, write something for the Mayor. Mickey, let the Commissioner know what he has to do."

Moran: "There's something else I think I'll have to do as well, Frank. Michael, advise me here. I know the Mayor's press secretary, Andy Infantino, pretty well. He'll write the press release, talking about how tough the Mayor is and how the NYPD will take care of this. He will talk about what a coward Prophet is and how he, the Mayor, knows how to deal with cowards."

Goldberg: "That would be a disaster. She'll will come right for him. She's shockingly immature. The video clips from the gangsters' toilets, the fake accents, it's childish. She will look at any comment as a challenge to be beaten."

I pointed out, "The Mayor is really well protected. We all know how good Spencer and his team are."

Matty: "It doesn't matter how good they are. They won't know what hit them. Their pagers will direct them to call HQ and they'll get a message telling them they're needed at a place far from the Mayor. They'll realize their mistake within minutes, but it will be impossible for them to travel back because the traffic light sequences will be messed up, creating a traffic jam on every corner. A series of emergencies will happen all at once as subway cars crash, computerized alarms go off in every building in the city, fire alarms ring, sending millions into the streets. The Mayor will be a sitting duck."

Moran: "Jesus, is this possible?"

Matty: "It's what I would do if I wanted to kill the Mayor."

I asked, "Matty, could you actually do all that?"

"Yes."

"Then we have to assume Prophet can too."

Matty looked sullen. He was quiet. Then he said, "Yes."

"Good catch on your part, Mickey." This from Dr. Goldberg. "Tell Infantino to emphasize the Mayor's deep concern, and to note respect for the daring of this murderer who feels comfortable to reveal her face, if not her name. Tell him that the Mayor should express confidence in the NYPD. Tell the Mayor to say, *We're all in this together.* That's important; it will do two things. It will counteract

Prophet's trying to keep us from working together. That's why she killed that poor woman — to create a sense that it's every man for himself. But it will also diffuse who Anna Prophet can blame. I have some thoughts about a gigantic and immensely strong woman who is clearly a genius that I'm going to follow up."

I took my phone and called Arnie Schultz on the Organized Crime Task Force — one of the oldest detectives on the force, and one of the smartest. "What's up, Frank?"

"Can you come to my office right now?"

"Did your Dad get the Mayor to make you Commissioner?"

"Not a joke, Arnie. Come now."

"You on this new thing?"

"Just come."

"Anna Prophet, right?"

"I'm hanging up." I did.

In less than five minutes Schultz had joined us. "Arnie, I'm not going to show you the whole video. We'll go to the part where all the mob bosses get killed. Okay. Look at each of the guys standing behind a Don. Take your time. Any look familiar?"

"Familiar, yes. This young guy, he reminds me of Irish Albano. Looks like him. Even holds his piece like Irish, a little sideways. I think that's Albano's kid, whose name is...Salvatore. They call him Sally. Pretty sure that's Sally Albano."

"Where's the dad?"

"Attica. I can bring him downstate or go upstate if you want."

"Let me think about it."

"Lemme know. Happy to be on the case, Frank."

"I never said what case it is, Arnie."

"You didn't have to. The video is all over the news. Ten minutes ago, the Mayor and the Commissioner announced they were sending New York's finest criminal justice mind to catch Anna Prophet, our own Sherlock Holmes, the legendary Frank Scott."

II

We were quiet for a long minute.

"Fuck." I wasn't sure if I said it or one of the other guys. It could have been me. Maybe we all said it, because Schultz was looking at all of us like we were a sister act in a freak show.

"What's the problem?"

"Anna Prophet is a homicidal genius that Dr. Goldberg figures will kill the person she perceives as her nemesis. Sort of a Hannibal Lector on steroids and with a gang."

"Sorta like Wolfy Schwartz."

"Worse."

"Shit. Worse than Schwartz."

Goldberg said it: "Worse."

"Fuck," said Schultz, becoming the fifth sister in the freak show act.

"All right, let's get to work."

"Frank."

"Yes Dr. Goldberg."

"The only person known to be close to you is your father. He's now in mortal danger. And Prophet has a 10-minute lead on you."

"Oh my god. I've got to call him."

Matty: "Your call could be traced. It'll make it easier for them to find him. I can do something."

"Do it." He took my phone, brought it to my desktop, connected it through the USB port and did stuff. Then he handed it back to me. Call him. This can be cracked, but it would take me 24 hours."

"Will my number come up on the caller ID?"

"No."

Shit. Dad rarely picked up the phone if he didn't recognize the number.

"What will come up on the caller ID?"

"A string of random numbers."

Would my father pick up the phone if he saw that? I prayed he would. I dialed his cell. It rang twice and he answered it.

"Dad, it's Frank."

"Thought it might be, after I heard the Mayor's announcement. What's with the funny number? The caller ID doesn't have your name, just a string of random numbers."

"Encrypted. Did you see the video?"

"Yes. The Mayor's office released it to the public. It's horrible." Dr. Goldberg cursed softly under his breath.

"You've got to get lost. Dr. Goldberg thinks Anna Prophet will be coming for me, which means she'll be coming for you."

"Oh Jesus. What should I do?"

"Drive someplace nobody would ever think to look for you." Matty cut in, "No! His car has more Intel processors than your desktop. It can be associated with your father and tracked."

"Dad, don't take the car. Take my old dirt bike and get far from the house. Pay for everything with cash. Don't use a credit card. I reckon you have about 15 minutes to get out."

"I don't know how to drive the dirt bike."

"It's pretty straightforward. Don't call anyone. In fact, turn off your phone. Turn it back on in two hours. I'll call after I figure out how to reach you without being traced."

"15 minutes?"

"Yeah. Can you tell me where you're going to go in a way that no one else will understand?"

"Yes. You haven't enjoyed that scenic spot since you were 15."

I thought for a couple of seconds. Then I said, "Good Choice. Take the cash and get out. Don't pack anything. I'll buy clothes and find you. Get out." Dad had a major safe in the house but only kept a little bit of cash in it. It was there to give crooks something to focus on. He kept $50,000 under the couch cushions in the library. "And Dad..."

"Yes?"

"Get out fast, but drive slowly. Don't kill yourself."

"Let's hope that neither of us gets me killed." That hurt. He hung up.

"Matty, is it possible for Anna Prophet to track every call I've made from this phone for the last several months?"

"It's not easy. She'd have to hack the phone company, figure out enough variables to identify you, then find the usage databases. It's possible, but she couldn't have done it in the last 15 minutes since it was announced you're on the case. Of course, if she anticipated that you'd get the assignment, she might have already done that work."

"I need to make another call. Will the next call be encrypted as well?"

"No. I'll need to do that thing again." He did. I took my phone back, left the room, and called Daisy Stein. Daisy is the lead crime reporter at the Daily News and the best crime reporter in the City, maybe the country. We were friends, though I tried to lowball that, and so did she. Fact is, I fed her scoops that led to reporting that made me look good and made her into a superstar. That we occasionally had dinner, occasionally had breakfast, and were with each other in between, was something we kept to ourselves. From my perspective, it kept her out of the line-of-sight of people who would have loved to get back at me, and it suited Daisy because I was one small part of her army of sources, but she would lose credibility if our relationship were commonly known. So we were careful.

I didn't need to worry if Daisy would answer her phone when the caller ID only showed a string of random numbers. That kind of mystery would be irresistible to her. She'd be more likely to answer her phone if she saw a string of random numbers than if she saw my name. She had a strong dose of monkey curiosity in her that made her a great reporter — the kind that advanced the knowledge base of the species, but was awfully unhealthy for the individual.

"Daisy, it's Frank."

"Why is a string of random numbers coming up on my caller ID instead of your name?"

"The call is encrypted. I'm sure you've seen the Anna Prophet video. I'm sure you saw the Mayor announce I'm on the case. This one is a special kind of crazy. According to Dr. Goldberg, anyone associated with me is in danger. You're going to need to get out of town."

"Get out of town when the most high-profile crime story of the decade is unfolding in the City? You need to get out of town, Frank, if you think that's going to happen. Anyway, I'm checking my Facebook page as we're talking and Anna Prophet has already accepted my invitation."

"What?"

"After I saw the video, I wrote an invitation on Facebook for Prophet to be interviewed for the News. She wouldn't be making videos if she didn't want to go public, so I thought I'd give her a chance and get the scoop. I figured someone that tech savvy would have a way of finding my invitation. Wait until Tommy hears." Tommy was her editor.

"You won't survive that interview. She'll do to you what she did to the doctor. Once she's used you up she'll kill you."

"I have a plan. I posted that I want to do an interview for a straight news story, but that I would return to work and write an editorial about her personally — her significance as the first super criminal who understands the power of technology and social media, what drives her, why she matters. I'm playing to her ego, Frank. A woman who makes a spectacle of herself like that will find the attention irresistible. She'll let me go in order to get the editorial."

"This is fucking harebrained and suicidal."

"Relax Frank. I covered the Wolfy Schwartz case, remember?"

"Goldberg says Anna Prophet is worse than Schwartz."

"Shit. Worse than Wolfy Schwartz?"

"I'm going to talk to Goldberg. Are you okay if I tell him about us?"

"Shit."

"Is that a *yes?*"

"I guess so. Yes."

"Don't go anywhere. I'll call you back."

I hung up and went back to my office. Moran said, "I'd better get back to my desk." He left. Matty and Goldberg got up to leave.

"Michael, would you stay a bit longer? Matty, before you go, would you do that thing one more time to my phone."

"Sure. I'll come back with a phone for you that will be totally encrypted."

Matty left. Now came the acid test for how good I've been at keeping my relationship with Daisy a secret. Goldberg paid attention. If he didn't know about it, probably nobody did.

"Michael, I just made another call on the Anna Prophet case."

"I figured you were calling someone you want to protect. But I have no idea who it was. I didn't think anyone was close to you except your Dad."

"It was Daisy Stein."

"At the News?"

"Yeah."

"Why'd you call the newspapers...oh. No kidding? You and Daisy. I can see it. Wouldn't have guessed it, though."

"She's put her foot in it. After the Mayor's announcement, she went on Facebook and invited Prophet to meet with her for an interview. Prophet accepted."

"Daisy can't do that. Prophet'll kill her as a finish to the interview."

"She says she has a plan. She'll tell Prophet that she wants to write an editorial on her significance as the first super criminal to understand the power of social media."

"That might work."

"Not taking the chance."

"What if you could trace Daisy to Prophet?"

"She'll check Daisy for bugs."

"Maybe Matty has a trick up his sleeve."

I picked up the phone. "Matty, can you come back." Here it comes, I thought, a wise ass comment that illustrates what a senile detective I am because I couldn't remember what I needed while he was there. But Matty just said, "Okay."

He seemed really effected by the video. Anna Prophet is scary. I'm 6'2" and trained to fight. I wasn't raised in the streets; I was a rich kid who just liked being a detective and was able to get connected in the world's most high profile police force. But like every cop, I'd faced down a lot of hoods. And like every detective, I go where the trail leads, even when it's scary at the end.

It was my nature to be a fighter; I got that from dad. You couldn't ask for a courtlier gentleman than my father, who was rich and well mannered. But you don't get to be governor of New York if you can't be a backroom, bare-knuckled fighter. His six months in prison were at Club Fed and he didn't need to break heads, but he was too tough to define himself as an ex-con and emerged from jail as the ex-governor. He was tough enough to make that image stick.

Same was true for me. I wasn't on the Force because I needed a job. I liked solving crimes. I liked getting into it with bad guys. It was my nature. I was social and well mannered, well read and generally appropriate. But I liked a fight.

Matty was a geek, a computer scientist who had become supreme in a very exclusive specialty. He wasn't used to dealing directly with the criminal. For him, Anna Prophet was something out of a nightmare. He liked dealing with things from a distance. For him, the job was more like playing a video game. Suddenly, the bad guy had stepped out of the computer and was in his face. I hoped he could hold it together.

"What's up, Frank?"

"If someone were to meet with Anna Prophet, is it possible for you to rig up a trace that she wouldn't find?"

"No. There's only a handful of technologies that provide a signal you can trace. Prophet will know how to find them and block them."

Damn, we weren't going to be able to out-tech her.

"Let's try a different direction. If I was as smart as Anna Prophet, what would I do about Daisy?"

Matty: "Daisy?"

Me: Daisy Stein, of the News. Anna Prophet is going to give her an interview."

Matty: "Is she fucking crazy!"

Me: "Michael, what is Anna Prophet thinking about Daisy at this moment?"

Goldberg: "She's thinking that Daisy is useful. But she wouldn't stop there. If she perceives that Daisy's useful to her, she'd feel proprietary, a sense of ownership."

Me: "I'm thinking she's having Daisy tailed. She figures that Daisy won't involve the police for fear of losing her scoop. But

Prophet won't take a chance that she'll lose the interview for any reason."

Goldberg: "It's more than that. In Prophet's mind, Daisy is her tool now. The only reason she hasn't kidnapped her is because she wants her to be in good psychological shape for the interview. I think you're right and she's having her tailed."

I called Schultz. "Arnie, come back." He was back in my office in a couple of minutes.

"Dr. Goldberg and I believe that Prophet sent someone to tail Daisy Stein of the Daily News."

"I like Daisy. She's fair to the cops. Always makes **you** look good, but other than that, she's fair. Why is Prophet tailing her?"

"You're not a Facebook user. Stein offered to interview her and she accepted."

"Is she fucking crazy!"

"A question for Dr. Goldberg, not me. You're as likely as anyone to recognize whoever is on her tail and follow him."

"Is Prophet going to kidnap Daisy?"

"We don't think so. But don't collar the tail. Wait for his relief. Follow him as far as it is safe."

"I get the drill."

"Who's your back up?"

"I'll get Dunne."

"Good. How about a third?"

"Semel."

"She'll be good. Chances are, if you're spotted you're dead, they're dead, Daisy's dead, and I'm dead. Maybe Matty too."

Schultz looked at Matty for a few seconds, then shrugged. "Did you say that Matty **would** be dead, or just **maybe** would be dead?"

"Get going."

I called Daisy and told her the plan.

"What did Goldberg say?"

"He said he wouldn't have guessed we'd be in a relationship, but he could see it."

"I don't mean what did he say about us. What did he say about my plan?"

"It might work. I can't stress heavily enough the danger you're in. Anna Prophet now thinks you're her property and we think she's having you tailed. You know Arnie Schultz. He'll be tailing the tail. Do not acknowledge him in any way."

"Duh. Hang up and turn on your TV, Frank. I just got a text from Tommy that the Mayor is going live on the hour."

I went back to my office and turned on the TV. Matty, Goldberg and I watched the Mayor deliver Goldberg's words. Mickey had gotten to Infantino on time. We were coordinating.

III

On my way out, I stopped at the Chief's office. Jack Mulberry is the Chief of Department, the highest-ranking uniformed cop. He's the City's second black chief, and the first in 20 years. He's probably the smartest guy in the NYPD.

"Quite a case, Frank."

"I need some help."

"Okay."

"She'll go after every one she thinks I care about." I didn't have to explain who "She" was.

"That would be your dad, as far as I know."

"She'll go levels below that. Daisy Stein at the News didn't do anyone any favors when she wrote that feature on me that lists my favorite bars and restaurants. I figure by tonight Prophet'll have gunmen there to make a point."

"Shit, you're right. I'll have SWAT teams there before the dinner trade." He refrained from saying that Daisy did **me** a favor with that feature.

"You need to get them there now. If Matty is right, I expect around dinner time there will be all sorts of alarms and emergencies going off across the City that will require SWAT teams. They will be bullshit and will prevent your teams from getting where they're really needed."

"How am I supposed to know what is real?"

"Anything to do with Anna Prophet coming after me or the Mayor is real. For anything else, send a patrolman. We probably will need SWAT at every place Daisy wrote about. But let me ask you something. What kind of power can we deploy undercover?"

"Not what I can do in uniform."

"A uniformed team will scare them away from their targets, which is good. But we need to get rid of her army. Are you tracking me?"

"Dangerous, Frank. You **want** them to come, and us to kill them. That puts too many people at risk. I won't do it. We'll deploy SWAT and keep them away."

"You're right, Jack."

"I don't blame you for being scared, Frank, but don't let it cloud your thinking."

"Right."

"Where are you going to go? If she's going after your favorite bars, she'll be waiting at your house."

"Yes she will."

"Seems like now would be a good time to deploy plainclothesmen at your place, maybe a half hour before you get there. People that look like your laundry service, your cleaners, a neighbor who keeps searching her pocketbook for the keys she can't find, right before you get to your door. I can coordinate that with Dolan." Dolan was Chief of Detectives. "Or you can go into hiding for the day."

"I like your Plan A, Jack."

"The neighbor has to be white, like you. It's a fancy building. I'll send Jackie Neal. Everyone else has to look like me. Suarez will lead that team. They'll be eight inside. We'll have the place surrounded."

It's amazing how fast Mulberry had put it together.

"She may have already had people break into my apartment."

"Good point. I'll have twelve on the floor, 50 on site. The team will be dispatched now and will go to your floor."

"It's 28."

"Wait a minute and I'll give you a list of everyone. Don't shoot any of them."

"Thank you, Jack."

"Frank, I think this one's worse than Wolfy Schwartz."

"Goldberg agrees."

"Shit."

I left Mulberry's office and called my father from the phone Matty had given me. Dad picked it up right away.

"How are you?"

"Fine Frank. How's the case?"

"Playing defense so far."

"So far?"

"I'm told this phone is encrypted but not to stay on too long. What can I bring you?"

"I'm okay for now. But how can I reach you if I need to?"

"If you are where I think you are, tell the second one what you need to say to me and tell her to call the other number." He digested that for a second, then said, "Got it. I am where you think I am."

We hung up. Dad had driven the dirt bike to the bus depot, bought a ticket with cash, gone to the Overlook Motel, which was the place I used to go when I wanted to run away from home. Overlook was owned by two sisters. The elder was miserable, the younger delightful. I used to call the younger sister *Number Two*, like the old Avis Rent-a-Car commercial: *We're number two; we try harder.*

That woman, Claire, would take in the bedraggled kid I used to be and calm me down before renting me a room. She was an angel to a 14-year-old. And she had an obsolete cellphone number of mine that I had gotten as a runaway with a made-up name. I haven't stopped paying the bill since I was a kid, so the phone company never turned off the service. It has been very handy for me to have a phone that isn't associated with my real name. It's actually listed in the name of Dante Alighieri. I was a dramatic kid.

Claire had that number because I trusted her. While Anna Prophet may be able to trace calls, there could be no connection to me with calls from a Duchess County motel to someone named Dante Alighieri.

Dad was safe. Now some action. It was 2:00 pm — time to head home.

IV

I got to the door of my building right behind Jackie Neal, who looked blondish-grey, middle aged and flustered. She didn't pay attention to me. Out of the corner of my eye I saw a man in a suit speak into a lapel. He had a wire running to his ear. He wasn't anyone I knew. I thought of all the names on the list Mulberry had given me. I wanted to run away. I wanted to grab him and beat him. I just put my hands in my pocket where I'd moved my gun and kept walking like I saw nothing.

Jackie got to the elevator and pushed the button. I arrived and gave her the faint smile of a neighbor who barely recognized her. She gave a faint smile back. We got on the elevator. A man who had been waiting in the lobby got on the elevator too — was going to have to speak with the doorman — and the man I saw in the street had jogged in to the lobby and also swung on to the elevator. It was me and Jackie and two of them. The elevator door closed and I didn't wait. I already had my gun in hand and shot them both. The first guy just fell dead. The second was reaching for his piece when I got him.

180

Jackie was shaken. "What the hell, Frank!"

Then she calmed herself. "Taking a chance. How do you know they're Prophet's? Could just be residents."

"You know better."

"Question is, what are we going to find when we get to the 28th floor?"

"They wouldn't have heard the shots. Have your gun in your hand and don't worry about the fumbling-for-the-key routine. These guys were told to kill on sight, me and anyone nearby. You saw the list of our people. Anyone else, just shoot."

"You're acting funny, Frank. I've never seen you like this. Fuck'in bloodthirsty. Never heard that you shoot first, ask questions later."

I was scared. Bottom line. When I saw her face approach the camera it felt like being stalked by a panther. It left me shaken. I wasn't used to that. This didn't feel like a case I was solving. It felt like I was being hunted and needed to kill the predator that was coming for me. Maybe I wouldn't have felt this way if the Mayor hadn't said on TV that it was me on the case. But maybe I would have.

There was something else disturbing me. I didn't want to meet her face to face. There was something terrifying about her perfect proportions, her gigantic size. She was like a creature out of a fairytale, the giant that ate children, the witch in the gingerbread house. And beneath that, something compelling— the witch trying to make Hansel and Gretel want to be eaten. But it wasn't sexual—at least, I didn't think so from the video. The way she killed, it was as if people were a lesser species that existed for her to hunt, not to mate with. I wanted to catch her without meeting her. I wanted someone else to kill her. But I wanted her dead.

We were getting to my floor. "Gun out. They may be waiting in front of the elevator or on either side. We need to catch them by surprise."

"What's gotten into you Frank? This is not how it's done."

"Did you see the video?"

"No."

"Mulberry should have made everyone watch it."

"I was making a collar when it hit the Department."

"I am not over reacting."

The elevator doors opened. I aimed right; Jackie aimed left. There was a man there with a gun pointed at me. I didn't get a chance to shoot. Neither did Jackie. As the elevator doors opened, undercover cops stepped from stairwells, utility closets, and empty apartments and shot, killing both men. This part of the team had clearly watched the video.

I said, "I think there are at least two in my apartment. They would have heard the gun fire. I'll knock on the door as if I'm one of their gang so that they open up. If this doesn't work, blow the door apart with the shotgun."

It was me, Jackie, and 12 other cops. We all took position on either side of the door. I reached over and knocked, trying to knock like a hood who had just done his job. Three bullets came through the center of the door where I would have been standing if I didn't suspect anything.

"Okay, let's go." One of the undercover guys hauled a big ass shotgun and in six shots blew down my door. I groaned inside. I like this apartment. Another cop tossed in a teargas grenade. My place would be unlivable for a month. Whoever was inside didn't run out, they just started coughing and shooting wildly. When the bullets stopped for a few seconds, the guy with the shotgun came back and used it to sweep my apartment, blasting in a semicircle from the doorway. Was this covered by my insurance?

The guy with the shotgun, a new detective named Covell, ran in first. I was right behind him and Jackie behind me. There were two men on the floor. One was dead. One was a bloody mess, groaning.

I opened the windows and turned on the central air. The place cleared out quickly. I worked hard not to look at the wall over the mantelpiece, where the painting my father had given me was hung. I wasn't ready to know what had happened to something that beautiful, that expensive.

The man on the floor was too smashed up to attack. I took a good look and recognized Salvatore Albano, whom Arnie Schultz had identified as the son of gangster Irish Albano. I walked up to him.

"Sally Albano." Through his pain he looked up at me. "Your dad would be so disappointed in you. Working for Prophet, turning your back on the family."

He didn't bother to answer. He was in pain.

"Sally, where's Prophet? He was muttering something that I could barely hear. It might have been *fuck you*.

"Sally, how do I explain to you this is life and death?" I went into my kitchen. It was ruined; everything in the house was ruined. I went to the fruit bowl on the counter and got a lemon. I like to cook and it's good to have lemons around. Then I got a paring knife and carried the knife and the lemon over to Sally.

"Your friends in the elevator went for their guns and I blew their brains out. There were six of you and you're all dead except for little Sally Albano. Where's Prophet?"

Nothing.

I found a huge wound on his stomach made by the buckshot. I sliced the lemon in half. With the tip of the knife I spread the opening of the gut wound and squeezed lemon juice in. Sally screamed. I found a cut on his face and squeezed in lemon juice. He screamed again.

"Tell me where I can find Profit or I'll keep watering your holes until you're unconscious from pain, then I'll kill you." I squeezed lemon into the cut near his left eye.

"What's he doing?" I heard one of the cops whisper.

"Trying to stay alive," another answered. "Didn't you see the video?"

I took the small paring knife and slowly started opening the gut wound, poking the peritoneum lining the inside of Sally's stomach. He screamed some more.

"Call her and tell her mission accomplished. If you don't, I'll kill you and 13 other cops will say it was self-defense. Take out your cell phone and call her."

He said his first words, assuming that screams aren't language. "Pocket. It's in my jacket pocket." I went back to the kitchen and got two pair of tongs. Dealing with Prophet, I wasn't going to take a chance that there was a poison needle in the jacket pocket. I used the tongs to fish around Sally's jacket. But his phone had been smashed by the shot he took. I called HQ. "Jack, how quickly can you put a trace on my home phone?"

"We'll need a warrant. This will take time."

"For Chrissakes! It's my phone. You have consent."

"Five minutes"

I waited five minutes, then handed him my house phone. "Use this. Call Prophet. Tell her you killed me or I'll kill you."

He hesitated about 4 seconds and took the phone. He dialed a number and I hoped HQ was getting the trace.

"Anna, it's Sally. We got him."

"Why are you calling me on his phone line?"

"My phone was destroyed. I got hit. I'm hurt."

"Where are the others?"

"I don't know. Dead or wounded."

"There were six of you. What the hell happened?"

"I don't know. Me and Tony were in the apartment in case Scott got past the elevator and the hallway. He was hurt, it took him a long time to open the door. His gun was in his hand when he walked in. He shot Tony and I shot him, but he got a shot off at me and it hit me in the chest." I was amazed at how creative Sally Albano could be. Or how terrified. He made up quite a story about how I could be dead, and so could five of the six sent after me.

"One man couldn't have gotten six of you."

"He's dead, Anna."

"Kill yourself, Sal." She hung up. Without any apparent thought, Albano reached for his chest holster. I believed if he would have found a gun he would have killed himself. Then he seemed to lose it all and fell unconscious.

I turned my focus away from Albano and realized that all the other cops in the room had backed away from me, were staring at me. I pulled out my cell phone and called Mulberry. He said, "We got a location."

"I don't think anyone will be there when we arrive. Have the bomb squad go first. It will probably be booby-trapped. But we may find some clues after everything blows up."

The trace actually led us to a brothel on the upper East Side that the former governor, the one that came after my father, was said to frequent. It was a joke. She knew we were tracing the call. Doctors were working on Sally Albano; if he lived, we would try to get some answers.

I got back to headquarters and sent an e-mail requesting a palaver with Mulberry, Goldberg, Moran, and Matty. I thought briefly about asking Matty to shower before coming to the meeting, but decided I was going to need him at the top of his game. The rest of us were going to have to deal with it.

We met in a conference room next to Moran's office. I turned up the air-conditioning.

Mulberry started. "What do we have?"

"She didn't kill me and she's down six men."

Moran: "She didn't kill you **yet**."

Matty: "You should have asked me to set the trace on Francis' phone. Give me access to the coding of the trace."

Mulberry: "We didn't get anything. It was a wild goose chase."

Matty: "I'll learn something from analyzing how the trace was baffled. But it's going to take some time to figure it out."

Mulberry: "Okay."

Matty left to go back to his lab and practice whatever witchcraft he employed.

Goldberg: "I had a thought about a woman who is 6'4", a genius, and is immensely violent. So I searched Ivy League application records."

Moran: "You found out where she went to college?"

Goldberg: "She didn't go to college. But her parents thought she should."

Mulberry: "Explain."

Goldberg: "Picture two Russian immigrants in Brooklyn. Married after they met at the genetics lab where they were both scientists. Brilliant, frustrated by the Russian controls on research, concerned that their work would only be used for warfare, they easily figured out a way to leave the country and come to the U.S. Here, they had a child. I don't know if she was so extraordinary because both of her parents were extraordinary, mentally and physically, or if these two geneticists were...experimenting with their own child. But she turned out to be amazing. Smarter than anyone around her. First dazzling, then surpassing her teachers. By the time she was 13-years-old it was clear she had nothing to gain from further schooling, even college.

"But her parents disagreed.

"They came to America to send their child to Harvard or one of the other Ivies. It wasn't about knowledge or connections. It was about status and ego. Their supervisor in the genetics lab in Russia wasn't bright enough to understand their work, yet he was their boss. He had the job at the lab because, stupid as he was, his parents had connections and the money to send him to America to attend college at NYU. His parents' money and the American credential landed him the job. He spoke incessantly about his education in America, how superior it was to anything available locally.

"The girl's parents had counted on sending her to a better school than NYU and rubbing the old boss' face in it. It's petty. It's small. I can't explain how two such brilliant people were motivated by something so absurd. But it was their central motivation.

"Imagine their anger and disappointment when their prodigy announced that she wasn't going to go to college but was ready to move on! So they ignored her wishes and sent out college applications. Not wanting to take any chances, they described her athletic prowess, great size and strength, and pointed out how she would be the anchor of any sports team at the university.

"She never knew they had done that. She left home before a single acceptance envelope returned. So she never knew that she had a trail to erase. Olga Olinskia did whatever she had to do in order to become Anna Prophet. The girl from Brooklyn, by way of Russia, is our game."

Me: "What are the parents' first names?"

Goldberg: "Serge and Sophia. Why?"

Me: "For when I file my report."

Moran: "When did this all happen? Prophet looks like she's in her mid to late 30's."

Goldberg: "She left home five years ago. She's 16. A girl who was 11 built a criminal enterprise in 5 years."

Moran: "That's impossible, Dr. Goldberg. The woman on that video isn't 16. She's at least in her late 20s. You got the wrong suspect."

Goldberg: "She has matured unbelievably quickly. I don't know if that's a function of genetic manipulation or psychosomatic stimulation of the maturation process."

Mulberry: "If you're right, we may be dealing with a genetically enhanced superwoman."

Goldberg: "Her parents said that she wasn't genetically enhanced. I can't tell if they're lying."

Mulberry: "Michael, we may be dealing with someone who is smarter than all of us. What the hell are we going to do?"

Goldberg: "No, Jack. She may be smarter than any single one of us, but she's not smarter than all of us put together."

V

"I'm starting to believe it's a mistake to let Daisy Stein do the interview."

"You're right Frank," Mulberry said. I pulled out my cell phone to call Schultz, but it was dead. "I don't get it. I charged the thing this morning."

Everyone pulled out their phones. All were dead. Then my phone rang, scaring the shit out of me.

"It's Matty. Prophet is beginning the Citywide hack. Shit is going to start blowing up."

"My phone was dead. How are you getting through?

"I can construct an alternative IP route using the internal IP Protocol and...never mind. I can make our phone work. But only the phones on our account at HQ." I told the others in the room.

"And Francis, I learned something from deconstructing her trace baffle." Dramatic silence followed.

"WHAT!"

"She's in a phone company central office building."

"How do you know?"

"The ease with which she was able to multiplex a POTS-based access call to a digital cross connect would require..."

"Okay." I cut him off. "Where?"

"Manhattan, south of 57th Street. Best I could do. But that was a pretty neat bit of work, don't you th..."

I cut him off again and turned toward the folks in the room. "Matty says she's in a phone company central office in Manhattan, south of 57th."

Goldberg said, "I'm thinking where she grew up in Brooklyn."

"Why?"

"She walked out on her home and parents, but maybe she needs to prove that she can be the best in the house, the best in the neighborhood, as well as the best in the City."

"Could she be in a central office in Manhattan that overlooks Brooklyn?"

"Looking down on the old neighborhood from a perch higher up the mountain. That sounds right to me."

"Verizon has a central office on Pearl Street that overlooks Brooklyn and almost all of Manhattan."

"That's the place."

Mulberry: "How we gonna get there? Look out the window."

The streets were already chaotic. It was the streetlights. They all turned green in every direction at the same time. Everybody went.

"Shit," said somebody. It could have been me.

At this, Arnie Schultz walked in.

"We tailed her like you said. We found her."

"The phone company central office on Pearl Street?"

"No. Why would you think that? She's a block away." I heard Matty cursing over the phone.

"Matty, do you think Arnie is wrong?"

More cursing. "Matty?"

"No motherfucker. I don't. Wait a minute." Silence, then, "Fuck. Here it is. A recursive loop inside the secondary pathway. She fooled me." More silence. Then again, very softly, "She fooled me."

None of us ever thought we'd hear those words coming out of Matty's mouth. The *fooled me*, not the *motherfucker*.

Arnie chuckled, looking pleased. "By the way," he said, she took Stein. I was close enough to hear the stooge say he was with Prophet and that she was being summoned for the interview. I remembered what you said about her not being in danger of getting kidnapped and I didn't blow the tail. Dunne followed. I came here."

Goldberg said, "Shit." I immediately knew why.

Goldberg: "The game has changed. She didn't kill you Frank. I don't know that she's ever been outdone in anything. She wanted you dead; six of hers are gone. She's going to switch to a short-term strategy. She's going to kill Daisy Stein and beat it."

Me: "Arnie, do you know her address?"

"16 Lafayette."

"Okay. Call Dunne, tell him to get back here. Jack, we need an army that can walk through the mess out there."

Mulberry: "On it. But I won't be able to get the heavy equipment to the site. Not with the streets locked down like this."

Me: "Double edged sword. We can't get assault vehicles there, but she can't escape in this mess."

Schultz: "Dunne's not answering."

Me: "Dunne may be dead. I'm going now. They're escaping on foot. Jack, get the back-up out there as soon as you can." I started running to 16 Lafayette. Schultz was running too, just a lot slower. In about 5 minutes a SWAT phalanx would be following and within 15 minute helicopters would be in the air. It took me seven minutes run four blocks. The whole time I was dodging people, stopped cars, and confused dogs held by upset dog walkers.

Then I heard the engines.

Motorcycles.

She was prepared to be discovered, prepared to get away. Twenty motorcycles were weaving their way through the blocked traffic. They made no accommodation for pedestrians, running down whoever was too slow to get out of their way. And they were getting away. Coming roughly toward me was a bike with a giant woman. There wasn't any red hair coming out from under her helmet, but her size and the way she dominated the bike marked her as Anna Prophet—Olga Olinskia. I didn't dare try to take a shot at her in this crowd. Behind her was a small figure on another motorcycle. I had no doubt it was Daisy Stein and I thought to myself, *What is that crazy woman doing, following Prophet? Why the hell is she still alive?* And while I couldn't explain it, I knew that she was still alive because she was following Prophet.

I was certain that I was going to lose Prophet when a shot came from somewhere in the crowded street. The shot missed Prophet but hit her motorcycle, which veered and went over on its side. Who the hell would fire at her in a crowd? Prophet came up with the .22 pistol in her hand and aimed in the direction of the shot and fired. I heard someone grunt, but didn't see who, didn't see where he fell. I was getting close to her now and had my gun out. Her men were heading in different directions; no doubt that was their plan to escape. They hadn't realized their boss was knocked off her bike. She must have signaled to them for assistance, because they all turned and tried to join her, though the crowds that they had created by screwing with the traffic light sequences was a sticky trap for them too.

I heard more motorcycle engines. But these were cops. Mulberry had seen and reacted. SWAT teams were arriving by foot and six helicopters hovered while SWAT teams lowered by rope to the floor.

Prophet looked around. She was brilliant, smarter than any one of us. But she was inexperienced and had never dealt with defeat. She had her gun in hand and turned toward Daisy.

I screamed, "*Olga!*"

She turned, almost looking startled. Saw me and smiled.

"Frank Scott."

As she spoke she lifted her gun but never had a chance to fire. Another shot came from the crowd. It was closer. It shattered her helmet and splattered the street with red. I turned in the direction of the shot, ducking and pointing my gun. But I didn't know who to shoot.

VI

Daisy had stopped her bike about 20 feet from Prophet's. I walked over to her. She didn't get off to meet me. As I got closer, I saw why. She was chained to the bike. She had a metal collar around her neck that was locked to the handlebars. On top of the gas tank was an electronic box with a blinking red light.

"Frank, clear the crowd! The bike is booby-trapped."

"Is it on a timer?"

"I don't know. She had a detonator. She said if I didn't follow her she'd blow me up."

SWAT teams arrived. I told them the story and they immediately cleared the street.

When the Squad arrived, they confirmed the bomb wasn't on a timer. They deactivated the device and the detonator and cut Daisy loose from the motorcycle. I stared at Prophet. She was dead. She was a giant, well-proportioned woman with a bloody helmet for a head. I was very relieved. Very relieved. My shoulders slumped and my head fell forward just a bit.

Daisy filled me in. "She was prepared for you guys to come. If I didn't follow her, she'd blow up the bike. The bike was all wired up with the bomb and with chains. She wanted her interview. She wasn't going to kill me until it was done. Oh, the building on Lafayette is wired to blow. Don't send anybody in there. Just fire a canon at it or something. She thought of everything."

"Daisy, this must be traumatic. I'll call Goldberg."

"I'll say it was traumatic. All that, and I never got an interview. But I was her prisoner for almost an hour. I'm the only reporter who actually met her. I've got to get to a computer."

Daisy, rhymes with crazy.

Matty had hacked Prophet's hijack of the street light and restored their regular algorithm. The streets were moving as well as Manhattan streets can move. I saw Arnie Schultz and waived him over to walk back to Police Plaza.

"Arnie, did you shoot Prophet? While I had no idea you were that kind of marksman, it was risky firing into the crowd."

"Wasn't me, Frank."

What the fuck?

We got to HQ and I looked up Mulberry. "Jack, that sniper was amazing. But risky."

"Snipers were ordered but not yet in position. When forensics gets through, I bet the bullet isn't one of ours."

VII

Who killed Anna Prophet?

I stopped off at Matty's lab. I thought very carefully about what I would say.

"Was she really as good at this stuff as she seemed?"

"She was good, Detective Scott. Just not the best."

"You seemed to think highly of her."

"Sure. But she wasn't as good as she thought she was."

"What do you mean?"

"Very few people are perfect."

"Not following you, Matty."

"Story of your life, Francis. Don't even bother trying." He turned back to his console, which I took as a dismissal.

I called Arnie Schultz back at the Organized Crime Bureau. "Arnie, it's Frank. At the scene, did you see any of your usual mobsters there?"

"Could have been a couple from the Calabria clan. Not sure. The only reason I thought so was because I saw guys wearing red ties and I know the clan likes them because Vinnie wore them. But not sure."

Why would there be a couple of guys from the Calabria family at the scene?

VIII

That night I visited Dad, back at home.

"So what are you thinking, Frank?"

"The Calabria's."

"How? How could they have known where she was? How could they have gotten their best marksman there?"

"Someone told them where to go and helped them get there."

"How is that possible? Even if someone knew where to send them, how would they get from their club at the pier to Lafayette? That's half a mile in impenetrable conditions."

"Who would know how to reach the Calabria's? Know where to send them? Know how to get them there? And cover his tracks so that no one could trace it to him?"

"You think it was Matty? What are you going to do? Are you going to tell anyone?"

"I didn't say that. But if it was Matty, do you think I'd squeal on a guy who can hack into my employment file, bank account, personal computer? For that matter, your stuff as well. I don't think so."

"Oh... If not Matty, who?"

"Still thinking."

"How is Detective Dunne?"

"Doing well. She shot him, but a .22 wasn't enough to kill that guy."

IX

Three days later, I stopped into Goldberg's office with a bottle of my favorite single malt, Longmorn. It's a wonderful scotch that is not in a hurry. It rewards you to hold it on your tongue for a second before swallowing. It tells you things about peat, about smoke, about land and stillness.

"Michael, we have a lot to celebrate. We are heroes. I have brought with me my favorite toast. Let us drink."

"I don't really drink a lot, Frank." I knew that.

"Take a sip, at any rate, and let me toast."

"Okay."

I poured a small shot for me and a bare sip for him.

"To the team! Our species would never have come so far if we worked alone."

I watched him. Goldberg put the glass to his lips, let the whiskey touch his upper lip, but never swallowed any.

"I don't blame you for not wanting to drink, Michael. If you're not used to it, you can lose control. In your business that wouldn't be a good idea. Anyway, I'm not sure that toast makes sense for you."

"Frank, just because I don't drink doesn't mean I'm not happy to be part of the team. And this isn't work. You're not a patient."

"And you're not a psychiatrist. Or maybe you are. But you're not just a psychiatrist."

"What are you talking about, Frank. I earned those degrees on the wall."

"I'm sure you did. In fact, you're an amazing psychiatrist. You instantly scoped out Anna Prophet, predicted what she was thinking, how she would act. It was amazing. And you're a detective too, tracking down her parents. That was brilliant, checking college applications to the Ivies."

"You don't sound grateful."

"I visited Olga's parents, the ones who you tracked down. I guess maybe godparents would be a better term."

"Really?"

"Yeah. They wouldn't say a word to me. They were big and threatening, but very quiet. After the cold shoulder they gave me, I was amazed at how much they shared with you."

"We learn how to get people to open up in psychiatry school."

"Do you know where their paychecks come from?"

"Frank?"

"The Defense Advanced Research Projects Agency—DARPA. They were involved with the government's genetic soldier program. It's why the CIA facilitated their escape from Russia."

"Where would you come up with that?"

"I'm a detective, Michael. People don't like to talk to me, but I find things out anyway."

"What else have you found out?"

"There are limits to how super a superman is."

"Not following you, Frank."

"Funny, I said the same thing to a superman just the other day. I knew the conversation was over when he turned from me to his computer. Sound like any supermen you know?"

"Frank, as a psychiatrist, I'm thinking you need a break. Your conversation is disjointed and you're sounding like you need a rest, which is perfectly understandable after the strain you've been under. Take that bottle home and do it justice. Take tomorrow off. It'll do you a world of good."

"Michael, I'm thinking if I go back to my dad's house, where I'm staying while my place gets fixed up, and I drink this bottle of scotch, I won't be alert enough to deal with the visitors who will be stopping by."

"I'm going to add paranoia to stress for this diagnosis."

"How did you get such startling insight into Anna Prophet?"

"I'm good at my job."

"How did you do the research into the Ivies? You couldn't have made so many calls and gotten so much information in the short period of time we had."

"Matty helped."

"Ah. Computers. Let's hold that for a minute. It was you who identified Anna Prophet as Olga Olinskia, a 16-year old girl who built a sophisticated criminal enterprise starting at age 11. How could Olga's parents have applied to colleges when their daughter didn't have a high school transcript?"

"They sent letters to the admissions offices."

"Those wouldn't be in the universities' admissions databases. The databases only hold standardized information that is scanned from admission forms. They have notations if letters are received, but not the contents of the letters. You couldn't have done a computer search of the Ivies' admissions databases and there wasn't time for you to call the universities and speak with their admissions offices. So you knew about Olga Olinskia already.

"But I agree, Dr. Goldberg, you are good at your job. I checked your performance at each of the institutions that issued those degrees on your wall. Medical school, your residency and fellowship — every mentor you had thought you were brilliant. Everyone expected you to go into academic research and practice."

"I liked forensics."

"Lucky for the NYPD. And lucky for you that you received military scholarships for your education. Except, no matter how hard I looked, I couldn't find any record of military service. But I did learn that DARPA gives scholarships. DARPA doesn't give birth certificates, unfortunately for you. They do keep a record of home addresses of the students whom they fund. And what a surprise to find that your home address was in Brooklyn, at the house owned by..."

"Okay Frank. Nice work. Serge and Sophia told me you visited, but I didn't know about the rest of your research."

"Surprised, aren't you. Why didn't Matty let you know? I'm guessing that people like you and Olga don't get surprised very often."

"You'd be amazed. Olga surprised her parents. Shit, that's what America is all about, isn't it! You come from the old country and think your kids will follow the same patterns that you did. And then damn, the kids go and marry outside the religion, or don't go into their parents' business, or won't go to college, or disappoint you in some way you'd never expect. Olga was truly an American, she rebelled against everyone."

"And you're telling me this because..."

"Because you're not going to survive past tonight, Frank, which I really regret. I like you. I like working with you and I like talking to you more than any other nomod I've ever met. And I love working at the NYPD. I really do like forensics. I like the idea of helping you folks and working for justice. I hate everything that's going to happen next. But the government can't allow its program to go public. I was personally rooting for you not to discover us, but that was something that had been considered. It's going to be hard for you to stay alive, so it doesn't matter what you hear now. Damn."

"Nomod?"

"Non-modified. It's what we call you people. Whatever you think you've done with Matty, I assure you he's not your captive, and if he is, you'll be hearing from Washington very shortly telling you to let him go. Matty found the bug you left in my office. I deactivated it before speaking."

"That right, superman? Where's the bug?"

"Between the top drawer and the frame of my desk." He pulled out the drawer and detached it from the desk, reached his hand into the frame, felt around, and pulled out a listening device. "Again, I'm sorry Frank."

"What about on the other side of the frame? The drawer on the right?"

Goldberg looked surprised. He pulled out the drawer on the right and found another device.

"What about under your seat?"

He felt under his seat and pulled up another bug.

"There's also one in the light fixture. Maybe a couple of others."

"What did you do to Matty?"

"Before I say, let me just check to see if our conversation carried. Let me make a couple of calls." I took out my cell phone. "Hello Jack, did you get it? Good."

"That was Mulberry?" I didn't answer Goldberg. I hit speed dial again.

"Hello Daisy, did you get that? Good." I hung up.

"What the fuck! Daisy Stein? Are you out of your mind!"

"You tell me, Doctor. You asked about Matty. Matty's on board."

"What do you mean?"

"He didn't like being part of the experiment. He didn't want to breed with Olga. Honestly, I understand that completely. She was beautiful, but she was horrifying."

"You have no idea. My God, she's magnificent. It's not just that she was beautiful. No woman feels like her to touch. No woman smells like her. Every ounce of her drives me wild with the desire to breed with her. I was furious that Matty was picked, that it was going to be his germline that would breed the next generation. We all have variations, it's part of the project. Matty's was deemed superior to mine. Olga was everything that any of us wanted. The urge to breed with her was something we all felt."

"Not Matty."

"Impossible."

"Imagine a male black widow spider that was a self-aware genius. It shouldn't be hard for you, Michael.

"That fat, pulsing, black death machine turns you on, but you don't want to get eaten. That's how it felt to Matty.

"You all lost control of Olga. Matty realized it. He didn't want to get eaten. He even realized that Olga may not have even wanted to breed with him. Like I said, you all lost control."

"We lost control."

"And Matty likes police work. Like you."

"Of course he does. We were created to be smarter than everyone else for the purpose of war. But America isn't in a war right now. And a lot of us thought about our destinies and didn't like them.

We're not machines; we're people. Matty and I both felt lucky to be sent here to keep an eye on New York, the biggest point of entry into the U.S., for the really nasty criminals. It's challenging work and gives us purpose. We'll miss it.

"What now, Frank?"

"Depends on you. Mulberry likes you. The Homicide guys like you. Hell, I like you. Matty let your handlers at the Pentagon know where they stand. We like having two super geniuses in the NYPD. It helps raise the average IQ of the Department. You really did earn those degrees. It's not your fault that you're only 16, Michael. How many jobs are available to psychiatrists that have a pension? The way the City calculates retirement benefits, you'll be able to retire on almost full salary in 39 short years at the age of 55. If you want to stay we want to have you."

X

The Commissioner could not be more upset about the media coverage I got. And I got plenty. But not from Daisy Stein. She was an all-star after her eye witness story. The News couldn't sell enough copies. But every other paper and TV network only had me as a source and they made the most of it. The Commissioner personally requested that the Mayor not throw a tickertape parade for me. When I was interviewed, I was as modest as a baseball player who hit the walk-off grand slam but just talked about the team effort. In this case, though, it really was all about the team.

The Pentagon called Matty and Goldberg in for a debriefing, but the military learned a lot less from them than the two of them learned from the military. Goldberg filled me in when he returned. "They questioned us about what went wrong, what the signs were. I spoke about unpredictability. We're genetically modified, but we are human, with human foibles. They didn't hear a word I said. They started planning for the next generation of mods. They like the Olga Olinskia pattern—which they're now calling the Anna Prophet model— and are going to make one of the replicates active, but less blood thirsty this time. I tried to explain that bloodthirstiness isn't a trait on the genome, but they were deaf to me. They had a question about you that I couldn't answer."

"What was that, Michael?"

How did you get so smart?

"Compared to what?"

"Put it this way, they'd like to breed you with the next Anna model."

I shuddered. Goldberg observed that. "Don't knock it. Once you get passed that different species thing, it's incredibly hot."

"There are more!"

"I have a number of brothers and sisters, Frank. Olga was the only one who could turn into an Anna Prophet."

"Have those fucking idiots at DARPA ever seen a science fiction movie!"

"I'm going to try not to take that personally."

"This is a conversation for another day, Michael. I have another interspecies fight to take on now."

I was referring to the eternal battle between cops and reporters. I had to get together with Daisy for the next round of fighting her to make sure she didn't write the story about government-created super humans gone wild. Our deal was that I would let her in on the story of the century but she couldn't publish it. I needed her for an insurance policy. She had to write the story, attach it to an e-mail, get ready to hit send if she didn't hear from me, and delete it if she did hear from me. Predictably, she did not want to delete the story. But she hadn't pushed send yet either. At least as of now, the experiment was a success; she was still listening.

ଓ ଞ

*In 1984 **J. David Liss** received an MFA from Brooklyn College. Trained in writing, inclined to politics, he worked as a speechwriter and lobbyist for causes that allow him to earn a living but are worthwhile. Liss published poetry and fiction in a number of places, including a recent anthology from Between the Lines Press.*

EVERYTHING YOU SEE AT THIS MOMENT IN TIME IS MADE OF IRON AND SALTWATER
- NATALIE KWAN

everything you see at this moment in time is made of iron and
saltwater,
trapped in a small infinity of black and a whirlwind of magnificent
colour—of blue or brown or green or grey!
oh, the things you will see with those silly green eyes!
how they laugh when you smile and dance when you sing,
and sting when you weep and bark when you shout.
oh, the tears you will cry with those pretty brown eyes
as tiny drops of saline run off filling oceans in your collarbones.

everything you touch is made of flesh and bones,
fixed in place like the characters of a Shakespearean tragedy
because sometimes they shake among the cold stage and sometimes
they break under tremendous pressure.
and the flesh that encloses you,
the flesh on your hands that can say so much wrong and do so much
worse
and can act like muted strums of a tactical guitarist,
can behave like a million lovers and love like a thousand years.
your flesh and bones speak in ways of musical instruments and 16th
century theatre
you are iron and saltwater
mixed within a spectacular machine of sorts, creating a beat that lasts
a thousand miles.

CR   BO

*Natalie Kwan is an aspiring poet from Unionville, Ontario who is currently
working towards a Bachelor of Arts at Queen's University. Her style of
writing is heavily influenced by that of poet E. E. Cummings. In her spare
time, Natalie enjoys reading, writing, and figure skating.*

I DREAMED OF A FESTIVAL OF BIRDS ON FIRE
- MIKEY SIVAK

The altar fire must always be kept burning - It must never go out.
– Leviticus 6:13

In some pre-medieval town,
robed supplicants had built a great
scaffold, a steeple made
of wood & bone like
an antenna to god.

The bones of every creature
of the earth & the sea were used,
& the bones of men, women, & children
of every age & race were mingled
in strange ways among the joists,
all tied together with fruiting vines
& flowers & thorny branches
of ziziphus & briar.

At sundown the priests set it ablaze
with flames they had carried down
in a procession of torches from
a great bowl of fire atop
the highest mountain.
Ten-thousand communicants
dropped to their knees
in great circles around
the tower.

Birds of all kinds flocked in
swarms around the burning structure.
Sparrows, kingfishers, mourning
doves & falcons
all formed a great spiral
reaching out beyond the city
to the encompassing
forests and hills as far
as could be seen.

Through the burning pillar
the birds flew in turn, each catching fire
& flying on, each trailing smoke
behind itself like a little
meteor descending.

Pheasants and peacocks,
and all the species of flightless
fowl were released by the faithful
from wooden cages in stone tower
parapets, and these too soared
like gliders through
the monolithic
fire.

There were also pilots
within the ribs of skeletal
DiVinci machines, wooden,
almost birdlike, with wings of papyrus
upon which secret symbols
were inscribed.

There were also balloons
of stitched parchment & vellum, each
raised by a fire of bones in a basket, each orb
inscribed with a codex:
the words of every scripture
of each religion ever written
by men, women, or gods since the start
of time incarnate in all the alphabets
of every language ever
conceived.

Beneath the baskets
long scrolls dangled dancing
like pennants in the hot fire wind,
& upon these were written
endless maths & equations,
calculations of Creation,
each one contradicting
the next.

& as the burning birds flew,
landed in the framework
of the machines, or alighted
atop the great balloons,
these all caught fire too,

Until the airships crashed
to the cobblestone streets
among the shower
of encrusted & smoldering birds,
knocking over structures,
smashing into kiosks,
crushing supplicants
to bits.

Among it all, stray dogs lurked
picking up cooked birds in their teeth,
swallowing them in gulps, & rats scrabbled
from the gutters to nip off the blackened fingertips
of dead pilots. The scaffold burned
on into the night

Until the vines were gone, the bones black
& brittle, & finally it all collapsed, falling
beneath its own weight, bones of every species
plummeting aflame to the cobblestones, bursting
apart in glowing shrapnel, spreading
to everything there

Within the city walls, people kneeling
still as corpses as their cloaks
caught flame, remaining
totally motionless, as they
slowly burned
to charcoal.

Vultures
& ravens
that had not flown
through the fire but circled
high above the smoke & flames

in the cold clear air among the night stars,
waited & watched with hungry
black eyes for the feast
to finally
cool.

෴   ෴

Mikey Sivak is a writer and visual artist from New Haven, Connecticut. http://mykls.tumblr.com/

When the boys cut their first fish from dorsal fin to lower lip they were not prepared for so much wine-grey fluid, both runny and viscous like a clogged drain. They reeled back as it spilled out over the blade and between their slender fingers browned by summer; cadence of saltwater brushed over the need to be worthy. The fish twitched violently until the tall boy severed the head, hesitantly so that it remained attached, and then with indignation, wounded pride. The asphyxiated head leapt over the shore leaving a trail of sludgy matter, its flat pupil-less eyes at rest by the lapping water. Between their clumsily masculine hands, the split body convulsed as if still submerged, its jagged lattice of bones prehistoric against warm flesh. An examination of the inseparable. Scales littered their hands, the sand, in the little tide of death and water signifying a draw close of childhood. The dark responsibility each bears to relinquish himself to the tide that has left them at the maw of change, unaware that there is not a way back; that they could not withhold their spirit's departure into age.

∞ ∞

Hannah Wells *is 27 years old and graduated with a BA in English from Wayland Baptist University. Publications to date include Anima Poetry Press, All the Sins Literary Magazine, The Big Windows Review, Avatar Review, Peeking Cat Poetry Magazine and Del Sol Magazine. She strives to capture the specificity of visceral moments found in nature through a spiritual perspective.*

"And now, like the monks, you will take a vow of silence. No talking as we walk to the abbey, starting...now." I made eye contact with my friend across the room and we shared a smile. We were wearing bland gray robes over our clothes, tied at the middle with slim rope. I wondered just how in-character they expected us to be.

We exited the Fountains Abbey information center and made our way to the beginning of the path, a silent group of about thirty teenagers dressed as monks. It was a soggy kind of day, the sky a uniform, pearlescent gray. Icy mist clung to our skin and clothes, and made the grass pale and glittery. I caught up to my friend, trying to telepathically communicate with her about how bizarre this was. Being in England was already strange enough, but dressing up as monks and exploring the ruins of an old abbey seemed like the kind of thing that only happened in stories.

"All right now," said one of the two guides, "From this moment until I tell you to stop, you are monks, so you're going to act like monks. Hoods up, everyone, heads down. Hold your hands together in front of you, like so." The guide demonstrated. "We'll be walking in a line two by two so get yourselves organized."

My friend rolled her eyes at me, but we both complied, making sure to situate ourselves next to one another. There was a bit of shuffling as we all tried to get into a line without communicating. A few girls next to us stifled laughter as they rushed around and squeezed between people to get in line.

The hood of my robe was big and fell down to my eyes when I put it up. The sleeves were oversized as well, and it didn't take much to shake them down over my hands, protecting them slightly from the hostile air. I clasped my hands together and waited for the bustling to cease.

After standing still for a moment in a formation that loosely resembled two parallel lines, we followed the guides as they set off down the gravel path. I glanced quickly at the window of an old building to my right, catching sight of our reflections, but for a moment I couldn't recognize them. In the dark, warped glass of the window, we seemed to take on the form of medieval shadows, apparitions of the past that were unidentifiable in formless robes. Before I could marvel at the transformation, we had moved beyond the window and the ghosts disappeared.

The grounds of the abbey were sprawling, and the gravel path we traversed wound through the grass like a snake, constantly turning corners and revealing a different view. We walked by a crumbling stone bridge over a small stream. Trees bowed over the path as if in prayer, leaves brushing the ground. Birds chimed out flitting, ephemeral hymns; the only other noise aside from the crunch of footsteps.

Our solemn procession eventually made it to the ruins. They were dark silhouettes towering against the gray sky, wreathed in green. Shattered stone walls arched upwards as if trying to crawl away from the ground, sticking out of the earth like the fractured ends of broken bones. Some parts still held an original imprint of what the building must have looked like when it was constructed in the twelfth century, but most of it had yielded to the weight of time. Gaping holes peppered the walls like a botched execution.

This ruin was like life support for the past, trying to keep history breathing even though its heart had stopped a long time ago. There was a stale sort of hope that it would return, would open its eyes and continue on as if nothing had happened.

We split off into two groups with one guide each so we weren't cramped in the small corridors of the abbey. I approached the ruins cautiously, keeping to the back of the group. Our guide explained that the roof of the abbey had been taken away during the dissolution of the monasteries in the fifteen hundreds and had been melted down for the lead. The stone walls that still stood formed an outline of where the roof should have been.

Even after the guide gave us permission to talk, I remained silent, shivering in the frigid air. I gazed up at the towering walls, feeling like a mourner at a funeral despite the happily chattering students surrounding me. I was walking were medieval monks had walked, had lived their lives. They might have once stood in this same exact spot as I was standing, their feet would have touched the same ground. They couldn't have known that eventually their grand abbey would be dismembered and hollowed out.

The grave of an abbots was still visible in the floor of one of the main chambers. It was a life-sized plaque in the ground, placed between two rows of cracked pillars. Resting in the middle of it was the carved form of the abbot. Grass crept over the edges of the hewn stone like outstretched fingers, trying to banish the abbot from sight and pull him further into the ground. Had he been standing, he would have barely been taller than the shortest teenager in the group.

Without a roof and most of the walls, the abbey was more like the suggestion of a building, the scar tissue, the bones of a carcass. It felt dead, like the stones themselves were bodies left to moulder. I closed my eyes for a few seconds, concentrating on the cold air and the rustling leaves. Perhaps if I just took a moment and stood still, my mind would compensate for the centuries that had passed and I'd be able to see it the way the monks had. But when I opened my eyes the abbey was still decaying.

Our group marched up a winding staircase and into a small tower chamber with windows that overlooked the core of the abbey. "The monks used to sing from up here. The acoustics are fantastic! Would anyone like to give it a try?" asked the guide. We all shuffled awkwardly, none of us saying a word. The guide chuckled. "All right then, we'll carry on."

The abbey was a strange configuration. Hallways were filled with grass, walls stopped at odd angles, the ceiling was the sky. None of it seemed to add up to a place that could ever have been lived in. And yet it had. That was the room that the monks would get their blood drawn with leeches. This was the room that they would sing in. These were the halls they would walk through.

I shuddered and crossed my arms, trying to retain some warmth as we walked back into the open air. The guide kept talking, throwing facts at us that I would never be able to completely remember, but that didn't stop me from trying as hard as I could. I didn't want to forget a single moment. I wanted to soak in the history and keep it with me even after the two week school trip was over so I could revisit it whenever I wanted. There were no great ruins like this back home.

As we moved through an arched hallway, close to the grave of the abbot, a sound floated towards us, carried by a numbing draft of air. It was something other than bird song and the soft chatter of the students. I stopped and looked up, my eyes scanning the sharp edges of the abbey.

When I recognized the sound as singing, my breath froze in my lungs. The monks were singing. Their songs must have sunk into the stones and were now emanating from the walls around us. My eyes flickered around, waiting for the manifestation of ethereal spirits to emerge from the surrounding fog. Perhaps our robes had fooled them into rising and joining the people they thought were their brothers. I listened to the ancient voices drifting through the mist.

"... wooooorld, she took the midnight train goin' aaaaaanyyyyyywheeeeeere."

Oh.

We turned a corner and came into view of the tower. Through the bare windows I could see the gray robes and blue sweatshirts of the other group. Their guide must have convinced them to test out the acoustics. It was the song that had somehow been chosen as the anthem for our trip, it was sung during bus rides and while walking around cities. And now it was being sung in a decrepit place of worship, bouncing off of the same stones as Latin hymns once did.

Air escaped my lungs in a quiet huff, sparkling in front of me for a moment before evaporating. I glanced around, this time trying to find my friend instead of the ghosts of people who had died so long ago they were now most likely nothing more than dust in the ground. The monks did not appear, the dead remained silent, and I was no longer waiting for the impossible to happen. But at least the guide was right about the acoustics.

03   80

Julie Guerra is an undergraduate senior at the University of Maine at Farmington. She is majoring in both Creative Writing and English, with a minor in Theatre.

UNWANTED VISITOR - AGGIE SANTILLANES

I lived in a small village in Northern New Mexico. Our farm was in the outskirts of this village. It was late November 1943 and a storm was brewing.

Wind had picked up and was very cold. My father, my two brothers and I locked up the animals for the night and gave one last round securing the farm for the night. My mother had supper on the table. We prayed before we ate. It was a blessing because my mother always served us a good and warm homemade meal, breakfast, lunch and supper. We sat around the fireplace after supper and we would read or play games.

That particular night I could hear our dogs barking. They seemed very restless. My father said it was the wind. I had an uncomfortable feeling.

It was a weekend night so I stayed up later than the others reading a book I had brought home from school. The fire was dying down and I was growing tired with heavy eyes. I could hear the wind. It had picked up quite a bit.

I decided to look out our living room window. As I pushed the curtain open I felt chills run up my spine and I looked out hoping to see the trees sway back and forth with the wind, but there right before me was a face-looking back at me-the only thing that separated us was the window.

He had a long hooded cape and his eyes were set so deep in his face. I tried so hard to scream but nothing would come out, as I was trying to scream I closed the curtain, and ran for my father. I ran, without knocking, into my parent's bedroom and with sweat and shock on my face I told my father what had happened.

He jumped out of bed and ran to the living room window and opened the curtain and there was the face still looking right back at my father. I became short of breath and the chills on my spine were still there. My father yelled to my older brother to get his shotgun and scrambled to put his boots on. At the same time my poor mom holding her rosary and praying the Hail Mary as loud as she could. My dad and brothers ran for the door and opened it and ran out yelling "Who's there?" as my mom and I stood at the door. The only thing answering was the wind. One of my brothers ran back and said, "There is no one there anymore." My father fired a shot from his rifle just to scare whoever it was. We all came back inside and my mother made coffee and we all sat around the kitchen table waiting to see if this person would return, wondering how close by he was. I could see the scared look on my father's face.

The next morning we all went outside to look around by the window and there were no footprints or any sign of anyone being there. As my father walk to the front gate that leads to the road, there outside the gate were two hoof prints of a goat, not four. My father and mother called for the priest to come and bless the farm.

We never spoke of this to no one ever.

CR SO

Aggie Santillanes is from Northern New Mexico. (Las Vegas, NM). She just began to write short stories and poems. She is a retired Middle School Language Arts teacher. She is a proud wife and mother of 4 children, 2 boys and 2 girls. She and her husband have 7 grandchildren.... They are their life.

GOOD STORY – GALE ACUFF

When Miss Hooker dies I hope I'm there to
mourn, and I mean as her widower–I'm
in love with her, my Sunday School teacher,
even though she's already old, I'd say
25, to my 10, but I can wait
until I'm 16 and she's 31
and maybe by then age won't matter much,
not that it matters much to me but her,
I'm not yet sure. When I'm 75
she'll be 90 and when folks get that old
I guess they can do as they damn well please
only they probably do it slower.
But after she's buried I'll visit her

and talk to her and not just her stone and
not just the dirt and the grass beginning
to cover her up, her gravesite I mean,
and I'll remind her about the Sundays
when she told those Bible stories and good
ones, as if she had been an eyewitness
to the ladies with all those lamps, and that
Prodigal Son and Good Samaritan
and David and Goliath and Moses
parting the Red Sea and turning his rod
into a snake that swallowed up Pharoah's
magicians', or God did, and Joshua
making the sun stand still, or God did, and
Jesus raising Lazarus and raising
Himself, or God did, but Jesus was God
so I guess it doesn't really matter,
that's if I've paid attention every week.
I'll bring her flowers, too–maybe candy

as well, but since she can't eat it and not
just because she lost her teeth but her life
I'll help myself to it and tell her how
it tastes, and then I'll get up off the ground
and say something like, Well, Baby, it's time
to go now, and wonder if they have that

up there in Heaven like we know it here,
time I mean, and See you tomorrow–be
here, ha ha, then walk back home and look back
two or three times to see how she looks from
afar, and on a dreary day to see
if I can spot her ghost back there, or spy
her walking, even, resurrected and
following me but I won't be afraid

too much because I'll be old myself and
ready, more or less, to join her. I can't
wait but still I'm patient and we'll be
together forever if I merit
Heaven but if I go to Hell we'll have
a problem ever seeing each other,
not that I deserve to see her but I
pray I'll get at least a look before God
casts me into the Lake of Eternal

Fire, which is probably like a sewer
in flames, but if I can see she's happy
and all in one piece and maybe even
younger, then I think I can take it, all
the moaning and groaning and frying skin
and muscles and fat and bones–I'll keep her
last look in my mind even though my brain
is boiling and roiling in my skull and
there's no relief from the punishment for
all my sins and the shame I'll feel that I
had babies with a woman much too good
for me and I hope that God won't hold it
against her and change His mind and throw her
in after me but at least we wouldn't
be alone, but then again I'd watch her
being tortured by devils and she me.

I wonder if in Heaven she'll have red
hair still, and green eyes and that mole on her
nose and all those freckles or if Heaven
has no color but looks more like fog or
those back and white photographs when someone
shook the camera when he pressed the button

or someone he was shooting trembled or
moved otherwise. She paints her toenails does
Miss Hooker, almost a different color
for every Sunday morning so I love
her from top to bottom. When I say my

prayers I say a special one for her,
that God will help her fall in love with me
and we'll be always happy even when
her red hair turns white and her green eyes go
blank and her mole becomes a cancer and
her freckles cover her head like the mange.
Then life will have been too much for her and
I'll come back home from a walk one afternoon
and find her dead on the couch but alive
in a way that you've got to live a life
to understand and when you do you don't
have long yourself. That's why they say God's good.

CR   BO

Gale Acuff has had poetry published in many journals and is the author of three books of poetry. He has taught tertiary English courses in the US, China, and Palestine.

Fifty Percent Cotton

Francis Francis of West Virginia
gave birth
to eleven children
four of which
made it to adulthood
and the ones who died
she buried one by one on the hill
by her house
one died when his nightgown burned
as he walked by the fire pit
another died when she coughed herself
to death
the four who had survived
made it to Ohio
Zelah whose name was from
a bible story
went to school with
the famous writer Toni Morrison
who was named something else
at the time
Francis was married to
Golden Mills, an alcoholic
and every week she went
down to the coal mine
to get his paycheck
before he could cash it
at the bar
and I tell you this now
before I am too old to remember
or maybe
no longer here to tell you

Unexpected Happiness

Still alive? I ask her,
through the silence

Yes, they are all gone
(the kids)
and I finally get to sit on the toilet
for a minute

kids are a lot of work, she
tells me

Uh, yes, like never ending
and happiness comes in
sitting on a toilet

As I Walked

The sun was humming through the clouds
just enough that
this particular morning
felt brighter but still gray
and the snow was in piles
touched with dirty footprints
the people looked miserable
and rightly so
clumps of ice and dirty snow
fell around me
as I walked
all was calm yet
dull
and steam was rolling off the rooftops
the coffee was settling in
tomorrow would come
without fanfare
without punctuation
but it would come,
none the less
and I would greet it
as any other day

with as much enthusiasm
as it did me

On This Particular Morning

Two birds were arguing with each other
as I walked, half asleep
to nowhere
lovers in a drunken quarrel
dancing on the bar top for all to see
I say this because it was loud and
boisterous
rumbling above the other sounds
above the noise of my own footsteps
above the rattle of the coming train
and the booming airplane engines
in the sky
they were in two separate trees
on two separate streets
the air was cold
the kind of cold that settles into the bones
and makes its home for days at a time
with no intention of leaving
the sun was coming up
as it had been doing so earlier and earlier
and I could tell just by staring into it
how it reflected from every branch
in the spider web of trees
how everything was lit just so
Spring would soon be here
the sunrise had that look to it today
sometimes in the Fall as well
but this sunrise doesn't come with a
sadness
the awareness that every living thing
will start to wilt and crumble
but instead be born again
so they argued
in the naked branches
of the separate trees
unaware and indifferent
to the idea that I was listening to everything

I pulled my coat tightly around my neck
adjusted my hat for the hundredth time
felt for my house keys
stepped over a tree root
squinted from the sun
and walked on
letting them continue their disagreement
I let the wind blow through the branches
I left the squirrels to forage
stepped aside allowing the waking life
to reach up to the rising sun
watched the feral cats prowl
watched it all fade behind me
until everything was silent once again
except for the sound of my footsteps
thumping in tune with
my own beating heart

The Things Well Hidden

We thought she was half-baked
from the medication
control had become overrun with
madness, forgetfulness
all those little pills to kill
the overbearing cancer
little objects found in odd places
left us wondering
'Why would she do that?'
a ring hidden on a shelf
no one would ever find
unless they got an itch
to dust a shelf no one ever paid
attention to
an old bus pass underneath a basket
on top of the piano
we have since come to believe
to understand, rather
it was all done with purpose, not madness
as little reminders of her because
she was so afraid we might forget

感 ∽

Ken Tomaro *is an artist and writer living in Cleveland, Ohio. His work has been published in The Light Ekphastic, Tipton Poetry Journal and Sincerely Magazine. He has published two collections of poetry and most if his work is the result of living with depression.*

Links: https://www.amazon.com/gp/aw/d/1549779699/ref=tmm_pap_title_0 ?ie=UTF8&qid=&sr=

https://www.amazon.com/Your-Dog-Called-Wifes-Fire/dp/1520793448

LARS BREAXFACE AND THE TREE OF BONES – BRANDON GETZ

Lars tossed another empty bottle at the oozing, twinkling tree in the corner of the cargo hold.

Solstices didn't mean much in the emptiness of space, and the wolfman had long ago stopped counting days and months by the Terran calendar, but Sheila, his stalwart starcruiser, still rang a gong for all the major holidays of his junked and haggard planet. The night before, as Lars snoozed half-blitzed in his bunk dreaming of the white wonderland of a certain vampire princess's lumps and nethers, Sheila had blared a black-metal "Jingle Bells," her signal that Hot Cosmic Christmas had reared its merry head. Out of habit, or maybe because he finally had someone to celebrate with besides a full keg and an indifferent starship, he'd steered course for the nearest planet, trudged into a shimmering swamp with his new shipmate, the cyborg amphibian called Fish, and yanked a serviceable tree from the muck to decorate with holiday cheer. Fish had daisy-chained a string of wires from the cigarette lighter in the pilot house, and an old hologram projector threw a haze of twinkle lights on the alien tree. Atop its roughly conical shape, a five-pronged sex toy slouched, blinking red and green from some internal LED.

The wolfman was lounging in human form, as he usually did, no threats in his own ship requiring a wolf-out. He grabbed another bottle from the mini-fridge – last one in the stash. After that, he'd have to tap one of the kegs crated up in the middle of the hold. He popped the cap, watched it stick silver side up in the tree's ooze, and took a long pull from the bottle. Nothing like the spiked egg snot he used to chug back in the flood town of his barefoot youth, but he didn't mind. Festive or no, the beer was better. If he'd had a cinnamon stick, he would've dropped it in, just to add some holiday spice.

A flush erupted from the head, and Fish stumbled out, his scales a shade greener than their usual hue.

"Beer?" Lars offered, holding out his bottle.

The amphibian pressed his cybernetic hand to his lips and looked ready to retch again. It'd been a long time since Lars had seen somebody so space-sick. Fish slumped against a wall near the slime-covered tree, limbs splayed in defeat.

"What is this for, anyway?" he said, nodding his finned head toward the tree. "Do you eat it?"

Lars shrugged. "You got me. It's just part of the shtick – haul a tree into your home, fancy it up with lights and tinsel, throw some presents under it at some time or another."

"And this is what the Jeezus did on their birthday? I mean, I know it's traditional to dress a tree in drag and engage in ceremonial inebriation, but –"

"Basically, yadda yadda the deity congealed from the cosmic ether to wish the Universe a happy new year and give us all a fine excuse to get drunk, yell at our families, and give other people the old shit we don't want anymore, wrapped up with a bow on top, and if nobody gets punched in the teeth, it's a happy holiday. Merriest time of the year." Lars took another swallow off the beer. Maybe it wouldn't have been so bad to have a little nog. So long as it came with a lot of whiskey. "Anyway, that's the quick version. Visit a chapel if you want it unabridged."

"Back on my home world," Fish started, "we have something like that, a big holiday, the Feast of Frogsgulch, to celebrate the moment the Frog Mother laid the infinite egg strands that became the stars and worlds of the Universe." A nostalgic sheen fell over the amphibian's eyes. "We all gather in the temple and pass around the ceremonial jelly, which we spread on our cloaca as the priestesses recite the liturgy of the Mother. Then we hum the ancient hymns into each other's holy regions, breathing in the fumes of our brothers and sisters."

The fish-man closed his eyes, licking his lips slowly.

Lars realized he was staring. "So, you mean to tell me your big holiday is you grease up and sing into each other's sex holes?"

"There is also a feast."

"No kidding."

The beer was empty. Sheila was still playing death-metal versions of Hot Cosmic Christmas classics. On the sound system, somebody was growling through "O Tannenbaum." Time to tap the keg. Lars felt something wet hit his beard and worried, for a moment, that Fish had gotten space-sick in the hold. Or that he was uncapping a jar of Frogsgulch jelly.

"Fish, the fuck is –" he started, wiping his face with his forearm. He stopped short, looking at the slime on his skin. "Fish. You just toss a slimeball at me?"

"A what?" came the amphibian's reply, but the tree was already reaching.

"Fish, look out!"

Still twinkling with holographic starlight, pentadactylic dildo wagging on its top, the sludged-up tree was rearing for attack. Lower branches lifted, revealing a maw of bony tentacles, each one twitching toward Fish. Slime dripped along the bones. Fish seemed frozen, a space-sick cyborg frogsicle, the tech tucked into his cyber-parts doing him no good if he didn't use it. The boughs of muck slithered closer to the fish-man, and Lars felt his knuckles begin to bend and break, reforming into claws, his whole skeleton cracking as wolf flowed through him.

"Fishman," he snarled, "Roast his chestnuts."

As the tree's grotesque tentacle teeth touched Fish's throat, the robophibian shook loose of his trance and thrust his cybernetic hand forward, the fingers disappearing to reveal the glowing ellipse of a laser chainsaw. Zip, and the slimy tips of the tentacles clattered across the floor. The long teeth sucked back into tree's mouth, and the creature screeched. Fish crawled backward, trying to stand. The tree shook itself like a wet dog, and ooze sprayed everywhere in the hold – kegs, crates of canned meat, Lars' grizzled fur. The five-pronged dildo whirled through the air, blinking its festive red and green, and landed square in the werewolf's eye.

Lars howled.

A bony tentacle-branch wrapped itself around his ripped pant leg, and he was dragged to the floor. He thrashed, wolf-talons scraping against the bone. The tree was hunched in the corner of the ceiling, looking more like a skeletal anemone than a swamp tree, now that the slime had been splattered all over his cruiser. It dangled the werewolf in the air, prodding him with its myriad ossified limbs. A few twisted around his wrists, but he broke free with his wolf-strength. He kicked at the thick bone rope around his leg. No luck. He couldn't get leverage hanging up there like Rudolph's ball sack. How was this for a jolly holiday – no stockings, no nog, and the tree was about to gobble him down like a Christmas ham. He sure as shit wasn't drunk enough for this.

And then he was tumbling down, hitting the ooze-spattered floor with a hard thud. Fish was standing over him. The amphibian flashed his laser chainsaw and grinned.

"Owe me one, Breaxface." Then it was Fish who was dragged, a tentacle around each of his robotic legs. As he was hauled across the hold, his chainsaw hand whipped wildly, slicing open crates of gravy, bags of cargo netting, and a single keg of beer.

"The beer!" Lars roared.

The werewolf crouched. His ankle ached and his eye still stung from the dildo's insidious poke, but there were more important things to worry about. Precious lager splashed across the floor, frothing up with the tree's discarded slime. Lars launched himself toward the writhing bone creature. The tree tossed Fish across the hold and spread its maw. Tentacles twitched and reached, a twinkling circle of finger-teeth. Its conical top bobbled like a dunce hat of death. The tree screeched, and Lars howled, a full-on moon-drunk werewolf howl.

He crashed into the first of the tentacles and kept on crashing. The teeth scraped like brambles, and he felt blood in his fur. He clawed, chewed, and wrenched, pulling bony bits out from the inside. The tree convulsed, and tentacles grabbed for his ankles. The werewolf dodged and kept yanking. Finally, he found what he was looking for – a thick column of gray, grinding vertebrae. The trunk. He grabbed the spine with both claws and sunk his teeth into it, chewing through bone while the tree flailed and shuddered. When at last he tasted fluid among the shards in his mouth, he felt the tree fall limp and slide down the wall, what was left of its appendages rattling against the floor.

A doom metal "Deck the Halls" rang through the cargo hold. The smell of spilled beer and bone dust hung in the air, a far cry from cinnamon and evergreen. Lars shook the slime and blood from his fur. His wounds were already healing. As his body broke back into human form, he searched the hold for Fish. The amphibian crawled out from under a toppled stack of ammo boxes, all of them empty or nearly enough. His nose was bloodied, and his cyborg arm looked a little dinged up.

"Got your fucking halls decked," Lars said. "You good?"

Fish cracked his neck and checked some beeping thing on his robo-arm. "Good."

Sheila banked, and the remains of the tree rattled again. It was a sad-looking thing, cracked in half at the trunk and splayed like strings of old bone. The hologram had finally kicked off, and the twinkle lights were gone.

"Looks like we picked the wrong tree," said the wolfman.

"Animal response," Fish said. "It must've woken up here, reacted out of fear."

"Yeah," Lars said. "But it wasted my beer."

As Fish made his way to the head, he stopped and looked back. "You know, that tree-thing reminds me a little of –"

"Save it," Lars said. "Ain't nothing like him."

Fish nodded, then disappeared into the interior of the ship.

From the slimed and trash-strewn floor, Lars found the five-pronged dildo, still blinking red-green. He walked over to the dead thing, stepping carefully through its limbs. With the slime off the skeleton's top, the sex toy slide onto the point easily. He plugged the hologram projector back in, and the twinkle lights made the osseous corpse look almost merry. A fresh keg tapped and a mug of ale poured, Lars sat back in his spot near the locker of lunar batteries, watching the lights and listening to Sheila's playlist of holiday metal tunes.

When Fish limped back in, he was carrying a package. A small bundle wrapped in toilet paper. Thankfully, it looked to be unused.

"You said this celebration featured gifts," Fish said, offering the wad of paper.

"Ah, Fishman, you didn't have –" Lars started, unrolling the bundle.

Fish grinned.

"These are my socks," Lars continued. "That I already had. From my bunk."

The pair was mismatched, and especially stiff. If his shipmate were going to rifle through his drawers for a fistful of treasure, he might've at least grabbed a set of stockings Lars hadn't stuffed. The wolfman offered an affirmative nod. "Thanks, Fish."

There was something in one of the lockers that he'd figured he might pass to Fish on account of the holiday. What do you give a half-cybernetic amphibious humanoid who's lost his home and livelihood twice, both times being more or less your fault? Lars dug deep in a canvas pack till he felt glass.

"Close your eyes," he said. "I didn't wrap this shit."

He set the gift in Fish's hands, the cyborg's metal fingers clinking against the glass dome. Fish opened his eyes and gasped.

It was a small glass ball on a base carved to look like an ice floe. Inside, a fat white beast sat in the middle of a snowy plain, sucking on a bottle of black liquid.

"Just some kitsch from home I picked up at a spinner near Earth a while back," Lars mumbled. "I don't know, thought you might get a kick out of it."

Fish gave the ball a small shake. A confetti of snow whirled and fell around the globe's drunk beast. In his wide, fishy eyes, the scene reflected in duplicate – two ghost globes, two beasts, double the falling confetti.

"I've never seen snow."

"It's cold," Lars said. "And light, like ash. But clean."

The snow settled, and Fish shook it again.

"Thanks, Breaxface."

"Don't stress it." Lars stood up, found his way to the keg, and poured a second mug, then topped off his own. "Here," he said, "a cup of Hot Cosmic Christmas cheer. It ain't a holiday if you're sober."

Fish took the mug in his free hand and sipped at the froth. In his other, the globe shook again, and again.

Lars sat back and watched the snow fall. He raised his glass to the tree of bones, and to his cyborg shipmate, and the long-gone vampire princess, her stalwart tremuloid bodyguard, the minotaur monk, and all the other friends who had come and gone in the ever-churning infiniteness of space and time. 'Twas the reason for the season, he figured. To slow down, to halt the grind. To remember. He drank long and slow from his mug, and decided this one, dark and heavy, had in it just a hint of festive spice. Not half bad, he thought, gulping it down. Happy fucking New Year.

Lars Breaxface Werewolf in Space is coming Fall 2019 from Spaceboy Books LLC. Experience the preceding and continuing adventures of Lars, Fish and Sheila as they tear ass through the universe!

CR SO

Brandon Getz lives in Pittsburgh, PA. His work has appeared in F(r)iction, Versal, The Delmarva Review, and elsewhere. Read more at www.brandongetz.com

WHEN I LISTEN MORE - SRAVANI SINGAMPALLI

It's strange that I can listen more when the world is asleep. When there is complete silence I can listen to the sound of the food churning in my stomach. I listen to all the nighttime singers. I listen to the chirps of crickets, the 'eh eh eh' loud, pulsing noise of katydids and the buzzing sound of mosquitoes actively searching for a blood meal. Sometimes I can listen to the songs of the frogs, squeaking, gnawing and fighting sounds of rodents and the mating song of a mouse. I can also listen to the sound of dripping water and howling wind. While they all keep me awake and leave me contemplating many stories, the voice of my soul dominates them all. It is this time when I listen to myself more and bid adieu to the hustle and bustle of daytime.

CR SO

Sravani Singampalli is a published writer and poet from India. She is presently pursuing doctor of pharmacy at JNTU KAKINADA university in Andhra Pradesh, India.

BONED: A Collection of Skeletal Writings is a project started by Nate Ragolia in 2016. Each Tuesday, a new story, poem, play, or essay posts. The common theme is that all content features either bones, or a skeleton, in some capacity.

Read each week at bonedstories.wordpress.com,

ABOUT THE PUBLISHING TEAM

Nate Ragolia was labeled "weird" early in school, and it stuck. He's a lifelong lover of science fiction, and a nerd/geek. In 2015 his first book, *There You Feel Free,* was published by 1888's Black Hill Press. He's also the author of *The Retroactivist*, published by Spaceboy Books. He founded and edits BONED, an online literary magazine, has created webcomics, and writes whenever he's not playing video games or petting dogs.

Shaunn Grulkowski has been compared to Warren Ellis and Phillip K. Dick and was once described as what a baby conceived by Kurt Vonnegut and Margaret Atwood would turn out to be. He's at least the fifth best Slavic-Latino-American sci-fi writer in the Baltimore metro area. He's the author of *Retcontinuum,* and the editor of *A Stalled Ox* and *The Goldfish,* all for 1888/Black Hill Press.

Antoine Valot, Graphics Bot is a 2015 Nexus™ series Replicant from the Tyrell Corporation, communications/design model. He enjoys designing book covers, nitpicking about words, functioning within his operating margins, and making the most of the two years he has left to live.

Learn more about Spaceboy Books at readspaceboy.com

This book features the font Skullphabet by Noah Scalin (Skull-A-Day). Learn more about Skull-A-Day at skulladay.blogspot.com

www.ingramcontent.com/pod-product-compliance
Lightning Source LLC
Chambersburg PA
CBHW020606180626
46810CB00007B/2676